The Killing Cards

A Novel By

Lou Campanozzi

Published By
Hollis Books, LLC

VA CA NY VI

Dedication

This novel is dedicated with love, to Nancy, my wife of 33 years. Her belief that it was possible, along with the appropriate amounts of support, encouragement, and scolding, brought it along from an idea, to paper, and finally to publication. Without her, I would still be saying that someday I was going to write a murder mystery.

ISBN: 1-928781-48-9

Published by Hollis Books

Cover by Hollis Books

PROLOGUE

The rookie, having attended his very first roll call, left the squad room and walked a respectful one full step behind the veteran cop to whom he had been assigned. When they reached the squad car the older man finally turned to his charge and said, "I'm Bob Jokovich. They call me 'Trapper'. You can call me Bob, Trapper, or Jokovich. Just don't call me Officer Jokovich like they taught you in the academy."

With that matter settled, the senior man stowed his gear in the trunk and slid into the driver's seat of the car. Once in the beat up vehicle and in motion, the lecture began.

"I don't like having a rookie with me, but I got ya so I'll take care of ya and teach ya. You don't listen to me and I'll put ya out on a beat so fast you're pants will still be in the unit." He paused long enough to see if his words had received an affirmative nod. He then continued, "Until I say otherwise, everything to the right of the glove box is yours and the rest is mine. Ya don't touch the radio, the reports, the emergency controls, and ya sure as hell don't drive. Ya watch, ya listen, but ya don't speak. I tell some street asshole he's going to jail, ya don't interrupt with all that legal crap. All ya do is obey everything I tell ya and maybe, if ya make it through the next month, then I'll teach ya more."

The rookie went home in disillusionment, suspecting he would never make it through the next four weeks under his assigned mentor. The relationship was not what he had expected once he finally hit the streets. He had sought a brotherhood, a job where each man looked out for the other, where each man treated the other with respect, where senior officers talked to, not *at* the rookies. He had done his time in boot camp and in Viet Nam, and he didn't expect the FNG (Frigging New Guy) treatment back in the States, on the Police Department.

A few days became a week. One week became two. Slowly Trapper Jokovich allowed the shiny young recruit more and more space and more involvement. One quiet night, when the dispatcher was unusually absent from breaking into the silence, the two cops stopped for coffee and then brought their Styrofoam cups back to the car. Trapper appeared to let the car almost drive itself to a secluded spot behind the Genesee Brewery. Once there, the car was stopped and both men exited the vehicle. Jokovich unfastened his leather belt, carefully rolled it up around the gun and holster, and laid it on the hood of the car he announced his agenda for this rest break.

"I'm gonna give ya some rules, kid, and I want ya to listen up."

By this time the rookie knew the older man was not just an angry old cop with axes to grind. The past few weeks had made it clear that his trainer with the huge feet, busted up nose, and muscles earned in part time construction and landscaping jobs, was a no-nonsense sort of man who had quick hands to deal with crooks and a wide streak of generosity and empathy for the casual citizen they encountered.

"Ya watch their hands all the time. Forget their lips and the bullshit they're givin' ya. Their lips and face ain't gonna kill ya, but, their hands will."

The kid gave a nod.

"Just as important is that ya never throw away the lid to your coffee cup. If ya throw it away, just sure as hell, the dispatcher will give ya a hot call and you'll have to dump the whole damn thing. You keep the lid on, just like you're expectin' a call, and ya won't get one, and you'll be able to drink you're coffee in peace."

The rookie smiled and nodded. The incongruancy of the two rules being held so closely together was apparently lost on the older man...or so it seemed.

"And most important, kid, is that ya latch on to what I'm tellin' ya now. The first thing I told ya will save your life. The second thing will save ya money. This one here will save ya your sanity."

Jokovich checked to ensure he had the kid's attention. Then he pointed a beefy finger straight up at the sky and began.

"From now on, for the rest of the time ya spend on the job, ya ain't never gonna be right. Ya got it? If ya win a fight, you're a bully. If ya lose a fight, well then you're a whimp. If ya give a ticket to some asshole, then you're a dick. If ya give a guy a break, they will say you're on the take. If ya can't solve a case, they'll think you're stupid or lazy, but if ya solve one, they'll say ya just got lucky. Everyone will want ya enforcin' the law against everyone else but them. Ya bust a burglar and he'll tell ya that ya oughtta be after the drug dealers. Ya get a drug dealer and he'll tell ya that ya should be gettin' the murderers. When ya get a murderer he'll tell ya that ya should be out there stoppin' the drunk drivers. And, the drunk driver will tell ya that ya oughtta be grabbin the burglars. People will demand ya stop the speeders in their neighborhood and as soon as ya write a ticket against one of their kids, they'll be in the Chief's office tellin' him you're pickin' on their people. Bosses who never was at the scene will criticize ya for what ya did or didn't do. Ya have to shoot some mug, and there will be more Monday morning quarterbacks comin' out of the woodwork then ya ever known existed. Every friggin' citizen who is too friggin' scared to leave their house will call you a murderer and a coward. The Blacks will say you're afraid to lock up the Whites and the Whites will say you're afraid of the Blacks."

"Kind of hopeless, huh?" the rookie asked before he drew a swallow of coffee through the opening of the plastic lid that covered his coffee cup.

"That's the lesson, kid. It's hopeless if ya let it bother ya. The trick is that ya don't let it bother ya. Ya do the job as best ya can and ya let it go at that. Ya go home knowin' ya did the right thing and that ya did the thing right. Get it? Ya satisfy yourself, your standards, your ethics. Screw them and what they think. Ya gotta know up here," Jokovich said as he touched the side of his head with a thick digit, "that ya did the right thing and let all the other crap roll right off ya."

Seeing the quizzed look on his tutor's face, the kid nodded and said, "I got it."

"Bull! Ya ain't got it, kid. You ain't gonna get it until ya live it a couple of hundred times. The thing I want ya to do is this, every time ya start belly achin' and pissin' and moanin' about 'them' and about how they don't understand ya and don't know what the hell's goin' on, well, it's then I want ya thinkin' about what I'm tellin' ya right now. Ya do your job the best way ya know how, and screw everyone else. They ain't cops, they ain't lived it, so they don't know and they don't matter. You just make sure you do the job right and don't listen to them other stiffs."

The advice would be tucked in the back of the rookie's mind for the next 30 years, and many times he would reach back there and pull it up to the front of his brain.

CHAPTER ONE

THE END

Up until now, the worst days of my life had been in the jungles of Viet Nam. However, tonight, sitting here beaten, bleeding, and bound, I find the thought of a fox hole in that hot, muggy piece of hell to be an attractive alternative to my present situation. My life as a cop has surely been less than spectacular, and, by the looks of things, the future doesn't hold a lot of promise.

Over the past few months, since this mind-screwing case began, I've been messed with by my Chief, my own doubts and fears, and one very nasty killer. My career, what little there had been of one, is in the toilet. My reputation, such as it was, is shattered. The remnants of my sanity and sobriety are things of the past. My downfall and my imminent death are due to one man ...one vengeful and angry man.

Because of him, I stand here with my head split open, bound to a concrete pillar in this cold, wet, abandoned, rat-infested warehouse. The musty smells of puddled water and rotting concrete fill my nostrils and find their way to my gut. As my stomach wretches, I know my only hope for survival is that my host, the maniac with the gun, will be stricken with an immediate, and very fatal heart attack.

I watch the whacko pace back and forth as he rants about all the injustices in the world, the worst of which, at least according to him, appears to be me. My eyes are on him, but my mind keeps drifting back to what has brought me here, to this spot, this night. Maybe I got too close to this case, too emotionally caught up in it. It very simply may be that this last round of killings became too personal. Perhaps I'm getting too old, stupid, cocky, or crazy. Probably it's a combination of all of the above.

With my hands bound behind me, it's quite a chore to hunch up my shoulders enough to wipe the blood that runs down the outside corner of my right eye, but in making the painful effort, I am at least able to see my tormentor. My head pounds like a kettle drum doing the *1812 Overture*, and passing out seems to be a very attractive and viable option. At least, in doing so, I will be better off than sitting here, fully conscious, a witness to my own murder.

The sneering mental turns toward me, and I see his agony displayed in a twisted face. Anger, sadness, frustration, vengeance, and hate all mingle together to share the energy of the muscles imbedded in his brow, eyes, and lips.

Facing me now, my killer slowly rolls his head from side to side as if stretching his neck in a distorted, slow motion exercise. He extends his right hand toward my shattered body and soul. His thumb pulls back the hammer of the gun. Fear now comes forward to haunt and mock me. It is not death that I fear, for I came to grips with that demon in a jungle more than a quarter of a century earlier when I learned there were things worse than death. The fear I have this night is rooted in the knowledge I have failed to cage the killer. It is a fear that, in death, I will be ridiculed for my carelessness and stupidity. I fear that none will know how hard I tried, and all will suspect that ego has led me to danger and my death.

Fear, not death, is my villain. Death is sometimes a welcome visitor, a benefactor who resolves your other fears, the ones that have pushed you toward a bottle...and away from everything else. I wonder to myself if it is better to be alive and alone or dead and alone.

I look up to glare at the man who is intent on killing me. I try to look him in the eye but my attention locks on the sight of the gun's barrel and I can picture the copper-jacketed bullet that will soon rocket through the tube and blast its way into my skull.

For better or for worse, it's time to die.

CHAPTER TWO

THE BEGINNING

It's not much of a town, but it's my town. I was born and raised in this berg of a quarter million souls, and when I left to join the Marines, I swore I would never come back. However, after a tour in 'Nam, I found there were places a lot less attractive than Rochester, New York. So I came home, joined the cops, fell in love, and got married. The job worked out fine, but the marriage didn't make it.

I've been carrying around a badge for almost 25 years. For the last five years it's been a Lieutenant's badge. As the Commanding Officer of the Violent Crimes Unit, I get to see the worst efforts of my fellow citizens. Over the years I found that whenever I want to say I've seen it all, a new animal pops up and shows me something brand new. Gore and depravity seem to be limitless when left to the minds of man. That's what I do for a living. I investigate man's cruelty to man. And, the way it shapes up, I'm going to have more than enough business to last me a lifetime.

My town sits on the southern edge of Lake Ontario, some 50-odd miles from Toronto, Canada. Consequently, the winters are brutal and the summers are uncomfortable. Cold, biting wind coupled with 10 feet of snow mark one season. Heat and humidity mark the other.

When this case began, it was February 2nd. Winter was getting its second wind, and, as far as I was concerned, was being too successful in the endeavor. I got called out at 2:10 in the morning. As I arrived at the scene thirty-five minutes later, the all-too-cheerful disc jockey announced we were enjoying a balmy 18 degree morning. I found myself resenting the buoyant spirit of the DJ. While the radio voice rambled on with his nonsensical patter, people were dying, and the rest of us were fencing with the petty problems that life brings. Perhaps the gabby announcer had never seen and smelled what human beings do to other human beings. Maybe he lived in a utopia where kids didn't hang themselves, and men didn't open their wives' guts with 12-gauge shotguns, and women didn't slit their lovers' throats with straight razors. I knew he must live in such a wonderland. I sure as hell didn't.

Our most recent homicide victim had been found on the far west side of the city, in an area filled with vacant warehouses and small factories. The flashing red lights from a couple of cop cars marked the particular building, among a row of dilapidated buildings, where our stiff had been found. I pulled the unmarked vehicle behind the two patrol units. Once I shut off the engine and made sure the keys were in my pocket, I grabbed my notebook, flashlight and gloves. As I blew into the gloves to warm them, I began to walk in the direction indicated by the cop who was just finishing his job of decorating the scene with yellow crime scene tape. My collar did little to keep the bite of winter wind and a few thousand swirling snowflakes from giving me the shivers.

I followed the narrow, broken walkway up to what had been the main entrance of the building, and let it guide me around the long south wall to the secluded rear of what used to be a prosperous factory in this used-to-be-prosperous city. The wide, brick building was now home to a half-dozen or so homeless people, several hundred rats, and one very dead murder victim.

There was a time when a murder like this came in, and half of the squad would be called out to start the job right so it would end up being solved. Those days were gone. Now we were being managed by bean counters and MBA's instead of real cops. Running the Department had become a matter of austerity budgeting, down-sizing, and right-sizing. Nobody was worried about doing police work, about locking up mopes, or solving crime. Affirmative action, political correctness, and meeting the bottom line were the watch words of the day.

Our present Chief of Police thought it would be proper that I respond to each and every homicide. Once I was at the scene, I was supposed to evaluate the situation and make a decision to either turn the case over to the district cops, or, if absolutely necessary, order in one team to handle the case. Consequently, here I was, freezing my butt, and about to venture into the strangest murder case I had ever investigated.

I took one look at the body slumped against the loading dock door, and said, "Forget about it!" to my coat collar and to all the conditions and variables the budget people hold sacred. I used a young copper's radio to instruct the dispatcher to notify the on-call detective team. In the morning, my boss would be chewed out by the Chief for my brashness, but my first look at the corpse told me this case was not a smoking-gun murder that was going to be solved in an hour, with time out for commercials.

What we had here, based on my first impressions, was a mob hit. History, being what it is, had taught me two things about mob hits. One, they aren't easy to solve. And two, when there was one, there was a better than even chance more would follow.

The best thing that could be said about our fat little victim, Frankie "Ten Times" Lanovara, was that he never murdered his mother. Okay, so he slapped her around a couple of times, but he never actually murdered her. Coming up with a list of people that would want to see this 350 pound tubby, sub-human killed would be easy, primarily due to the fact that Frankie was probably near the top of the list when it came to the most hated men in the world. This blob of mankind was so unpopular, his testimonial dinner could be held, if he ever had one, in the phone booth at Main and State Streets, and there would be a lot of room to spare.

Officially, on any public record, Frankie "Ten Times" Lanovara was a carpenter. In the real world he was a leg-breaker for the mob, with some sideline endeavors as a gambler and a loan shark. As a vocation and a hobby, he enjoyed pounding the stuffing out of anyone who got in his way. However, citizen Lanovara was more than just run-of-the-mill scum. In the opinion of most cops, he would be considered a legend among citizens who are consider to be scum. A brutal man, he took great joy in his role as an enforcer for the mob. It was said that Frankie usually gave his contractors a two-for-one special, breaking the offender's right leg as part of the contract, then breaking the left one just for fun.

I hated the guy when he was alive and fouling the air by his mere existence. Now, in his death, I hated him for getting killed on such a miserable, nasty, cold night. As far as I was concerned, Frankie was a feared, hated, and disgusting fat man when he was alive. In his present condition, he was simply a hated, disgusting, fat corpse.

Lanovara's short, dumpy body was in a seated position, with his back resting against a loading dock doorway that was presently minus the door. His hands, resting at his sides, were open with palms up, in kind of a, "Why me?" death pose. I stood about twenty feet from the body and made two more notes before looking up to the portly, middle-aged, uniformed Sergeant who was now standing beside me.

"What've you got, Sergeant?" I asked, not making any attempt to hide my dislike for the man.

"What we got, Lute, is this," the Sergeant said in a drone voice. "A 9-1-1 call from some wino came in at zero-one-fifty-seven this date, saying he had stumbled on a fat guy who was bleeding and dead. First officer on the scene was Harris. He jumps to a snap decision, based on the bullet to the head of Mr. Lanovara, that this is a homicide. So, he calls for the bosses, the tech guys, and all that. Our citizen caller, an ever-popular wino-type, is secured in Harris' car, where I am sure he is challenging the Officer's deodorizer. Questions?"

"Yeah, two of them. First, who's been up to the body so far?"

"No one but Harris. The technicians took their location photos and snapped a couple of shots of the victim from outside the tape. We awaited your timely arrival for the close-in stuff." The Sergeant folded his arms, cocked an eyebrow and asked, "Question number two?"

"Do you always have this cruddy attitude or is it something you save just for me?" I asked the question as I walked away, not bothering to wait for an answer that really didn't matter to me.

Making my way over to Officer Jon Harris, I noted the location of Lanovara's Cadillac, which was parked some twenty or so feet from the body. It appeared Frankie had pulled around the rear of the building and went past the door opening where he was now seated and deceased. Evidently, he had parked the car, exited the vehicle, and walked to the location of his murder. Due to the fact that I doubted that anyone would want to drag the fat blob around after he was dead, it was a fair assumption the head shot had dropped the fat pig on the spot. I carefully moved in to take a closer look at the body. The bullet had entered Lanovara's head just below and behind the right ear, and apparently built up enough force and mass to take out the left side of his skull from just above the left ear to the corner of the left eye. The large, messy hole had leaked out more brains than I had thought Frankie Ten Times had stored in his head. "Always a pleasure to see you, Frankie," I said to the body as I crouched down next to it. After scanning the body one more time I entered a few more lines of notes in the spiral pad.

"Good morning, Lieutenant. Sorry to drag you out so late," Harris said as he extended a formal salute. "Did Sergeant Berkland brief you?"

"Yeah, he gave me the basics. You got the call at 1:57. Some intox found it. You got the intox in your unit. Technicians have gotten some over-all photos. Nothing else. What have you got, Jon?"

The officer smiled at the mention of his name, somewhat impressed, or maybe concerned, that Ace Amato, the supposed hard-hearted homicide commander, even knew his name. Actually, the only reason I remembered the kid's name was because he had screwed up a homicide scene a few months earlier. Harris was first at a scene where a six-year-old girl's body had been found. Out of compassion for the victim, something I can't fault, Harris covered up the body. I chewed the young copper's ear for a full ten minutes about his stupidity. I don't mind compassion, but I won't tolerate someone messing with my crime scene. It was easy enough to end up looking incompetent on these cases. I didn't need cops adding to my problems

"That's about it, Lieutenant," Harris reported. "Except that I kind of looked around inside the place, you know, real careful not to screw anything up. Nothing in there...nothing that I saw anyway! I asked the dispatcher for the bosses and technicians to come down, to notify you, and to see if you wanted anyone else called in. The black Caddy over there belongs to the victim. We ran the plates and they came back to one Francis Anthony Lanovara."

"Nice job." I smiled as I rubbed my gloved hands together in a useless attempt to generate some heat. "I got Paskell and Verno coming in. By the way, who's the intox, and what's he got to say about all this?"

"Yeah, right, Lieutenant. Sorry, forgot all about him," Harris stammered as he tried to sort out whether I was smiling at him because he forgot to include the obviously important facts in his briefing, or if I was smiling because I understood his nervousness. "The intox is John Martin Goreman, 43 years, white, male, no known address. Goreman says he sleeps here, on and off anyway, and was doing so tonight. He was up near the front of the building. He says there's fewer rats up there. Anyway, he hears voices back here in this area. He first thinks he is just hearing things and when he doesn't hear anything more, he rolls over to try to go back to sleep. That's when he hears, 'Crack, crack.'"

"Two shots?"

"Two of them. He's positive. Two shots, Lieutenant."

"Voices talking, or voices arguing?"

"He's not too sure on that, Lute. He says they woke him up, but he doesn't think they were shouting at each other. Anyway, he comes back here, sees the body, and freaks out. He says he ran up to West Avenue to a bar in order to make the call."

I indicated to the young patrol officer to follow me as I moved back to the body. Using a pen, I lifted the left side of Frankie Lanovara's blue, quilted vest, and then the right side. My flashlight ran up and down the fat legs that strained the brown fabric of the dead man's pants. I then worked the flashlight back up the entire length of the body.

"You see a second wound, Jon?"

"No, sir. Sure don't. But he's emphatic, Lieutenant. Two shots."

"When the Medical Examiner's people get here, we'll roll him over and look at his back side. A guy as fat as this character could have the second one stuck in a flab fold, and it wouldn't even bleed externally. The M.E. will strip him down and have to look for it during the autopsy...if it's in there."

The next half hour or so got killed as we waited for the Medical Examiner's ghouls to show up. I checked things out with the crime scene technician as we kicked around a couple of old cases and assorted war stories. Harris had started his report and came up to check a couple of things with me. Having his questions answered, he popped the usual question that young cops asked when they encountered Frankie Ten Times.

"Lieutenant, can you tell me something?" Harris asked. "Why do they call him 'Frankie Ten Times'?"

"In a minute, kid," I said as Detectives James Paskell and Al Verno approached us. "I need to take care of something first."

"Morning, Lieutenant," the two said almost in concert.

"Darn near noon," I snorted. "You two ladies have to catch a bus in order to get down here?"

"It's less than an hour since we got the call, Boss!" Verno pleaded. "Besides, the car is acting up, Lute."

"Save that bull for your wives. I don't want to hear that old, 'car trouble' line. If you guys can't make it to the scene in less time than this, I sure as hell don't need you." Without waiting for a reply I gave them the run-down of the crime. Paskell volunteered to interview the wino-witness and attempt to get an intelligible statement from him.

"Fine," I agreed. "After that, I want one of you doing a neighborhood check for any other witnesses, and the other one in the warehouse looking for the second bullet."

"Ain't much of a neighborhood to find witnesses, boss," Paskell noted.

"Never know what you might find, Jimmy. Start looking," I said without the slightest trace of a smile. "Check all these other warehouses, factories, whatever they were once, and see if you find any other sleeping winos. The other one of you, stay here on the scene. See if you can find the other bullet and any signs of a car coming back here, that is if we haven't trampled whatever tracks that were here. When you get done, meet me back in the office. I got some things to take care of."

Sergeant Berkland stepped up behind the two detectives and said something as he clamped his meaty hands on the shoulders of Verno and Paskell. Then he added, "I don't know how you guys put up with him."

The comment was said just loud enough for me to hear. I tried, but just couldn't fight the urge to respond. Stopping in my tracks, I turned to face the Sergeant, and then began to slowly walk toward him. "They put up with me for three reasons, *Sergeant*. One, they know I'm right. Two, I'm demanding, but I'm fair. And three, I'm not an incompetent boss who's standing around with my finger knuckle deep in my nose while my man does all the work."

Verno, with a short nod of his head, smiled at the red-faced Sergeant and said, "That kind of sums it up for me, Sarge!"

Following my critique, I began telling Harris about how Frankie Lanovara earned his nick name. "He was 10, maybe 12 years old at the time, the way I hear it. His family goes to one of these buffet places, you know, one of these, 'All you Can Eat' restaurants. Little Frankie there, goes up again and again and fills his plate with shrimp, ribs, all the good stuff. The owner of the place goes over and asks old man Lanovara to tell the kid to ease up a little. Mr. Lanovara tells the guy to bug off, and says his kid is a growing boy who needs nourishment. The way the story goes, the old man told Frankie to go up ten times if he wanted to, and, sure enough, Little Frankie did. The little pig filled his plate ten times and ate it all down. Then, having eaten all the guy's profits, as the family is leaving, Frankie goes and pukes it all up by the front door. I tell you, kid, this mope never had any class. Not then, not now."

Before I left the scene, I stepped back into a corner of the building's parking lot and surveyed the entire set up. An old-time detective had taught me the trick some 20 years earlier. His point was, a murder scene is like a fine painting...you have to step back in order to appreciate it. From the position of Frankie Ten Times' car, the present placement of his body, and the lack of a second set of tire prints in the icy snow, I could only guess that Lanovara came to the scene to meet someone who had secreted themselves in or near the loading dock door.

Lanovara may have arrived early, parked his car twenty feet from the doorway and then moved over to the door to await the arrival of his cohort. Maybe he suspected it was a hit and didn't want to be a sitting duck in his car. Maybe he had to take a leak and went over to the building to do it. Probably the killer was already there, concealed in the warehouse, and maybe after the victim showed up, the suspect stepped forward and slammed a round into the head of Mister Ten Times. I let the possible scenarios run through my head for a few minutes and finally decided the answers would not be forth coming until we had the killer. However, one thing was for sure. Frankie was not an accidental victim, like a robbery victim, or a drive-by shooting. No, it wasn't a matter of him being in the wrong place at the right time. This was not a crime of opportunity. No way! This was a planned, cold-blooded killing.

Fifteen minutes later I was letting my car glide by the Sicilian-American Club on the city's east side. I took my time scanning the cars parked on both sides of the street, as well as the small group of men engaged in an animated conversation in front of the gambling joint. I noted, with a smile, that it could be thirty below zero in a blizzard and there would still be a half-dozen of these idiots out on the sidewalk, talking and stomping their feet. From there I drove over to Johnny's Bar on Lake Avenue and then over to the Tutto Bene Restaurant on North Street. At each location it was the same. Normal. Normal. Normal. If Frankie Ten Times was the victim of an approved hit, things were too quiet, too routine, too ordinary. And, if this was an outsider's, unauthorized hit, there was going to be hell to pay!

At 4:55 A.M. Paskell and Verno came into the Violent Crimes Office. In a nutshell, they had turned up very little. The second shot heard by the wino had traveled straight up and lodged in an overhead beam about ten feet above the warehouse floor. It had been recovered and appeared to be a .9mm slug. The hard-packed cinder driveway covered with old, hard-packed, snow and ice gave no readable signs of a car or truck having recently traveled along the side or behind the warehouse. So, maybe our killer was without transportation, or, just maybe he was smart and parked on the street or around the corner before walking to the back of the warehouse to make his meeting.

"Put it together in a report, start a case folder, and grab the tech sheets for the file," I told the two detectives as I pulled on my overcoat. "I'm going to go grab some breakfast and be back for roll call. You guys get some eats or some sleep and then be back in here by ten o'clock."

Three blocks away from Headquarters, I pulled up to an intersection that would be loaded with office workers in just a couple of hours. I stepped into the corner phone booth, dialed a number, and then turned my back to the street, getting into position so I could see a reflection of any movement on the roadway.

The phone at the other end of the call rang twice, and then a partial third before it was answered.

"Yeah?" the voice asked.

"Yo, Fast Eddy there?" I inquired in my best New York hood tone.

"Who's asking?"

"Wadda you care? Is he there?"

"No, he ain't."

"When he comes in, you tell him to get a hold of Artie. Got it? Artie!"

"Artie who?"

"What are you, his mother? You just tell him like I told you." I said in exaggerated annoyance, just before banging the phone down into the cradle.

Getting back into the car, I drove west on Main Street, right on State Street, past the Eastman Kodak Office, past the lights of a small all night diner, and down to Lyell Avenue. Three blocks later I made a U-turn and returned to Sophie's Cafe. There was no sign of traffic yet, but in a half-hour or so, Kodak workers would begin making their predictable, mindless way to their jobs. I parked directly in front of the small restaurant. Sophie's Cafe was the sort of place that caters to blue collar workers who crave a fast, cheap meal with a crowd unimpressed by good manners or highbrow conversation. The place was empty except for the robust owner-cook and her waiter. I nodded a hello to Sophie and, for my effort, received a wide, gap-tooth smile coupled with a seductive wink. As was my habit, I dropped two quarters into the cup on the counter and picked up a morning newspaper. Walking past the eight counter stools on my right, I slid into a booth at the rear of the diner. The position gave me a clear view of the front window and all who passed in front of it.

The smell of coffee and semi-burnt toast told my head what my belly already suspected. It was time for breakfast. I pulled out the sports section and smiled at the sullen waiter approaching me with a coffee pot.

"What brings you out so early, Lieutenant," the thin, young man asked.

"Another deceased citizen, Andy. How you doing?"

"Getting by, Lieutenant, just getting by," Andy replied with a slight shrug of his shoulders.

"The death of a loved one is a difficult thing to absorb," I consoled. "I know you and Danny were together a long time. He was a good man. It's not going to be easy, but I want you to know my prayers are with you."

"Bless you, Lieutenant," the waiter said as he laid a bony hand on my wrist. "You are so thoughtful."

I nodded to the sad man. We had a few seconds of silence, which I broke by ordering the usual, poached eggs on a toasted English muffin, and then, pointing to my cup, I asked the grieving Andy, "Do me a favor, will you? Whenever you go by, just fill it up."

"Don't you worry, Lieutenant. Andy is here to take care of you."

Over the next hour I ate my breakfast and read the paper from start to finish. Getting up, I dropped four bucks and some change on the table and made my way back to the Detective Bureau.

The Public Safety Building—simply referred to as "The Building" or "PSB" by the cops—will never win any architectural awards. It's a cold, gray, concrete-slab, six-story, unimaginative structure that came out of the city's 1950's urban renewal efforts. The PSB houses the Rochester Police Department, Fire Department, and city courts. It's one of three buildings that form an L-shaped combination of city-county criminal justice structures. The other two buildings are home to the Monroe County Sheriff's Department, the county jail, and county courts. To say the buildings are drab would be an understatement. However, the outside of the buildings did much to cover up the true drabness of mis-matched desks and odd assortment of chairs found in the Detective Bureau.

At eight o'clock in the morning Paskell and Verno were already seated at their desks in the Violent Crimes Unit's Squad Room. I was not surprised to see they had not taken advantage of my suggestion that they come in a little later in the morning. Each did his part to brief the squad on the murder of Frank Lanovara. Following the update on our most recent case, each team of detectives then briefed the other members of the unit on the status of their individually assigned rapes, robberies, and homicide cases. Forty-five minutes later I was briefing my boss, Major Charles Novitski, on each of the cases.

I don't care for too many bosses, however, Charlie Novitski is an exception. The guys is probably 15 years older than me in both age and police experience. His full mane of white hair attracts attention from those who meet him for the first time, but it's his savvy for the job that attracts the respect of those who have known him for years.

I have a special liking for the guy. In order to get me my present assignment, Novitski had fought long and hard with the former Chief of Police. Back then, I was considered to be a renegade with a very short fuse that usually exploded into trouble. Novitski assured one and all he needed me for the job, and that he could control me. A year or so later, when I ended up getting into the bottle on a regular basis, it was Novitski who pointed me straight, and then assured I stayed straight. I owed the man a lot. Loyalty was small portion of that debt.

"A hit?" Novitski, the master of short sentences asked about the Lanovara killing.

"Don't know," I answered. "Sure looks like it. One shot to the back of the head, behind the right ear. Nice, neat, quiet. Then again..."

"What?"

"I took a look around at all the joints last night. Everything was too normal. Usually when they whack a guy, things are very quiet. No one's around. But last night, everyone who should have been out was out and about."

"The slug?"

"It's a .9mm. I don't know what kind of condition it's in." I responded.

"Autopsy?" Novitski asked as he jotted a note.

"Later today. The Medical Examiner has two traffic fatalities he is doing first. Lanovara is batting third."

"Let me know what the M.E. comes up with."

"Will do."

I got up and was about to leave when Novitski got up from his chair. He leaned forward, his hands balled into fists, with his knuckles pressed down on the desk top. This was not normal, and I do not like things that are out of the norm.

"Anything else, boss?" I asked cautiously.

"Westfield called me as soon as I got in this morning. He wants a briefing on this Lanovara case today...and every day until it's closed."

"He's the Chief," I shrugged. "He wants to be briefed, you have to brief him. No big deal."

"He wants *you* to brief him, Mike. You personally."

"Me? Why me?"

"Don't know," Novitski said as he moved behind his chair and rested his beefy hands on the back of the piece of furniture. "Do you?"

"I don't have the foggiest notion, Major."

"Is there something going on that I should know about, Mike? Something between you and him? Is he focusing on you real tight because of some new problem?"

"You know the story about me and him, boss. He hates me and I wouldn't give a fat rat's ass for him. Our feelings go way back. You know better than anybody what that's all about."

"I do," Charles Novitski said. Then he paused and looked down at the seat of his chair, as if he would find the words he needed there. "He usually wants nothing to do with you, and he's one for sticking to the chain of command. Now out of the blue, he wants you to go directly to him every single day. It don't make sense to me, Mike."

I thought about mentioning the car that had been following me around lately, and my suspicion that Internal Affairs was tailing me for some reason. I thought about it, but didn't mention it. Paranoid cops are not a good thing to have in one's command. The Major expected his detectives to be sure and confident. He wouldn't feel too comfortable about having one of them, especially a supervisor, seeing ghosts in the background. Instead of mentioning the possible tail, I offered, "Okay. Every morning I brief you just like usual and then I go up and brief him. It don't bother me."

"Keep me close on this one, Mike. I know you always do, but on this one, keep me closer than usual. I want to know everything as soon as you know it. Everything!"

"No problem, Major. You got it." The unspoken order was clear. Novitski wanted to be briefed before the Chief got briefed...and be briefed more thoroughly.

Leaving the Bureau Commander, I took the elevator up two flights and sought out the office of Chief of Police Benjamin Westfield. After being kept waiting in the Chief's reception area for over a half hour, I was admitted into the large inner office.

While the city haggled over every pay raise the cops got, they had no problem giving each new Chief of Police a generous allotment to decorate his office. Looking around the place, I figured Westfield must have pocketed most of the money. The large office was sparse on furniture but bloated on books, magazines, and paper work. The man's desk was loaded with neat stacks of papers, folders, and assorted pads. The bookcase behind him was in precise order, with the shorter books near the left side of the shelves. The office was neat, but that's the most that could be said for it.

I walked the 10 paces from the door to his desk, offered a half-hearted salute, and sat down in one of the three straight-back chairs available to me. Chief Westfield didn't bother to give me the courtesy of looking up from his morning mail as I jumped into the briefing. I didn't bother to give him the courtesy of inviting me to start.

When I was done with the briefing in less than a minute, Westfield finally looked at me with an expressionless face. While he stared, he tapped the eraser end of his pencil on the desk pad in front of him in a steady, annoying, cadence. I kept a slight grin on my face as we looked at each other. I don't know what he saw, but I was focused on his expensive suit, starched white shirt, and silk tie. The fact that Ben Westfield had several inches on my 5 foot, 10 inch frame was not lost in our sitting positions. It bothered me that he was looking down at me—literally and figuratively—but I tried not to show it.

Finally, after a full thirty seconds of staring, and perhaps realizing he wasn't going to get a conversation starter from me, Westfield stated flatly, "This is a mob hit, you know."

"Could very well be, sir," I allowed.

"Could be?" Westfield asked in a half-laugh. "It sure as hell *is*!"

"Is that all, Chief?" I inquired instead of getting into a verbal battle of wits with this man who I believed was only half-equipped for such a fight.

"That's all for now, Lieutenant. You be up here tomorrow at 9:00 A.M. sharp, or sooner if something comes up. I want to be kept up on this, post haste. You understand? The mayor doesn't want any problems like this surfacing at this point in time."

"Understood, sir," I said with an accompanying salute that was too snappy, too exact, too sardonic...and hoped the guy was sharp enough to know it. If he did perceive my attitude, he didn't let on.

I headed back to the Detective Bureau wondering what that was all about. Once I got into the Chief's office, the entire thing, with dramatic pauses and all, took less than three minutes. So, what was the big deal in having me go up there? Was the message one that the Mayor was not too happy, or was I being told that Westfield was watching me? I played with my thoughts as the elevator descended the two floors, but as I stepped off at the Detective Bureau, I set the puzzle solving aside and got back to the business at hand.

Al Verno gave me the news as I got off the elevator at the Detective Bureau. "The Medical Examiner just called. They got something weird."

"They do the autopsy already? I thought our guy was coming up third in this morning's line-up?"

"The ghouls were doing a preliminary check of the body before they cut him," Verno said as he gave me a you-ain't-gonna-believe-this gesture with his hands up beside his shoulders in a surrendering position. "They found a Ten of Spades in Lanovara's mouth!"

"A what?"

"A playing card. The Ten of Spades, you know, from a deck of cards."

If I didn't know it before, I knew it right then. This case was about more than mob guys and vendettas. The guy who did this killing wasn't in it for the money or the organizational rewards that came from filling a contract.

This was the worst type of murderer cops will face. The guy who tapped Frankie Lanovara was in it for fun!

CHAPTER THREE

THE MOB

The news of the playing card and the following autopsy, made it necessary for me to make two more morning trips to see Novitski. After each one, I headed up to the Chief's office. Each time I had to meet with Westfield, I slipped into my suit coat and made sure I appeared to be the Chief's idea of what a detective should look like. The guy didn't have the foggiest notion about what a detective did, but he sure had a lot of opinions about their dress code and behavior. I personally saw no harm in walking around the cop shop in rolled-up sleeves and an open collar. However, that was just another thing about which the Chief of Police and I disagreed.

The fact that Frankie Ten Times' killer had the motivation and the patience to stuff a playing card into the fat man's mouth before leaving him seemed to be wasted on the Chief. It was futile to try to convince the dapper man that it was not too likely the mob would take such an action on a hit. I wondered what had suddenly made him an authority on homicides. After all, he hadn't spent more than five years on the streets in his entire career, and if the truth be known, crime fighting was not his strong suit!

Half a lifetime ago, Benjamin Westfield and I had been classmates at the old Police Academy on Scottsville Road. The guy was a bookworm who was more comfortable arguing law cases than he was down in the gym with the rest of the class. For our first assignment, both of us went to work the midnight shift in the Downtown Section. Westfield, who even then was predicting he would make Chief's rank someday, made few friends among the veteran cops.

While I moved on to the Tactical Unit, Street Crimes Unit, and assorted patrol assignments in the city's gut, Westfield worked his way into a three-piece suit job up in Research and Development. After making Sergeant, he went to Internal Affairs, and later, as a Lieutenant, he bounced over to the Training Section. Eventually, he made it back to Research and Development. When he received his Captain's bars, Westfield found himself back in patrol, commanding a precinct on the city's east side. He was there a year before he was rescued by a new Chief of Police, and with little surprise to one and all, became Deputy Chief Westfield.

All of this was running through my mind as I waited, for the third time in one day, to see the Chief. Mingled with those thoughts were concerns about why Westfield, out of the blue, recently became so interested in homicides. When I finally got in to see him, he showed a little of his hand.

"When I spoke to Ed Delany about this case this morning," Ben Westfield said as he sat erect in his chair with his arms folded across his chest, "he clearly hinted to me that this was a mob thing. Those guys have their stuff together over there, Lieutenant."

"Chief, with all due respect to our brothers in the world-famous FBI, Ed Delany, and the rest of those clowns couldn't find their back pocket with both hands. This thing looks like the mob on the surface, but to anyone who knows what they're doing, and that just about eliminates the FBI, it's real iffy this killing is a hit." Then I threw in, "And, what does, 'he clearly hinted' mean?"

"I personally think the Mafia goons are messing with us, Lieutenant!" Westfield said as he slapped his manicured hand on the desk. "They're trying to throw us off, or, as Delany sees it, they're sending a sign, a message, that this is over a gambling matter." He hesitated for a second, gave another of his trademark half-laughs and added, "Do I have to do your job for you? This is mob all the way! I know it, the FBI knows it, even the Mayor knows it. Everyone knows it, but you, Lieutenant."

"Right, sir," I conceded rather than wasting my time with this professional desk rider. "I'll pursue that line of investigation. Everybody who wasn't down at the scene freezing their butt and dealing with this thing first-hand knows it's a mob hit. Right. I'll make it a mob hit because you, the mayor, and those other jerks at the Federal Building think it's a Mafioso thing. I'll start pulling in all the mob guys. Okay?"

Naturally, the conversation went down hill from there, and subsequently ended on somewhat of a sour note with Westfield reminding me I was coming real close to losing thirty days pay. Hey, why not? I thought. We're so short on personnel now, what's one less detective? However, I remained silent on the subject.

By one o'clock in the afternoon I had calmed down enough to go through the complete autopsy report. Death was caused by a single shot to the head. That was no news bulletin! The slug was a .9mm, in decent but not great condition, that could be matched if we found the murder weapon. The weapon was almost in direct contact with Frankie's head when the round was fired, and the death was instantaneous. There were no other signs of violence. Out of curiosity I looked at the box listing the body's weight and found that Frankie Ten Times weighed in at 368 pounds.

Once again I made the Novitski-Westfield tour to let them know that our victim did, indeed, die from a bullet to the head.

It was well past four in the afternoon when my private line rang.

"You called?" the voice in my receiver asked.

"About twelve hours ago," I answered with just a tinge of sarcasm.

"I couldn't get away," Fast Eddy said in his nonchalant manner.

"We have to talk."

"It's gonna have to be later tonight."

"No way," I said through clenched teeth. I was close to the mouthpiece of the phone, talking quietly so others could not hear, but my tone was firm enough so my caller would be sure to get the message.

"Forget about it!" Eddy Cavaluso stated flatly. "It's gonna have to wait. There's a meeting later. We should get together after the meeting."

"Nine tonight," I said after absorbing the meaning of his last bit of information.

"Make it later."

"Later? How much later?"

"Honest, I ain't busting your chops. I'll know more later, after 10, maybe 11 o'clock tonight."

"Okay," I gave in again, but hated allowing my informant to control the meeting. At least, I was going to set the location. "Make it for one in the morning. In the box."

"One o'clock in the box," he repeated. The phone went dead.

After hanging up the phone, I took care of some of the administrative work that had been cluttering my desk. Then I started to wrestle with the budget modifications I was suppose to have been working on since January.

Before I knew it, the Detective Bureau was empty and night was overtaking the city. I got up from the desk, stretched, and was trying to decide how to best kill the next six hours before the meet with Fast Eddy. Sure, I could get back to the reports piling up on my desk, the personnel evaluations, the budget, or a hundred other bureaucratic odds and ends. Or, I could simply go home and catch the Knicks game I taped last week and still hadn't seen. The Knicks option was winning the minor mental tug of war when Major Novitski walked in, poured himself a cup of stale coffee from the hot plate next to the file cabinets, sat down opposite me, and propped his heels up on the desk.

"So, how's it going?" he asked in a way that suggested he didn't really expect a response.

"This is going to be a rough one, Major," I commented.

I doubt he even heard my answer. The stout, grandfatherly-looking, command officer looked at the tips of his shoes and said, "I got a problem, Mike."

"Can I help?" I asked, and as I spoke the words I knew the use of my first name meant this was going to be a private, man-to-man conversation, rather than a discussion on police matters.

"I hope so," he said. He didn't look away from his shoes. "My problem is you."

Instead of responding, I got up and topped off my already three-quarter filled cup with the hours old coffee that tasted like burnt asphalt. I needed the few seconds to think. My only comeback was a rhetorical question. "Me?" I asked with a little throat chuckle. "You mean me and the thing with Westfield, right boss?"

"You, Mike. You! You're pissing off everyone on the department. You have a chip on your shoulder that's a yard wide and weighs a ton. It's been making problems for you right along, and now, well now it's making problems for me, son."

It was unusual, not rare, just unusual, that Novitski would call me, "son." We had had these heart-to-heart chats before, and a few times they took on a father and son air. The old feelings of fear rose in the pit of my stomach as I realized that I had in some way failed this man. "Pissed off who, Major? The Chief? He's always upset with me."

"The Sergeant at the scene last night complained to his Captain about you calling him incompetent in front of his men. The crime scene technicians said you went in making demands and barking orders at them without so much as a, 'how do you do.' Yeah, and the Chief, too. You're angry, Mike, very angry," he commented and then paused. I was speechless, so he continued. "I know under that anger there's a lot of pain, a lot of frustration, but you have to learn to deal with it, Mike. Deal with it and control it."

"I'm just, you know, going through some, some stuff right now, Major. I'll make it right. I'll talk to these guys and apologize. I don't want any problems...for you or for me. I'll handle it."

"It's not just last night, or those few guys, Mike. You've been this way since before you and Diane split up. I'm no shrink, but I'm telling you, you have to get past this, get over it. The world isn't out to screw you, so quit acting like it! You made some choices in your life, and now they're coming home to roost. You have to take accountability for what you decided to do with your life. They were your choices, and right or wrong, good or bad, you got to deal with them. You decided to allow this job to take precedence over every other thing, so you can't go around blaming everybody else because you don't have anything else in your life but this job." He paused long enough for the points to sink in. Then he went for the heart. "You're drinking like a fish again and you look like hell. You have to pull yourself together, son, or I'm going to have to take some action that I really don't want to take."

As a grown man at forty-six years of age, I felt like a scolded child. Sure, I knew that was not Novitski's intent, but it did little to calm my insides. We sat in silence for a minute as I reached into my bottom drawer and pulled out a bottle of Sambuca. Both of us used the time of silence to take a couple of swallows of the strong, stale coffee now laced with the sweet, anise liquor.

"If it's about the guys in here, boss, I had to chew out Paskell and Verno last night for taking their sweet time in getting to the scene. If this thing is about me and the Chief, well, I don't know what to say. I've tried to put that thing to bed more than a few times, and, well...now we don't even pretend to get along."

"It's not about the guys in here, Mike. The detectives working for you would march through a brick wall just to follow you into the fires of hell."

"Then, it's the Chief," I reasoned.

"Listen to me, Mike, damn it!" Novitski said as he slid his feet off my desk and slammed them on the floor. "Yes, sure, part of it is the Chief. He had my rear end for a snack this afternoon. He wants you out of here on the express train. You're sarcastic and insubordinate with him. But don't worry about him. I can handle Westfield. It's you, Mike!" The white-haired man leaned forward with his massive forearms on my desk, and said, "I brought you up here to do this job because you're bright and dedicated as all get out. I knew you could get the job done. You're as loyal as a hound dog and twice as tenacious. I liked you then because you had the intestinal fortitude to take charge, to walk into a massive scene of confusion and put it in order. Back then you were a good boss, a natural leader. But now, now you're consumed with this anger, this hate, this frustration in you. It's making you mean and nasty toward everyone, even yourself...*especially* yourself!"

"What do you want me to do, Major. Just tell me, and I'll do it," I surrendered.

"Mike, I'm going to tell you something, and I know you well enough to trust that it stays right here," he said as he looked me in the eye and waited for the nod he didn't request, but both of us knew was needed in conversations such as this. "I've been through this, Mike," he confessed. "Back a few years ago, maybe even ten years ago, when I was sitting right where you are, me and Ruth split up for awhile. It was probably the same thing that did it to you and Diane. I lived and breathed the job. I wasn't home nights, weekends, holidays. The phone rang and I was off to go see another stinking, rotting body. I lived with the sights, smells, and sounds of death, just like you do now. And then, when I got home, she asked what I had been doing. I always told her like we all do, 'Nothing.' When she finally had enough of it and moved out, I had to do some soul searching, and I had to make some decisions, some choices."

"Such as?" I asked.

"Such as do I choose the job, or do I choose her. Luckily, we got back to talking and we both opened up a little, and well, here I am. But the thing is, son, I had to come to grips with the fact that the job demands a lot out of us. But damn it all, we still have choices to make, and sometimes we pour of ourselves into this job and give it more than it expects out of us." Novitski stopped long enough to drain his cup. Standing up he said, "You just have to realize you made a choice to give this job more than you gave your wife. That's not good, nor is it bad. It's just a choice. You have to recognize it, and move on, Mike. You can't take out on everyone else what you, yourself chose."

"I guess I chose the job, huh, Major?"

"I guess you did, Lieutenant." He nodded with a smile.

"And you? You chose Ruth?" I smiled back.

"I chose the job, Lieutenant. I also chose the job. It just worked out differently, that's all."

Novitski gave me a wave, and moved down the hall toward the elevators. I leaned back in my chair, put my feet up on the desk, and then reached out to set my desk alarm for midnight. As I tried to take a nap before meeting Fast Eddy, my mind replayed Novitski's conversation. My feelings ran from remorse to anger. The remorse came on because my big mouth had made it necessary that he have that talk with me. The anger came from....well, it was just there. Finally I gave up on the nap idea and headed for a bar over on Thurston Road that would provide my evening meal and a couple of beers to wash it down.

As I aimed the car toward the fringes of Rochester's downtown, my mind drifted between my talk with the Major and the conversation I was about to have with Eddy Cavaluso. I decided it was best to keep my mind on the business at hand, rather than business already transpired.

The Mafia, Cosa Nostra, Mob, Organized Crime, whatever you want to call them, and cops have a lot in common. Therefore, I don't consider it strange that guys from my old neighborhood tended to end up in one of the two organizations. Members of both groups are almost Peter Pan-like in their reluctance to grow up. As adults, we both still enjoy the cops and robbers games of our young years, we both use nicknames, and both of us still cling passionately to being a part of something...part of our respective gangs. In the privacy of my mind I acknowledge these similarities, and hated the fact that they are true!

On the other hand, the mob represented everything my old man had fought against. It was because of all the Italian names in the newspapers that my father had a hard time getting his name on the payroll of one of the city's better companies. The Mafia was filled with the dagos and wops with whom the rest of us were generically and automatically included by the general public.

I grew up with the mob. Tootie's, the corner grocery store, was a numbers' bank. Old man Sinestra, our neighbor, was rumored to have killed over a dozen men in his younger years. Tiny Tony Pentora, my best buddy in school, was now doing life in Attica for a hit he did for the mob. Danny Martin, a kid I tried to recruit for the Department, was a degenerate wannabe that hung around the mob guys like a dog following a bitch in heat. As a teen-ager, I have to admit, I was much more attracted to the glamour of the mob than I was to the uniform of a cop.

After Viet Nam my old man urged me to seek a civil service job rather than return to the streets. The Great Depression remained a very strong reality rooted in his mind. He believed the security of a civil service job was the only guarantee to keep his son from suffering from the next economic depression, which by the way, surely was just around the corner. Truth be known, I was going to be a fireman. I figured if you could pull down ten grand a year for playing with a fire hose one day of the week, while watching

TV the rest of the week, it couldn't be too bad of a life. Anyway, I took the police and fire exams the same week. Then, the police department called me first, so, here I am.

I thought about these things as I drove to meet a man my father would have instinctively liked as a person, but would just as instinctively hated him for what he was.

My relationship with Eddy Cavaluso goes back over 20 years. Before I even began walking a beat, Eddy already had reputation for being an adventurous thief. In fact, his nickname, Fast Eddy, was earned based on his quickness and stealth in stealing large items out from under the nose of the rightful owner. The particular event that earned him his moniker came from an incident back during the mid-1950's, in which Eddy was able to steal about 30 quality paintings from the walls of Saint Mary's Hospital. The boosting was done, in typical Fast Eddy fashion, in broad daylight, with staff, administrators, and patients as witnesses. Cavaluso simply walked into the hospital, laid out some tarps and paint cans - which were also stolen - and announced he was there to paint the hallways. The paintings were removed from the walls and were never seen again. Fast Eddy Cavaluso had struck!

One day, back when I was still pushing a patrol car around, I managed to grab the thief with a couple of hundred record albums he had just boosted out of a record store's warehouse. It was a less-than-legal bust. The fact of the matter was I really couldn't prove, beyond my own common sense, the albums were really stolen. The Sergeant made me turn Eddy loose. However, having been blessed with a gift of gab, I convinced Eddy I was the one who was turning him loose. After that, we would run into one another now and then. Cavaluso had, by then, become a made soldier in the local mob and was moving up the ladder in his chosen field of endeavor. Eddy would usually slip me a piece of information about so-and-so doing whatever. It was obvious that Eddy Cavaluso's information was always about one of his competitors and never about any of his associates. That didn't matter. He was using me, but regardless, the information was usually pretty solid and it was helping my career along nicely. As is the case in most cop-informant relationships, Eddy and I were using each other...and both of us were prospering.

As I rose in the Department, Eddy was moving up in his organization. He began a little gambling venture that developed into a formidable enterprise for him and the local mob. From what I hear, a couple of years later he was officially given his own crew in *La Cosa Nostra*. Just as things were going good for the hood, Fast Eddy Cavaluso got busted for doing a hit on a Buffalo mobster. I'm sure it wasn't his first or last hit, but it was the only one which landed him in court. After being found guilty of Manslaughter, he did a stint in Attica. Cavaluso completed about six years of his 25-year sentence, and then was back on the streets of Rochester, right back in the middle of action.

Seven or eight years ago, a cousin of Eddy's got into a dope deal with the son of a city councilman. The long and short of it is that Eddy's cousin threw a couple of shots around and ended up wounding the councilman's kid When the shooter took off, a lot of cops were thrown into the case. After a pretty good alibi was built for the suspect, Eddy talked his younger relative into surrendering. He then called me to go with him and pick up the kid. He told me I was the only cop he trusted to arrest his cousin and deliver him to court without a beating. Naturally, the bust earned me the thanks of the councilman, and my career took a little boost. After that, from time to time I would call Cavaluso and we would get together for a little chit-chat about things that were going on around town. The rules we lived by were simple. I would not give him any inside information about the Department's operations, and he would not talk about anyone who was a friend or associate.

I guess, in the true sense of the word, Fast Eddy wasn't a real *Informant,* but really more of a source for background information. After he gave me his cousin, Eddy would never mention any names. He would simply give me a sense of direction. You know, kind of tell me if I was barking up the right or the wrong tree.

It was about quarter past midnight when I made my way from the bar to meet my friendly adversary. I was not too happy to see the city being treated to another snow flurry. A couple of inches of the white stuff had already blanketed the streets, and the weatherman on the radio was predicting another couple of inches by the time our seldom-seen sun rose.

Because both Eddy and I knew our respective organizations would not approve of our relationship, we took precautions to have our meetings in some out-of-the-way place where we weren't likely to be spotted. I was 45 minutes early for the rendezvous, but I liked being early and having the opportunity to check things out before going into a meeting such as this. I cruised a few blocks of State Street, Brown Street, and Plymouth Avenue. On the last swing up State Street, I eased the car through Kodak's parking lot which was directly across the street from our meeting site. There were five cars and a pickup truck in the lot that was made to hold a couple of hundred cars. Each of the vehicles was covered with the fresh layer of snow. I could only assume the vehicles belonged to the security guards or to workers who couldn't get them started after completing their shift. Exiting the parking lot, I drove directly across the street and entered the six-level parking ramp that serviced area businesses, as well as the summer crowds that filled Frontier Stadium during the Rochester Red Wing baseball season. Checking each level, I made my way up to the sixth floor, then back down to the third level. I drove around the third level and was pleased to see it was void of any vehicles or life forms.

After backing the car into a slot against the west wall, I got out of the car and checked the stair wells on both ends of the parking garage. Confident there was no one around to interrupt or observe the clandestine meeting, I lit a cigarette and looked out at Kodak's main office building. My thoughts drifted to the workers who, in a few hours, would fill the empty parking lot across the street. I could never live their lives. It would drive me stock-raving mad to have to face the same setting, the same filing cabinets, the same routine, the same people, day after day. At least the cop job, with all of its obvious drawbacks, provided a break from the mundane. However, in all truth, I had to admit our jobs weren't all that dissimilar. The "Dackers", as they were referred to by cops, had their politics and their Ben Westfields. I wondered how many of them were alcoholics and divorced because of their job, and reasoned there were probably more than just a few. I finally settled on the fact that the only real difference between me and them was that they made a product, something tangible, and I made nothing...not even a difference.

It was about five minutes after one and three cigarettes later when Eddy Cavaluso's blue Lincoln pulled into the ramp. As he came up the ramp from the second level I flashed my parking lights. His car slipped by mine, went up a couple of more floors and then returned to pull in silently next to mine.

He swung his legs out of the car and planted them firmly on the ground. Then, using his arms, with one pressing on the back of the seat and one gripping the door frame, he pushed and pulled his large body our of the car.

"*Come sta, amico?*" he asked as he stood upright with some noticeable difficulty.

"Not too bad, Eddy," I responded, offering him my hand. "*E tu?*"

"Other than this damn arthritis, can't complain, I guess."

I opened my third pack of cigarettes of the day and offered him one. He refused it with a wave of his massive hand. "Forget about it! Those things are gonna kill you!"

I lit the cigarette, took a long drag, and exhaled as I looked out at the parking lot below us. "You know why I had to see you?" I asked.

"Sure. This Lanovara thing," Eddy said with a shrug of his shoulders.

"I don't want to put you on a spot here, Eddy, but, I got to have some way to move on this thing. You know what I mean?"

Eddy pulled his collar tight around his throat to protect himself from the wind that was whipping around the ramp garage. "Don't even bother asking, Mike. It wasn't our thing," he said flatly. His customary, "Forget about it," was added for emphasis

"What makes you so sure?" I asked as I turned to face him.

"The meeting I told you about, you know, on the phone today?"

"Yeah."

"Well, it was with the Old Man. He's up in arms over this thing! Big time pissed!"

The "Old Man" he referred to was Vincent Ruggeri, Rochester's answer to the Godfather. I remained silent, deciding to let him tell me what he knew in his own way, at his own speed.

"Mike, you know the rules as well as I do. You don't hit a made guy without permission. Forget about it! The Old Man is on fire. He says no one came to him for permission. He gave orders that all of us gotta get off our duffs and find out if one of our people did it. If someone did, there is gonna be another hit. He wants whoever whacked Frankie to be whacked now. And I do mean, now!"

"Lanovara was made? When?"

"Two, maybe three years ago. His uncle, you know, Petie Fisheyes, pushed the kid along and called in some favors. The Old Man authorized making Frankie and he grabbed a lot of heat about it, you know, from us older guys. Frankie was a trouble guy and we all knew it. We all told the Old Man the kid was trouble, that he was off the deep end. We all knew the kid was gonna do some stupid stuff and pull us in with him."

We both stood silent for a minute, each one trying to figure out his next move. I thought about popping in a question or two, but decided against it. Fast Eddy was trying to decide if he was saying too much. I decided to let the silence do its own thing.

Finally, he continued. "The Old Man figures one of us hit Lanovara, or had someone do it. He thinks maybe someone's trying to send him a message, and naturally, he considers it a slap in the face!"

I decided to show some good faith and give up a little information in order to get more back. "I'm not all that sure it's a hit, Eddy," I confided. "On the surface it looks like it, but there are some things, things I can't go into, that make me think otherwise. But, let me ask you this," I proposed, and allowed for a long pause. "Was Frankie in any dispute over gambling? You know, was he trying to muscle in on someone's action? Maybe running a game in somebody's backyard?"

I watched Eddy's lips press together in thought as he processed perhaps a thousand thoughts and filtered out what not to say, what to say, and how to say it. I suppose he was also trying to give meaning to my question.

"Gambling? Sure he gambled. But was he running a game? Forget about it. The kid's business was collecting on bad debts," Eddy said in a tone that accused me of being stupid for even asking the question. "But no, he wasn't doing any action himself. Not that I know of, anyway."

"Any reason a guy would kill him and leave some dice on him?" I asked trying to prompt him, but not wanting to give up too much information.

"Dice?"

"Dice."

"Forget about it. Don't make no sense to me."

I looked back over the parking lot and caught a flicker, just a quick shot of light, from the pickup truck parked in the Kodak lot about three hundred feet from us. I counted the cars again, and now there were five cars and two pickup trucks in the lot. Did I miss something when I passed through the lot? There was no sign of life around any of the vehicles when I rode around before the meet. But now...? I turned my left side to the parking lot, but kept myself in a position to watch the pickup truck without the occupant or Eddy sensing I was watching it.

"You ain't being straight with me, Mike," Eddy was saying as I tried to concentrate on the truck. "What's this you're trying to tell me about this dice thing? You ain't being up front with me, my friend."

"Fact is, Eddy," I stalled, trying to think of what to say without angering the man. "There was some gambling stuff, I can't say what, found around Frankie. I really don't know if it was his or if the killer left it as a message," I lied.

"Look, all I know is that Frankie Lanovara was a loose cannon. All of youse guys would have loved to see him dead and probably 90 percent of our guys would have loved to oblige youse. But, long and short of it, if we did him, it was not an authorized hit."

There it was again! A reflection of light inside the cab of the pickup. I turned and leaned my elbows on the railing of the garage after I lit a fresh cigarette. As I blew out a plume of cigarette smoke, I tried to focus my almost 50-year-old eyes on the truck. It was too dark, and too far away to see if there was someone in the truck, but there sure was something moving around inside that truck. Also, due to the lack of snow on the truck, along with the presence of the tracks leading up to it, it was obvious the vehicle had moved into place after I had made my sweep of the lot.

"Well, look, Eddy," I offered casually. "You know I'm going to appreciate anything you can give me on this thing. If it was one of your people and you can help me with the bust, I would appreciate it."

"Hey, Mike, if I hear anything, and I can do it, you're gonna hear about it. But you know, heads up going into this, if it was a friend of ours, well then, forget about it. You're on your own. If the guy that done it ain't one of ours, then you can have it. If he is one of ours, you're gonna have a fresh case to worry about."

"Fair enough," I said as I removed my glove and offered the big man my hand. I stood there watching the parking lot as Fast Eddy made his way to his car, slid into it, and started to glide down the ramp. I looked down as the Lincoln turned left onto the street and waited to see if the pickup truck moved. It didn't. After a minute I moved away from the railing and then crept back to it in a crouch. The truck remained motionless as I watched it for two more freezing minutes. Keeping low, I went back to my vehicle, started it, and let it move slowly down the ramp without turning on the car's lights.

As I exited the garage I hit my headlights and almost instantly saw the truck come to life. It lurched forward and began to turn toward the far side of the parking lot. Gunning the motor of the lazy cop car, I entered the parking lot just as the truck rolled onto the side street and turned west, toward Frontier Stadium. The truck's tail lights went around the corner onto Plymouth Avenue, and at the same time I went into a 360 degree turn on the ice and slid into an eight-foot snow bank. By the time I straightened the car out and made it to the side street, the pickup was nowhere in sight.

I cruised the side streets for a half hour looking for the pickup truck. With no sign of the phantom vehicle, I pointed the cop car towards home. My mind tossed around a couple of hundred thoughts about the night's events. Over a few shots of Southern Comfort and a TV dinner, I finally settled on three basic scenarios regarding the truck. My wishful thinking side said it could have been a couple of kids or some adults having an affair and using the parking lot as a cheap motel. However, my more pragmatic self tossed the idea. If it was just lovers in the truck, then why did they find it necessary to leave so quickly when I rolled out of the parking ramp? And, why wasn't the truck's motor running in this thirteen degree, freezing-your-butt-off night? The second choice was that it was the feds, or my own, dearly beloved Internal Affairs, keeping tabs on me. If it was the feds, it wasn't any big deal, because most of those pretend cops couldn't find their way out of a phone booth. After all, it was a common belief among local cops that FBI really stood for Famous But Inept. Internal affairs was another matter. Westfield had a long-standing dislike for me that went back a decade or so, and he wouldn't be all that shy about using the cop spies to put my soul in a jam. The third choice gave me some grief. The mob. What if it was the mob tracking Fast Eddy and they saw him meeting with me in a cold, empty, ramp garage late at night? They weren't much brighter than the feds, but then again, they needed a lot less proof in order to find someone guilty...and execute him.

I dragged myself out of bed around seven in the morning, showered, and got ready for another day of fun and games. It was one of those days when it was good to be a bachelor again. The towel was laying in a heap on the bathroom floor, my clothes from the day before laid spread on and around the unmade bed, and there were two days of dishes in the sink. Diane would go nuts if she saw the place. I guess my sloppy living habits was one of the reasons, one of the very minor ones, we were no longer together.

The Detective Bureau floor was coming alive with early morning chatter, but I only stopped long enough to grab a cup of coffee before I headed down the tiled hallway to Major Novitski's office. The best plan I could come up with all night was to provide cover for both me and Eddy Cavaluso. It wasn't a great plan, but it was the only one I had. I could lose my job for meeting with a known member of the Mafia. Eddy, could lose his life for meeting with a cop. I wasn't about to let either happen.

"Morning, boss," I said in an upscale way to Novitski as I literally ran into him at the coffee pot located in the reception area of his office. I knew our conversation of the night before would not come up today. In fact, it would never be mentioned again by either one of us.

"Back at you, Lieutenant," he said in his usual, less than cheerful manner.

He motioned to the pot, offering me a cup, but I raised the already full one I had grabbed in my pass through the Detective Bureau floor and signaled that I was all set. Our silent conversation over, he turned toward his office, and I followed him. Funny, I thought to myself, I just talked to this man last night, and I see him almost every day of my life, but suddenly he looks so old! His shoulders were beginning to droop slightly, but noticeably, and his walk was less than what one would call "perky". As he slid behind his desk, and sat in his chair with an audible, "Ahhh," it dawned on me, he even sounded old.

"News?" he asked.

"Nothing much newsworthy," I responded. "More of an update."

"Yes?"

"I don't think we have a mob whack, Major."

"And, you base that on...?"

"I had a talk last night with a guy, a mob guy, an informant, and he says they're as baffled as we are. Vincent Ruggeri is, as my guy reports it, up in arms about it. The CI also says if it was a hit, it was not an authorized one. He says Lanovara was a made guy and, according to the Old Man, no one had permission to take him out."

"And this CI, this confidential informant of yours, do we know him?"

"If I was to say his name, you would."

"But you're not saying it, I gather, hey, Lieutenant?"

"I can't do that, Major. All I can say is that he's right up near the top and I've had this guy in my pocket for a number of years. He's reliable. One hundred percent."

"Are we paying this confidential informant or yours?"

"No way, boss. We couldn't pay this guy enough. He's pulling down in a week what our entire CI budget is for the year. So, seeing how I don't funnel him any Department cash, I never registered him."

"But you will report the meeting, right?" Novitski asked, reassuring himself he was not going to be left holding this bag.

"The report is on your desk now, Major," I lied and offered an exaggerated wink.

"But so much paperwork gets laid here, I lose half of it," he lied back.

"That's not a bad thing," I noted with a big smile.

Our stories now straight, and more importantly, our collective butts covered, Novitski had me assure him I would brief the Chief post-haste. With a quick nod and grimace, I assured him I was on the way.

I made my way to Chief Westfield's Office, and as usual, was kept waiting for the customary forty-five, fifty minutes. I passed the time talking basketball with Sergeant Pete Polsen, Westfield's aid. Pete and I had worked together in the old Unit A Downtown Patrol District, back when I was rookie and he was barely out of the same status. He had been an outstanding street cop in his day, but one too many bloody bodies, along with one too many close calls, had taken their toll on the man. He reluctantly conceded to his wife that he would ride out his last couple of years in a safer environment than the streets.

"You and the man are getting awful close these days," he said with a sideways nod to the Chief's door.

"Yeah, Pete. It kind of starts the day off right. You know, a good, strong, cup of coffee, a good dump, and a heart-to-heart chat with Chief Whimpfield," I answered with a smile and short punch to his right arm.

"Yeah, right! I heard you two laughing and giggling yesterday when you were up here for one of those friendly little chats."

We both laughed, and went right back to a mid-sentence conversation about the Knicks as soon as the door to the inner-sanctum opened.

"Lieutenant, I believe the Chief is free to see you now," Pete said in his most impressive, Keeper of the Gate voice.

I stepped into Westfield's office and took a seat without an invitation to do so. These daily briefings were taking on their own routine. The Department liked routine and tried to build it into as much as it possibly could. Due to our newly established routine, I knew full well I would be kept waiting for another four or five minutes while the Chief played his role and flipped through reports and mail without looking up or acknowledging my presence. I picked up a Time Magazine from the table next to my chair, and began flipping through it until I heard my master's voice asking, "You have something, Lieutenant?"

"Nothing really new in the investigation, Chief. We really don't know anything more than we did yesterday." I paused, looked back at the magazine and pretended to read one more sentence, before closing it, and looked back at him. "However, I took your advice about the possible mob connection, and..."

"A very good possibility," Westfield interjected.

"And," I continued, as if his rude interruption had not really occurred, "reached out for a mob guy I know. I met with him last night. From what he tells me, they are totally surprised by this Lanovara killing."

"And you believe him?"

"Yes, sir, I do. He's never been bad with information before. He tells me the Old Man is about as upset as he can be about the hit, and went into orbit over it, saying if it was a hit, it wasn't an approved hit."

"Old man?" he asked.

"Ruggeri. Vincent Ruggeri, the local mob's chief," I responded somewhat dismayed that our own Chief of Police had no idea the city's mob boss was commonly referred to by one and all as "the Old Man".

Westfield leaned back in his chair and laced his fingers together over his chest as he looked at me with a wry grin. After a full minute he asked, "Who is this goombah friend of yours, Lieutenant?"

"Goombah? Was that, 'Goombah'?" I asked as I held my finger tips to my right ear. "I don't understand the term, 'Goombah', Chief. Is that some type of modern police acronym, or just some type of ethnic slur?" I said it, and I enjoyed saying it, but I instantly regretted it as my mind reminded me of my talk with the Major.

"Don't you get wise ass with me, Lieutenant!" Westfield snarled as he sat upright and slammed both hands on his desk.

"Sorry, sir," I said as earnestly as possible.

After ten seconds of glaring he leaned back and assumed his original pose. With a short nod and a thin smile he said, "Com-pad-re is a legitimate I-talian term. A word of respect I believe. Excuse me if, due to my long-time American heritage, I mispronounced a word of your language."

"My language is English, Chief. Maybe that's why I didn't understand you." Damn it! There I go again! Without waiting for the long-time American to get in a word, I continued. "Anyway, from what this guy assures me, if one of their people did it, it was not approved by the Old Man, Vinnie Ruggeri, and if they find the guy, he's going to be whacked."

Westfield took a few seconds to decide his next move. When it came, it was direct. "I want this informant's name."

"Chief, with all due respect, I can't do that."

"And, why not, may I ask?"

"I gave this guy my word. He's been good with information in the past, and, well, the arrangement we have is that his name never gets mentioned anywhere, anytime, to anyone."

The Chief leaned back in his chair, blew out a long low sigh, and said to the ceiling, "Let me see, now, isn't it General Order 97-16 that mandates all informants will be registered with the department?"

"It sure does, Chief," I said with a tone of amazement. "General Order 97-16, Section 2, paragraph B, says that, 'Any source of information to the Department who is paid, compensated, or remunerated in any way with department funds or assets will be registered with the department on Form RPD1278'."

"You sure know your policies and procedures, Lieutenant," the Chief said with mock admiration.

"I try, sir." My meek smile and simple nod were meant to be cute and annoying. They obviously did the job.

"Then I want a 1278 made out right now, right here, before you take one step from this office!"

"But, Chief, my guy isn't paid, compensated, remunerated, or even masturbated by the Department in any way, shape or form."

"Baloney, Lieutenant! You mean to tell me he gives mob information to the Department out of his sense of civic pride?" my leader bellowed. "I wasn't born yesterday, you know!" There was a clumsy quarter minute of silence when I didn't pickup the ball.

"I want his name! I want it correct! I want it now!"

"Is that an order, sir?" I asked in my best hint of innocence.

"You bet your sweet golden bars, that is an order, Lieutenant."

"Please, Chief," I almost whined. "I gave this man my word, as a sworn officer of this Department, that I would never mention his name to anyone. What honor do we have if we do not keep our word?" This was almost fun!

"I want that name, Amato. I want it in thirty seconds, or you are up on charges for insubordination. Now give it up."

I rubbed my chin, looked at Westfield with an altar boy look, and then picked up a piece of scratch paper off his desk. I violated his space once more and took a ball-point from his desk set. On the piece of paper I wrote in block letters, 'Phillip Villadante,' and pushed the paper across the desk. Westfield leaned forward, looked at the paper, and instantly looked up at me, his eyes wide. The second he looked up, I pulled back the paper and put it in my pocket.

"Phil..." Westfield began to say as he looked at me with wide eyes.

"Please, Chief," I interrupted with my right forefinger to my lips. "Now you know. I gave you the name in writing," I said for benefit of his recorder that was surely operating as we talked this day and every other day. "But please don't mention it. You never know who's listening," I said as I took my finger from my lips and pointed to the ceiling.

Ben Westfield looked at me with a blank look that slowly broadened into a smile. He eventually laughed out loud and shook his head. Most real cops wouldn't want a fearful cop around them, but for Westfield, who never was a real cop, my feigned paranoia was reassuring.

"You are one for the books, Amato. You are so paranoid, it's almost amusing. Okay, okay, I'll humor you. I won't mention your secret friend because the FBI, or the CIA, or the KGB, or some other part of the alphabet might be listening in. But, Lieutenant, this doesn't change one thing. This murder is mob-connected as sure as we're sitting here. I know that in my heart, and I feel it in my bones. Authorized or not authorized, one of those da..., one of those mob animals did this, and you better find out who. If you won't or can't, I'll find someone who will. Now get out of here!"

I breathed a giant sigh of relief and made for the door. "Amato," Ben Westfield bellowed as I almost completed my escape. "I still want a report on that meet! Paid or not paid, it still gets reported."

I gripped the piece of paper in my pants pocket and breathed a silent sigh of relief that he had not had the presence of mind to ask for the paper. "No sweat, Chief. It's on Major Novitski's desk as we speak," I said over my shoulder as I closed the door behind me. For me, the confrontation with Westfield had gone as hoped. The Chief got a name, and I could swear up and down I gave him Fast Eddy's name...if it ever came to that. Now my bars were covered within the Department. Unfortunately, it was still very much apparent that Eddy Cavaluso had to be covered with his people.

Westfield had ridiculed my behavior, but he didn't call me a liar. Evidently he didn't know who I had met the night before, and evidently it wasn't Internal Affairs watching me and Eddy at the ramp garage! The options were down to the feds, or the mob...a 50-50 chance for Eddy Cavaluso's continued survival.

I made it to my office with all good intentions of reaching out for Fast Eddy and giving him a heads up about the possibility of being spotted by his people. However, good intentions aside, the instant I got to my desk, the phone rang.

"Lieutenant Amato," I announced into the mouthpiece as I searched for my eye glasses.

"Lieutenant, this is Dispatch," Mary Anne Sweeny's 36-24-36 voiced cooed from her 52-58-60 body. "We have two of your teams at the South Avenue Ramp Garage with a homicide."

"What do they need?"

"They called by land line and said the victim is one John Landers, the labor guy. They're requesting you go to the scene ASAP."

"Tell them I'm on the way," I told the dispatcher matter-of-factly, even though my head hung low as I rubbed the back of my neck.

"Lieutenant," Mary Ann said quickly to keep me from hanging up the phone.

"What?" I shot back, wanting to drop the phone and get to the scene.

"Detective St. John is on the line again. You want me to transfer him?"

"Please do," I responded more pleasantly to keep on the good side of the dispatcher.

The phone clicked, and then clicked again. "Boss?" St. John's voice asked.

"Yeah. What have you got out there, Bobby?"

"Jack Landers, the union boss, caught two in the chest. Been here probably all night. The uniforms got a call about seven this morning and saw it as a heart attack. When the Medical Examiner's crew got here, they rolled him over and saw the blood."

I looked at my watch. "That's almost two-and-a-half-hours wasted on this thing already."

"Yeah, I know. And, Lieutenant, it doesn't get any better."

"What do you mean?"

"There's a Jack of Spades tucked in his belt!"

"Say again?" I requested, hoping the connection was bad and that I had not really heard what I thought I heard.

"The killer left a Jack of Spades tucked in the victim's belt."

Leaving the office, I took no solace in the fact that I had been right when I faced the Chief. It was now even more apparent the killing of Frankie "Ten Tines" Lanovara had not been a settling of some score among mob members. What was emerging, was evidence we had a serial killer on our hands. Evidently Frankie Lanovara's hit had not been an end to itself. It was only the beginning. And, unless I missed my guess, there was going to be at least three more killings.

CHAPTER FOUR

JACK OF ALL TRADES

The autopsy of John "Jack" Landers' gave testimony to the fact that he was no stranger to violence. In addition to the two, neat bullet holes in the center of his chest which were now several hours old, his nose showed signs of three or four fractures earned in assorted labor strikes decades ago. The ugly four-inch scar going from the corner of his left eye to the lobe of his left ear was courtesy of a whiskey bottle in the hands of a scab strike-breaker at a citywide trucking strike back in 1963. The longer, neater, scar, running across his bald head was delivered by a nightstick some fifty years before his death. His left arm, as well as his right shoulder, bore the scars of knife blades. Those two wounds were witness to his efforts to organize the construction workers. Eleven lesser scars of various lengths and depths marked Landers' legs, forearms, back and fingers. The X-rays of the body would reveal nine fractures dating back to the late 1940's. The old wounds were of little interest to us. For the moment our only concern was focused on the two bullet holes that caused his death...and, more importantly, who had put them there.

Where as Frankie Lanovara was a world-class jerk, Jack Landers was a prince of a guy. Sure, he had his scrapes with the law, but they were scrapes over matters of ethics and principles. I had known this man for most of my life, and knew him as a stand-up guy, devoted to the unions, and the members of those unions. Whether you were a Jew, Italian, Polish, Black, or whatever, was of no concern to Jack Landers. His only concerns in life were that a person had a job, got paid well for doing that job, and was protected from the whims of management. My old man had told me, when I was a kid, as he introduced me to Landers, "Michael, this is the only man in the entire city you can trust!"

Jack Landers entered the unions as a sixteen year old kid when he went to work in one of the old shoe factories that belched smoke and dollars into the city's environment. By the time he was twenty-two, he was organizing labor unions in the factories. Three years later he was the National Brotherhood of Workers' lead organizer for the Northeast states. The city's first labor unions were brought in under the guidance and fight of Jack Landers. The same was true for the county's refuse collectors and social service workers. By time the mid 1960's rolled around, Landers' leadership in organizing teachers, blue collar workers, clerks, and even the city police, had earned him the newspaper title, "Jack of All Trades."

At 1:25 in the afternoon, after being at the scene and then personally observing the autopsy, I was back in front of Novitski and the Chief. The brief meeting took place on Westfield's home court, the Office of the Chief of Police. Because I didn't like being in the place, I made my oral report short and to the point.

"Landers was last heard from last night. That's when he called his daughter at about eight-thirty or so and told her he was getting ready to leave the office," I told them as I flipped through my notes. "According to the daughter, her 82 year-old father sounded tired and was looking forward to catching the fights on cable television. At about six forty-five this morning, a parking lot attendant found Landers' body near the left, rear corner of his car which was in parking spot number 6 on the first level. That was the victim's assigned parking spot for the last five or so years. The body was partially covered with fresh snow that blew in during the night. There were no exit wounds on the body, and the blood that did spill, coagulated quickly on the victim's shirt in the nine degree air. The uniformed cops saw the thing as a heart attack or seizure until the ME showed up and rolled the body over to reveal the frozen bloody shirt. The two rounds that caught the victim in the chest were close contact wounds caused by .9mm rounds." Completing the concise briefing, I looked at Westfield and then turned my attention to Novitski.

"What's the condition of the bullets?" Novitski inquired.

"Good shape. Both were removed at the autopsy, and both are good enough to be compared to the round that snuffed Frankie Lanovara," I responded.

".9mm?"

"They sure are."

"The card?" the Major asked in his customary brevity.

"Same type, style and make as Lanovara's. Only difference is this one is the Jack of Spades. The techs are going to check for fingerprints, fibers, et cetera. They think the FBI lab may be sophisticated enough to tell us if it came from the same deck, but they're not sure about it. Anyway, it'll take the feds about a year to tell us anything."

"Stuffed in his pants?" Novitski again spoke as I waited for the Chief to jump in.

"Down the front," I answered. "Front, middle. Right behind the belt buckle. It was kind of folded in two, but I think that was due to the killer's hurry to get out of there."

Novitski's wrinkled forehead asked me to elaborate.

"Looks like the killer probably pushed the card in there with his hand," I said as I mimicked the gesture, sliding my right hand between my shirt and pants. "As he did, the bottom edge of the card bent upward. Still there was enough of the upper corner of the card sticking out so we would be sure to find it easily."

Ben Westfield stood and moved around behind his chair. Making a production of laying his two hands on the chair's arched back, he opened his mouth but said nothing, setting a mood for some type of important observation. A few seconds after the staged scene of silence, his tongue ran over his upper lip. He seemed to relish the appearance that his audience had patiently awaited his entry into the conversation. "You still don't see this as a mob thing, Lieutenant?" The question asked, he shifted his eyes to Major Novitski as if to say, "Listen to this!"

I wasn't about to argue with the man. "I don't know, Chief. I don't have enough to say 'yes' or 'no.'"

"Let's see," Westfield said in another staged pre-oratory observation as he shifted his gaze to the ceiling and allowed the thumb and forefinger of his right hand to stroke his chin. "Let's just run this out to see what it shows us." Another pause for the sake of drama. The theatrics were getting old, but he seemed to think they were necessary or effective. "Labor boss. Ties to the mob. Two close range shots. Evidence linking the killing to Lanovara's obvious hit." He punctuated his points by raising a finger of his left hand after each less than astute observation.

I really didn't want to waste the time or energy by arguing with the pompous ass. My let-it-ride side had a quick fight with my tell-the-jerk-to-buzz-off side. The let-it-ride side of my id won, and I said, "Good points, Chief. All I'm saying is, let's not go out on a limb with those thoughts as of yet. You know, an early theory can really sway the investigators to overlook something, or put too much importance on other things." As I concluded I stole a glance at the Major, hoping he would note I had presented my argument with the proper decorum.

Westfield looked at Novitski, then back to me, and again to Novitski. "What do you say about that, Major?" he asked.

"The Lieutenant has a point, Chief. You may be right on the mob thing, but then again, let's not lock on to anything too soon. Let's keep all the options open. It makes the investigators work harder if we aren't eliminating or targeting anything too soon. If we go public about it being a Mafia thing and it later turns out we're wrong, we look bad. Even if we're right, we're tipping our hand. Besides, the Mayor probably wouldn't like the publicity it would get in the papers."

The old boy knows what notes to play, I thought to myself. "Chief," I interrupted. "If I could interject something here, I think we better start looking at some of our future victims."

"Future victims?" Westfield asked with a wry grin. "You got a crystal ball, Lieutenant Amato?"

"No, Chief, I don't have a crystal ball," I said in a patient tone of voice. "All I have is some common sense that says this guy probably has some kind of list drawn up, and he's going to be checking off some names."

"Just what the heck are you talking about, Lieutenant?" Westfield asked of me as he looked at the Major.

"What I'm talking about, Chief, is this guy, for whatever reason only he and God know about, is going to keep this up until he plays out a royal straight flush."

"A what?" Ben Westfield asked me as he looked at Major Novitski in disbelief.

"A poker hand," I said in frustration. "This guy stuffs a Ten of Spades in Frankie Lanovara. Frankie Ten Times," I added, not trying to make my comments sound too much like a try-to-understand-this-you-dense-idiot tone of voice. "Then Jack Landers, the Jack of All Trades, gets nailed and ends up with a Jack of Spades stuffed in his shorts. Next is going to be some taxpayer, probably a female type. She is probably going to have something to do with queen in her name or life. Next comes the King. And then, as a grand finale, the Ace," I concluded, looking at Novitski for support. I hadn't run the idea past him, but it was a theory that had come to mind a day earlier and played out further as I stood at the end of the Medical Examiner's table this morning, watching Jack Lander's skull being sawed open.

The Chief stood there shaking his head back and forth for a full minute. Finally he snickered and asked, "And you think Ace Amato is going to be the Ace of Spades, don't you?"

"I didn't say that, and I do not have any reason to think it, " I responded in a flat monotone. Actually, the thought had passed through my mind, but I gave it very little weight. The nickname was an old one that was used only by my closest friends, or by people who wanted, very desperately, to get a punch in the mouth. Westfield was definitely in the latter category. I wish I could have obliged him.

Westfield looked from me to my boss. "What do you think about this, this, ah, this theory of the Lieutenant's, Major?"

"The Lieutenant and I discussed it, Chief," Novitski lied in his support of me. "We kicked it around a yesterday, and well, I think it has some merit," Novitski stated convincingly. "Our suspect started with a Ten of Spades, moved up to the Jack, and I guess it's logical there's a Queen, a King and an Ace in the planning." He then reverted, just for a minute, to his old, ballsy, self, and added, "In fact, I think we should act on it."

"Act on it? Act on it?" Westfield asked in a begging voice. "Act on what? Some hair-brained idea? Are we going to act on a hunch that some guy is out there playing poker with us?"

"Unless you have a better idea, Chief, it's all we have," Novitski replied.

"You guys make me laugh!" Westfield said with a theatrical, choked laugh. He looked back and forth between me and the Major a couple of times before asking with notable resignation, "How do you propose we act on this?"

"We start looking at who might be the next victim. Get a feel for who might be targeted by this guy." Novitski looked at me as he concluded the statement. I didn't know if he was looking at me to shut up or to jump in. I decided it was the former.

Westfield seemed to mull that thought over for a few seconds. Finally, with a shake of his head and a wave of his hand, he told me I was free to go. Novitski took that as his exit cue, but was told to hang back in order to discuss, "some other matters."

I gladly left the meeting and went back to the squad room. Detective Frank Donovan, whose robust, ruddy-face showed his 55 years of life and 30 years of police experience, greeted me with a thumbs down signal. I stopped in the doorway and asked him, "What's that mean?"

"Bobby and me talked to the daughter, but didn't get a lot," Donovan said as he stood, leaning the butt of his large, 6-foot frame against the edge my desk. "She tells us Landers was in a good mood when she talked to him. All he said was he had been waiting for a late appointment to show up, but the person never showed, so he was going to grab a sandwich on the way home, and then settle in to watch the fights on cable."

"Any idea regarding who he was meeting?" I asked, not really expecting the break that we could most certainly use.

"No idea at all," Donovan said. "But, she says Landers usually carried a planner, you know, an appointment book. She told us he wrote down almost everything in it."

"Make me a happy man, Frank, and tell me we have the appointment book."

"Yes and no, Ace," he said with a grin.

I shot Donovan a scowl that told him I wasn't in the mood for wisecracks.

He took the clue and became serious once again. "The book was not with Landers, or in his car, or around the scene. However, we just now called Landers' secretary, a Mildred Glatten. Bobby asked her about the book, and she told him she has it in the office. Bobby's down there now to meet with her and grab the book. I was hanging back here to get a jump on the paperwork. We're about two days behind in Supplemental Reports."

I nodded and Donovan returned to the typewriter he favored over the computers. I turned my attention to the budget that was suppose to be off my desk by the end of last week. I played around with some numbers, but found my mind wandering back to our latest murder victim. There was no denying Landers must have played around with the mob guys from time to time. To accomplish what he had, there had to be some deals made someplace, sometime. All the same, the guy was semi-retired now. If the wise guys had a beef with our victim, it must be years old. So, the natural question was, why whack the guy now? More than any other argument I could come up with, was the matter of the playing cards. I couldn't imagine the Mafia stooges hanging around after whacking a guy and trying to break our chops by playing a card game with us.

Screw you, Westfield! We got a whacko on our hands this time. This guy isn't killing guys because he's got a contract to fill. This killer is offing people because he's got a point to make! And, he enjoys it. He's breaking our stones and loving every minute of it! This guy is having fun doing the killings, and he's having fun toying with us. I know I'm not the world's smartest cop, but it doesn't take a Sherlock Holmes to figure out that if we don't get something shaking on this case we're going to get at least three more victims before our killer intends to finish his game. Then what? Where's our weird guy going after he fills out his royal flush? Does he play down to a four-of-a-kind? Maybe a full house? Or maybe he then shifts to a game of Monopoly and starts killing people named Marvin Garden and Park Place. Who knows? This killer has an agenda, and we better get with the program or we are going to have a lot of dead citizens out there.

I was still engaged in my internal conversation when Donovan filled in my door frame. "St. John is on his way in, Lieutenant. He's got the appointment book, and..."

"And what, Frank?" I asked impatiently, not being able to handle anymore pregnant pauses.

"Landers had a note in the book for a six-thirty appointment last night ."

"Good!" I exclaimed

"Not so good," Donovan said with a grimace. "He was going to be meeting with a cop."

"A cop?" I asked, hoping I had misunderstood.

"A cop," he confirmed. "It says," Frank Donovan said as he raised his notebook, '6:30 P.M., Meet D-E-T.'"

"D-E-T?" I spelled out the question.

"Right, Lieutenant. That's the way Bobby gave it to me. He says it looks like the abbreviation for Detective. He's coming in now with the book."

"Could be someone's initials, or initials for a business, or something," I appealed.

"Bobby doesn't think so. He says Landers told the secretary before she left that he was hanging back to meet with some detective that was hassling him about, what he called, 'some bogus thing.'"

Detective Robert St. John presented himself at my door less than twenty minutes later. The kid was an obvious up and comer. The fact of the matter is Bobby's about 30 years old, but it seems that lately I'm starting to call everyone a "kid." St. John is one of those college educated cops I usually shy away from, but this kid has shown everyone he has street smarts to go with his degree. St. John's a charmer with the women, and equally as smooth in the interrogation room. Although he's Black and a couple of inches taller than my five foot, ten inch frame, in many ways he reminds me of myself when I was 15 years younger and felt confident and invincible.

The kid also has a subtle, wise guy way about him whenever he chooses to use it. When I brought him into the unit, I asked him what he wanted to be called.

"What do you mean, Lieutenant?" he asked with boy-like innocence.

Trying to impress him with my, I'm-a-1990's-type-of-guy, routine, I said, "Do you prefer being called 'Afro-American,' or 'Black'?"

"Nah," he said with a big smile. "You can just call me Bob."

Editorial Reviews

Product Description

"Justice" is a work offiction that entices the reader to grapple with questions about what justice really means. Does a courtroom decision equal justice? Do two wrongs make a right? Does assassinating a killer make the act just? These are a few the questions raised in "Justice"... questions for the reader to ponder and answer. Police Lieutenant, Mike Amato and his squad of detectives are faced with the task of identifying and finding the person who has stalked, abducted, abused and murdered three young children in the streets of Rochester, New York. Following each murder, the killer torments the parents of his victims with details of the child's abduction and murder. With each murder, community hysteria increases and Amato and his squad feel the pressure to apprehend the killer. Although the killer is finallyapprehended and he readily admits to the killings and blames his own abuse-riddled childhood as the motive for his reign of terror the killer is caught again and not set free this time. But how can they make sure the killer doesn't slip through the judicial cracks again? As with the other Mike Amato novels, this work also contains a prologue and epilogue. In the prologue to "Justice" a rookie cop and his training officer discuss the concepts offairness versus justice. In the epilogue, Lt. Mike Amato finishes thediscussion and asks the readers to decide if justice was served.

About the Author

Louis Campanozzi was born and raised in Rochester, New York. After serving in the military he returned home and joined the Rochester Police Department. During his 22 years with the department, Lou worked undercover narcotics, commanded the homicide and robbery squad, and served as District Commander on the city's West Side. Campanozzi investigated some of the community's most notorious crimes and later wrote the sometimes-mean streets of Rochester as an author of mystery novels.Lou was one of the three founders of BowMac Educational Services, founded in 1980. BowMac is a police training-consulting firm. Lou taught hundreds of cops and now thousands of criminals use his techniques to this day. In turn, tens of thousands of criminals are put behind bars because of his teachings.After retiring as Captain from the Rochester Police Department Lou relocated to Albuquerque, New Mexico where he worked for the New Mexico State Police in addition to teaching for BowMac. He later took on the position of Chief of Police of an Indian Reservation in Albuquerque, New Mexico.Lou Campanozzi unexpectedly died at the age of 59 in 2002. His family takes great pride as they continue to distribute and keep Lou's ideas, words and characters alive through his novels. The first two novels in the Mike Amato Detective Series, "The Killing Cards" and ¿Ground Lions" have been well

Detective Robert St. John now confirmed what Donovan had relayed to me. He added, according to the victim's secretary, Landers didn't seem too concerned about the meeting, just kind of annoyed about it.

"When the secretary left it was about six last evening," St. John concluded. "Our victim was sitting at his desk working a crossword puzzle in the newspaper. That's it, Lute. That's all she had."

"She have any idea about who this cop is, what he wants?"

"Nothing. She says as far as she knows there's no investigation, no pending matters between the union and us. Only thing she knew was she took a call yesterday afternoon from a guy who said he was a detective with us, and he wanted to speak directly to Landers." St. John looked down at his notebook before continuing, "About ten or fifteen minutes later Landers tells her, after she asks if there's a problem, that some young cop was trying to make 'steak out of baloney' as he put it, and he was going to meet the detective that night. He told her he was going to meet the guy and 'set him straight.' She says that's a direct quote."

I let the information sink in for a couple of seconds. "Okay," I said finally. "I want you two interviewing everyone on the union staff to see if something, anything is hanging out there about a complaint, an investigation, maybe something with the feds, whatever."

"Done, Lute," Bobby St. John answered. "I already set it up for tomorrow morning.

"And..." I added, but was cut off by the detective.

"And, we start looking inside the Department. We poke around Intelligence, Internal Affairs, Organized Crime, the whole nine yards, to see if someone has got something pending with the union or its people."

"No! No way, Bobby! You leave that to me. We go nosing around and making too much noise, and if there is some cop involved in this thing, God forbid," I interjected with my hands pressed together in mock prayer, "he'll go underground on us. What I was going to say was, we let the Chief sniff around to see if some investigation is going on." At least it will keep the man out of my hair, I thought to myself.

Caution told me I better get in to brief Novitski and Westfield. However, the office was starting to feel stifling. I needed to get some air. I also had some important business to take care of. Eddy Cavaluso's life could be in danger. The briefings could wait.

Taking a spin around to a couple of the mob joints, I finally ran down Fast Eddy. He was standing around in front of the Sicilian-American Club with a couple of low level stiffs I knew from the streets. I got out of the car, and as I hassled the three of them with stupid questions and quick pat-downs,

I slipped a note into Eddy Cavaluso's overcoat pocket. We traded sarcastic comments for a few minutes. To seal our friendship, we threw each other the finger as I slid into my car.

By time I got back to the office and managed to get in to see Novitski, it was going on five o'clock. He called the Chief while I sat there and recounted the information about Landers' appointment book and the interview secretary.

"What did he have to say?" I asked.

"'Oh, no!'" Novitski related.

"It kind of let the air out of his Mafia killing theory," I mussed. "But what did he say about us doing any investigations into the union?"

"He says there isn't anything at all going on here, but he will check with the FBI, the Sheriff's people, and the State Police to see if they have anything in the works."

"That will keep him busy for a few days," I commented with a smile. "Especially trying to get any information out of the Feds."

I thanked the boss for backing me in front of the Chief earlier, and then briefed him on the investigative plans for the next day. When I got up to leave, Novitski asked me to hang on for a minute. He got up, went out to the reception area, and poured some coffee for the both of us.

"You still got your bottle of Sambuca in your desk, Mike?" he asked.

"Sure," I answered. "Why?"

"Go get it, and come back here. We need to talk."

A couple of minutes later I poured a long shot of liquor into each of our cups of coffee. Novitski then began to ruin the evening portion of my already ruined day.

"The Chief is assigning you two more guys to work with the squad on these killings."

"And, the bad news is?" I asked casually after taking a sip of the strong coffee. If Westfield was kicking me two additional guys for the investigation, there surely had to be a down side.

"The not-so-good news is that it's going to be two guys from the Organized Crime Bureau. Sergeants Jeff Bolson and Art Mancini are coming down. They'll be with you as of tomorrow morning."

"Aw, come on, Major," I moaned as I slammed my cup on his desk. "What do I need with two creeps from OCB?"

"Lieutenant," Novitski said, and just from the way he said it I knew there was a chewing out in my immediate future. "You listen to me now, and you listen good. Okay?"

He looked at me with his eyebrows raised, and I nodded back to him with a sigh of resignation. We both took a sip of the after-hours brew, and

Charlie Novitski ran his right hand through his white hair before continuing.

"Westfield wanted to take you off the case. He doesn't trust you with this thing because you keep fighting him. He's convinced these killings are connected to the mob, and right or wrong, he's the Chief. Now you may not agree with him, you might not like him, and maybe you won't be exchanging Christmas cards this year, but he *is* the Chief of Police, and he needs to be listened to...and respected." He waited for me to interrupt, but I decided to stand pat until he had his say. Novitski drained his cup, and then continued. "I argued the point with him, about taking you off the case. I finally got through to him that if we took the case out of your squad and sent it to OCB, it would raise havoc with the press and we would be telling the world we thought it was a mob thing. I finally made the point that if we're dealing with a mob war, then we're letting them know, and, if we are wrong, then we're showing our ass to the public. He didn't like it, but he saw the wisdom of it. So, long story short, the compromise was sending in two of the OCB guys to, 'help out,' as he put it."

"To snoop around is more like it," I said with disgust.

"Very possible, Mike," he conceded.

"There's more, isn't there?" I asked before I drained my cup.

"Yes there is. Westfield wants one of the two OCB Sergeants working directly with you. The other one you can assign to one of the teams."

"I'll take Mancini," I offered without a fight. Fighting this thing was going to take too much energy, and there was no way I was going to win. "At least I know him from back in the days when we both were in the Vice Squad. Bolson I don't like, and I don't trust. He's just going to be down here as a snitch for Westfield."

"I figured as much," Novitski said as he poured straight Sambuca into his cup. "So," he continued with just a hint of a smile. "I told the boss you would want Bolson in your car, and, of course, he insisted you take Mancini. So, you got Mancini. You are instructed by the Chief to use Bolson as your case coordinator."

"That sucks the big one, Major! The guy is going to be up on everything we're doing, and he sure as hell is going to be running back to the old man."

"Mike, what can I tell you? I tried to out-fox the guy, but he's no one's fool. He came right back and out-foxed me."

"Anything else?"

"He's asked the FBI to give us a hand with the case."

"He what?" I almost screamed.

"Shut up for a minute," Novitski said firmly as he slapped his right hand flat on the desk. "You know the Feebs. They don't break wind without checking with Washington first. They told him they will assist us with general intelligence for now, but they'll have to get the Justice Department people to okay their direct involvement. You know as well as I that will take weeks, if not months."

We sat there silently for a minute before we both poured more of the clear liquor into our cups. This time we skipped the coffee. Finally, I broke the silence.

"Okay if I let Bolson be the FBI contact? He's just like them, so maybe they'll recruit him and keep him."

The Major stuck his chin in the air as he thought that one over, and then, with a grin, agreed it would be a smart tactic.

"Now that's the thinking of the Mike Amato I know," he said as he extended a circled thumb and forefinger. "It'll show the Chief we're doing what he likes, and it will keep those D.C. suits out of here."

We sat in silence for a minute, and then agreed it was time to leave. As Novitski slipped on his overcoat, he asked me if I was open to a suggestion.

"Mike, have you ever thought about maybe sitting down with the Chief and resolving the thing between you and him?"

"Hey, Boss, what am I going to say to him? The entire incident is back there ten, eleven years ago. If he hasn't gotten over it by this time, he sure isn't going to let me off the hook now."

"I thought maybe if you sat down with him and laid it out on the table. You know, kind of tried to set the matter straight with him. Maybe if you let him say his piece and you eat a small piece of crow, well, maybe you could put the thing away once and for all."

"It's not going to change anything, Major."

"You may be right, Mike. You may be right. Then again, give it some thought. As long as that thing is hanging out there, he's going to be messing with you every time you turn around."

We sipped the last of the Sambuca in silence, shut off the lights to his office, and exchanged 'good nights.'

Returning to the quiet of my office, I filled another cup with strong, stale coffee and Sambuca. I needed time to think, to put the entire situation into some type of perspective. Here it was, the middle of February, and we were sitting on two very strange homicides with no resolution in sight. I liked detective work, but I hated mysteries...and this case was becoming one very large mystery.

The best we had done on Frankie Lanovara's case was to be able to trace his steps to where he was about six hours before we found his body. We had him placed at a small diner on the east side of the city, eating alone and going over racing forms. The waitress described him to a tee. "A real fat jerk!" She remembered him being obnoxious and trying to hit on her as he ordered almost three complete meals. Other than that sighting we had nothing. My best guess was he probably was around one or two of the mob joints after leaving the diner. However, nobody was volunteering any information about Frankie's comings and goings.

Now we have Jack Landers laying on a slab, with nothing to go on except that we may be dealing with a cop as a suspect in the case. I had never personally known anything about a police hit squad operating anywhere in this country, but for some South American countries, and in some Hollywood movies, the idea wasn't that far fetched. Could it be we have a renegade cop, or cops, running around here, settling up scores? In Frankie Ten Times' killing, I could easily imagine some copper being fed up enough with what we laughingly refer to as the Criminal Justice System, or with Frankie personally, to want to cancel the guy's ticket. But with Landers, it was another matter. What motive would a cop have for nailing the one man primarily responsible for him having a good, strong union?

The phone kicked me back to the reality of the darkened office.

"Homicide. Amato," I said into the mouthpiece

"You left me a note?" Eddy Cavaluso asked.

"Call me on the other phone in about ten minutes," I said, and placed the receiver back in its cradle.

About fifteen minutes later, the pay phone down by Headquarters rang. Although still in the police building, it was highly unlikely the Department would tap a public phone used by crooks every day as they came in and out of court. On the other hand, it was completely within the realm of possibility they would tap one of the office phones used by cops. After all, catching crooks had certain rules and standards for propriety, whereas getting cops was an endeavor without much regulation.

"It's me," I said to the caller.

"Like I said, I got your note," Eddy said with a degree of annoyance.

"I think we were followed the other night. Near as I can tell, it wasn't one of my people. My thinking is it could be some of your folks, or maybe the suits."

"If it was, there's no sign of it on this end," Eddy said. "My vote says if it was anyone, it was the feds.'

"It might be nothing, but then again, I just wanted you to know, and be careful." I was somewhat relieved to have him express a belief that it might have been the FBI and not the mob boys.

"Thanks for the thought," he said, and the phone went dead.

I left the building and headed for nowhere. I guess the car knew where to go, and in five minutes I was seated at the counter of Nick Tahou's joint.

Tahou's was the kind of greasy spoon found in most cities. The fare was hot dogs, hamburgers, fries, and bacon and eggs. It was also the kind of joint that was frequented by judges, lawyers, and business people in the daytime. When night time fell, the clientele switched over to hookers, pimps, and junkies. Cops were found there at any time of the day or night. No investigation or long night on the street was complete unless it was accompanied by a couple of white hots - a Western New York delicacy - so named because the bratwurst hot dogs take on a grayish-white appearance.

Nick Tahou, a Greek immigrant similar to the ones God had placed in every town in America to open such a restaurant, was a friendly, hard working man who greeted every customer with a handshake and a smile. His secret "Greek Sauce" was not only tasty, it did much to cover the sins an over-used grill left on his "sliders." Nick's hot dogs were referred to as tube steak, Greek steak, porkers, reds, or sliders. The last moniker made reference to the ability of the food to enter one end of the body and slide rather quickly out the opposite end.

I downed a couple of white hots loaded with Greek sauce and onions. Nick came over and slapped me on the back the way he usually did, and we passed a little time noting that in this day of racial enlightenment, his Black customers still tended to gather on the west side of his place, while the White kids from the University of Rochester, along with the suburbanite bowling teams gravitated to the seating area on the east side. After Nick drifted off to chat with other regulars, I suddenly found myself uncomfortable in this usually comfortable spot. Leaving there, I broke a promise I had made to myself. Without a conscious thought, I headed for a little neighborhood bar over near the Nineteenth Ward on the city's west side. At least I wouldn't be known over there, and wouldn't have to talk to anyone.

Once I had downed my first beer, and ordered my second one, I let my mind drift as I looked at my face in the mirror. The now-natural scowl on the face in the mirror told me Charlie Novitski was right, I was an angry man. Years ago, I would go to a bar where other cops hung out and I would be like the people here this night, engaged in animated conversation and laughing. Tonight I sat staring at a face in the mirror, a face I didn't know...and didn't really like. Perhaps even worse than the face looking back at me, were the thoughts spinning around behind the face.

For the first time since I dreamed up this little poker hand theory, I consciously acknowledged I had no idea how to approach the case. Added to that dismal outlook was a nagging thought back there in the folds of my brain, tugging on the sleeve of my mind. Maybe I was losing my sanity after all, just as Diane had said. Maybe the idea had been back there since I looked down at Jack Landers' lifeless body. I didn't know how the thought got there, or how long it had been floating around in my brain. The fact is, it had been there before Westfield brought it up. I didn't understand why it was there, just laying there, annoying me. But, as I drained my second beer and ordered a third, I brought the buried concept up to conscious thought.

What if this guy was making a point with each of these killings? Do Frankie Lanovara and Jack Landers represent something special? Yeah, sure the cards are connected to their nicknames, but was each of the two killings a single statement? Or, could it be the killer was in this thing for the long haul? Maybe the entire string of killings, all the way from the Ten of Spades through to the Ace of Spades, was his statement, his point, his creative work of art. But, what if the first four killings were only a lead-in, sort of a preamble to his final killing, the murder of the Ace?

I left the bar after the third beer. As I cleared the doorway and went out on to the sidewalk, it was more than the Rochester winter that sent a chill through me. Standing next to my car with the key in my right hand, the thought came back and tapped me on the shoulder.

Was Ace Amato going to be the killer's Ace of Spades?

CHAPTER FIVE

ENEMIES INSIDE AND OUT

The next morning I sat down with Sergeants Bolson and Mancini and brought them up to speed on the Lanovara-Landers killings. I spared nothing. However, for Bolson's benefit, I let on that we were seriously pursuing the theory that the killings were potential Mafia hits. The photos of the scenes were spread out on the table along with the autopsy reports, interview statements, and the forensic findings. If the case was going to get screwed up, it wasn't going to be because I held anything back. I even shared the poker hand theory with them, but emphasized it was only a theory. After they had a chance to absorb everything, I laid out the two dominant theories on the cases. The first being the killings were mob hits. The second choice was, we were dealing with a nut, and very possibly a police nut. I didn't say anything about who had what theory, and never brought in the Chief's name. When I got through, Jeff Bolson looked at his OCB buddy, and asked me if the two them could be excused for a minute.

"No, I don't think so, Sergeant," I answered soberly. "I don't know how you work down in the Organized Crime Bureau, but up here we don't keep any secrets from each other."

"No offense, Lieutenant," Bolson said politely, but with just a hint of a smug grin. "It's just that there may be some confidential OC matters that may plug into this, and maybe Art and I should discuss those things privately for now."

"If there is anything that may 'plug into this', Sergeant, then you should discuss them in front of me. My boss, your boss, and their respective boss, the Chief of Police, worked out this deal where you two were to come down here and assist in this case. The reasoning on that move is, I suppose, to get this matter resolved and find this bird. Now then, I just laid out the entire case for you two guys, and if you have something that ties into this matter I expect you to share it with me. Otherwise, there's no need for you two to be here."

Art Mancini lit a cigarette and blew the smoke up to the ceiling. "The thing is, Lieutenant, we don't have the faintest idea as to what's gong on with this thing," Mancini said through a blue haze. "Sure, Frankie Lanovara was connected. In fact, he was a made member as of about April almost two years ago. The word we have is he wasn't too well liked by his little playmates, but the Old Man, Vincent Ruggeri, was under some pressure to make him. We aren't too sure about where the pressure was coming from. When he got nailed, well, to tell you the truth, we kind of thought maybe the Old Man had him whacked just to get rid of him. As far as Landers goes, he don't figure in at all with the boys in the mob. We got a file on him, and I looked through it this morning before we came up here.   Other than some newspaper clippings, the last dated entry in the file was over eight years ago."

"Lanovara's uncle, Petie Fisheyes, pushed the Old Man to make Frankie," I threw into the midst of the conversation.

"Where did you get that, Lieutenant?" Bolson asked with some note of amazement. I was pleased he was surprised that I would have information about his supposed area of expertise.

"I know a guy who knows a guy," I responded casually. After it sank in that I was not going to elaborate on my information, I asked Mancini, "Anyway, getting back to Landers, was he connected?"

"Connected? If you mean did he know the wise guy crowd, yeah, sure he was connected. The old files, going back maybe twenty years, put him in face-to-face conversation with some of the old-time mob guys. His name came up on a wire tap or two back in the mid-70's. However, if you mean was he in tight with them, my assessment is, no way."

Sergeant Bolson watched Mancini and I as we talked. I guess he figured he might as well join the conversation with some tidbit and save some of his credibility.

"We think that back then he might have gone to the mob boys for some muscle on a couple of union strikes," Bolson threw in. "But like Art says, there's nothing firm, and sure as hell nothing recent."

I nodded at the information without looking at the source. Blowing my last drag of the cigarette across the room, stood up, and announced, "What I'm going to do is make Sergeant Bolson here, the case coordinator. Art, you're going to be with me for the duration. Jeff, I understand you're something of a whiz with computers. I want you to begin to catalogue this entire case, cross index it, plug it in so we can do day-to-day analysis. Then, have it ready every morning so we can update the Major and the Chief." I paused for a minute, had a quick discussion with myself, and decided to go out on a limb.

Without looking at either of them, I shuffled some paper around in the case folder and said, "I got a snitch in with the local mob crowd, and from what he told me the other night, they don't have a clue as to what's going on." I took a sneak peek at both of them, and could tell by the quick exchange of glances that the information was news to them. If I was being followed, it wasn't by either of them, and more than likely, not by anyone else in OCB.

"From what he tells me," I continued. "The Old Man is up in arms over Lanovara getting whacked, and he wants the head of the guy who did it brought to him on a platter."

Mancini spoke up. "Given all of what you just said, and what we know about this thing right now, who came up with the idea that this is mob score? No offense, Lieutenant, but speaking frankly, I don't see it." He looked over to his partner and asked, "Do you, Jeff?"

"I have to agree with Art on this, Lieutenant," Sergeant Bolson acknowledged. "I'm not throwing stones, but I personally think the mob thing is kind of lame."

I hid my smile behind my coffee cup before setting it down and answering, "It's the Chief's theory, and it is shared by the FBI office here. I think we need to respect that, gentlemen," I said seriously as I wished Novitski had been present to hear me give the official party line so convincingly.

After the briefing with the two new additions to our group, I took the opportunity of their arrival to reorganize the rest of the squad. I put Detectives Al Verno and Frank Donovan together to work on the two most recent killings as a primary task, but still to manage the other open cases they had been assigned. Detectives Paskell and St. John, along with their normal case load, were given the responsibility of trying to identify the next victim. Art Mancini and I would take the lead on the Lanovara and Landers cases.

Thank God, the next couple of days were relatively quiet. Some jerk kid decided it was time to move up to armed robbery from purse snatching, and hit a drug store. When the clerk moved to get the money that was demanded, the adolescent macho man panicked and fired a shot into her head. He was grabbed two blocks away by the uniformed guys, and our guys wrapped up the homicide in a couple of hours. During the lapse of those few days, Sergeant Jeff Bolson, the Chief's personal snitch in my camp, did, I am forced to secretly admit, a good job of entering all the limited information we had on the Lanovara-Landers homicides, cross-indexing it, or whatever one does on a computer, and printing out a nice, concise outline of what we had on the two murders. He also began to bug me with a personal theory he developed.

"The chances of two consecutive victims of a serial killer having their last names begin with the same letter is in the tens of thousands," Bolson told us at a morning briefing. "The chances of both of them having three letters the same, in this particular case, L-A-N, are almost astronomical." We looked at each other with an assortment of smiles, snickers, and bewilderment. "I'm proposing," the OCB Sergeant said after clearing his throat, "our suspect is following a personal agenda against people having those letters of their last name in common." The skinny, boy wonder hesitated and looked nervously at the homicide Detectives. "Really! Think about this," he insisted. "He's just attempting to throw us off with his deck of cards trick."

"You *have* got to be kidding," Verno said as he threw a balled up paper towel at the Sergeant.

"Or goofy," Donovan added.

"Knock it off!" I commanded over the top of my coffee cup. "At this point we take any and all ideas, and, we keep an open mind." The problem with my statement was that I half-way believed myself. Thinking that our whacko was killing people to make a poker hand might be just as much over the edge as believing he was pumping bullets into them because their names happened to begin with L-A-N. On the other hand, I thought Bolson was full of crap! I would like to believe I was being an open-minded manager by giving some attention to Bolson's theory, but the honest-to-God truth is I didn't want little Jeffrey running up to Westfield's office, telling him I wasn't playing nice in the sandbox.

The very same day Bolson presented his brain fart, Paskell and St. John laid their report on me. They had identified 132 possible victims our nut might target to fill in his Queen of Spades. Fifty-six had, "Queen" as a first or last name. Another 41 owned a business, or had some type of affiliation with an organization containing the name Queen. The remaining thirty-five had held the title of Queen of something some time in the past five years.

"We surely aren't going to baby sit a hundred and thirty something people," I told them.

"I know what you're saying, Lute," Paskell said as he waved my cigarette smoke away from his face. "And, the bad news is the number we gave you doesn't even include the homosexuals, whores, transvestites and cross-dressers who use the name Queen, plus the people who hang out at the Queen

Bee Bar, eat and work at the Queen's Tavern, and couple of hundred of other possibilities we didn't even consider. If we throw them into the mix and add all the high school prom queens from the past ten years, we're looking at upwards of a thousand frigging people."

While the teams hit the streets and Bolson fed his computer the facts, data, and circumstances, Sergeant Mancini began digging around any and all departmental records for anything that may have tied into the cases. I filled the vast majority of the day getting caught up on administrative matters, attending a strategic planning committee meeting, and finally moving the budget matters off my desk.

Late in the afternoon I passed on the day's information to Major Novitski, and he sent me up to Westfield with the developments. An hour went by while my heels cooled in the Chief's reception area, shooting the bull with my old buddy, Pete Polson. When I finally got in to see my Chief, I made it a point to lead off the questioning by asking him if he was able to make any determination about anyone in the Department doing an investigation into Jack Landers or the unions.

"Nothing to it, Lieutenant. I've had every Bureau Chief in here, had our Information System people search the computers, and the end result is that we are not into Landers or the unions. Nor is the DA's office, the Sheriff's Department, or the State Police interested in him or the unions right now." He let the information sit with me for a few seconds, and slipped in his commercial announcement. "So, I would say that leads us back to the Mafioso thing, doesn't it?"

"Sure sounds like it, Chief," I said in my best team-player tone. Then, not being able to fight the urge, asked, "What about the FBI? Do they have anything going on with Landers or the unions?"

"They're checking, Lieutenant. They have a fairly large organization there. It'll take a few days for them to get back to us."

I took his comment with a nod, and wanted to suggest he shouldn't hold his breath while he waited for the Federal boys to share information with the us locals. Instead of speaking my thoughts, a practice that was not widely accepted or practiced in today's modern crime fighting agency, I presented him with the recently generated L-A-N theory.

"That sounds like another far-fetched idea of yours, Lieutenant," he said with a patronizing smile. "Where do you and your men come up with these ideas?"

Silently, I thanked him for opening the door so wide. I took the opportunity to run right in. "Oh, it's not my idea, Chief. No, no," I commented with a serious look. "That's a theory Sergeant Bolson developed all on his own." It was a personal joy to watch the man try to deal with that bit of news.

"Well, all that aside for now," he recovered. "What else do you have for me?"

I gave him the update on Paskell and St. John's report concerning the next potential victim. When he heard the figure on the number of possible victims we had, Westfield went ballistic.

"Come on, Lieutenant, get serious! How the hell are we going to provide coverage on over a hundred people, around the clock, seven days a week?"

"Hey, Chief, I didn't make up these people," I said, letting anger get the best of me. Then, more calmly added, "And I'm not suggesting we cover all of them."

"Your people are trying to play some games here, Amato. They may want to rack up all kinds of overtime hours, but I'm not as dumb as you imagine I am! I sure as hell am not playing into their hands. That squad of prima donnas you have down there needs to be reigned in a little."

The past week had been too long, too laborious, and I didn't have the patience to put up with Westfield's posturing. "Look, Chief," I said coming up out of my chair and resting my finger tips on his desk as I leaned forward, across his desk. "If you got it out for me, then let's get it out in the open. But damn it, quit hounding my guys for busting their butts and for doing their job!"

"What are you talking about, Lieutenant?"

"I'm talking about you taking cheap shots at every thing we do down there. You got a problem with me, then deal with me. If you don't have the guts to do that, then just learn to live with it, and leave my people out of our thing. For the sake of God, it was ten frigging years ago!" Maybe this wasn't exactly what Major Novitski had in mind when he suggested I open up some dialogue with Westfield, but it sure made me feel good just to say it.

"You're about this close to having charges laid on your head, Amato," Westfield yelled as he held his forefinger and thumb about a half inch apart directly in front of my face.

Rather than punch his lights out, I turned to leave the office. As I pulled open his door, I heard him say something.

"You talking to me?" I spun around and asked.

"It was twelve years ago, Lieutenant. Not ten, but twelve years ago!"

I shook my head at him in disgust and completed my exit. Being less than ten minutes to quitting time, I didn't even stop by the office to pick up my coat. I went directly to my car, and before the hour struck I was on a stool inside Murphy's Mug, downing a beer. Ten minutes and two beers later,

Frank Donovan pulled out the stool next to mine and called for a draft.

"Rough day, Mike?"

"They're all getting rough, Frank," I answered without looking up.

"Well, it's probably going to get rougher tomorrow," he said almost as a condolence.

I looked over at him as he slid the evening paper to me. The headline just below the fold read, "Police Seek Serial Killer." Donovan gave me a wry grin and toasted me with his beer. I pulled the newspaper toward me and scanned the story.

According to the reporter, "a highly placed police official" confirmed the Department was viewing the recent Lanovara-Landers killings as being linked. The source, who was reported as being, "close to the investigation," was quoted as saying, "...the weapon was the same, the two victims bore similar evidence, and investigators are concerned by the fact that both men had a last name beginning with the letters LAN." Fortunately the, "source" didn't go into the cards that were found on the bodies. He, or she, had supposedly told the reporter there was more information, but for the sake of the investigation the source didn't want to jeopardize it by elaborating. I was grateful for his discretion on that matter, but still wanted to bounce this snitch off a couple of walls.

"This kind of crap is going to mess up the entire investigation," I said as I pushed the paper over the bar.

"You used the doo-doo word, Mike!" Donovan said with feigned shock. "I thought you were giving up swearing?"

"Yeah, well sometimes it's the only thing that fits," I offered with resignation.

We sipped our beers in silence. After a minute or two of silence, Donovan asked, "So who's the source, Mike?"

"Beats me. Westfield? Bolson? Some clerk reviewing the reports? Who the hell knows. Besides, what difference does it make? The impact's all the same, regardless of who our mole is!"

We drained our beers, moved over to a booth, and ordered a couple of hamburgers along with another round of "Jenny's," a local brew. Frank Donovan and I had worked around each other for probably the past fifteen years. Our careers had moved together although he was probably eight or nine years my senior. Truth be known, he was probably a sharper investigator than I would ever be, but the fact was I was luckier when it came to Civil Service exams.

Francis Xavier Donovan was about five or six years ahead me in coming out of the academy, but we made our Detective shields together. We were both subsequently assigned to the Department's Clinton Section Office. A few years later, Frank went to the gambling squad about the same time I went undercover in narcotics. When I made Sergeant and moved back into uniform, Frank got assigned to my new precinct a year or so later. He worked days and I worked nights, but our friendship built steadily through those years. When I made Lieutenant and went to Homicide, I sought out the hard-working detective, and brought him into the squad during my first year there. Even our divorces followed one after the other. When Diane left me, I hooked up with the lawyer who had represented Frank Donovan in his heated divorce. I tried not to let our friendship interfere with work, but, truth be known, I really liked the barrel-chested, easy-going, Irishman and I often went in search of his input on these rough cases...and some personal issues. He hadn't made the rank that I had, but he was sharper than me in many aspects.

Half way through our high cholesterol dinner, Donovan spoke up. "Has the thought struck you about our perp possibly having you in mind for his Ace of Spades?"

"What Frank?" I asked through a mouth of hamburger. "Are you working with Jeff Bolson in the Weird Theory Department?"

"That boy needs a reality tune up, Mike," he said with a laugh. After swallowing another bite of his food, he continued. "But, I'm serious, Mike. This guy is laying out a nice, neat pattern for us. All this mob stuff and the L-A-N theories aside, there's no doubt in my mind our next victim gets the Queen of Spades, then comes the King, and then the Ace."

"Yeah, well, there are a lot of Queens, Kings, and Aces, as we are beginning to find out. What makes you so concerned that he wants me?" I asked the question sarcastically, but I was truly interested in hearing his reasoning. If for nothing else, I wanted to see if it was consistent with my own mental wanderings.

"This perp is taunting us, Mike. He's enjoying what he's doing. He's got a personal thing here, and he don't mind taking on high profile people. If my guess is right, this L-A-N thing is a crock, and our nut is going become a very angry nut when he sees the paper."

"Angry? About what?"

"Angry that we're missing the point. He *wants* us to know he's putting together that straight flush! It wouldn't surprise me if he goes to the press with his own story, or somehow goes out of his way to get some notoriety so everyone knows what he's doing."

"If he does, we'll have hell to pay. Every fool that has anything to do with a queen, a king, or anything like that will be wanting police protection. Every parent whose kid played one of the Three Kings in a school Christmas play will want us escorting their kid around. It'll be a circus!"

"Yeah, well all that not withstanding, I still think this guy has got you in his sights. He hits the other four, and then, when he takes you out, it just looks like a serial killer thing. If he does get busted, he's laying out a nice insanity plea, and he still skates by."

"Still, all that considered, why me?"

"Ace Amato," Frank said as he spread his open hands apart as if displaying a headline.

"Don't bust my chops, Frank," I said, waving him off with my hands. "That was a long time ago."

"All in all though, it got you a lot of press. The news guys hung the tag on you, and, even now, you still get called Ace by some of the older guys. And, you know better than me, the headlines also made you some enemies along the way too, if I recall."

We both chuckled over his comment.

"The first time I saw you do it," Donovan said as he shook his head. "Was with that scum bag that was breaking into homes where little old ladies lived all alone. When you bet him you could read his mind, I thought you were nuttier than he was. Then I bust a gut when I realized what you were doing."

"Yeah, baloney!" I laughed. "You couldn't figure out what was going on when I told him to draw a card, and then told him he was holding the Ace of Spades."

"Well, damn it, Mike, give me some credit," Donovan laughed as he gave me a pretty fair punch on the right bicep. "I knew it was some type of card trick, I just didn't know until way later that you stacked the entire deck with Aces of Spades."

We laughed again, and then returned to finishing our burgers. We ordered another beer for dessert. After the beers came we both downed a long swallow.

"I haven't seen you pull that in probably five, six years, maybe longer."

"Yeah, well, after I pulled a fifteen day suspension for 'Conduct Unbecoming' when Judge Asher ripped me apart in open court for using deception with some poor, misunderstood stick-up artist, I kind of put that little act away. However, while it lasted, it was a nice entry into wearing a suspect down in the interrogation room."

We sat in silence for a few minutes, and finished our beers. The conversation drifted off onto other subjects, and we both considered another beer before deciding against it. Reluctantly, at least on my part, we called it a night.

"You be careful, Mike," Donovan called out to me over the roof of his car.

The next day began with my butt being eagerly devoured by the Chief. The reason this time for the chewing out was the leak to the press. I took it, figuring, after all, it was my responsibility to keep a lid on things. After leaving Westfield's den, I hooked up with Mancini and we made the rounds to most of the mob joints looking for the last few people we needed to interview. The day didn't amount to much. It just made me all the more convinced the Cosa Nostra crowd was the least of our immediate worries.

The following week gave us a break in the action. We fell back into somewhat regular eight or ten hour work days and all of us managed to get caught up with a lot of odds and ends. We worked hard but came up with nothing but dead-ends. Bobby St. John went nowhere with the information on the detective that was supposed to have had an appointment with Jack Landers. The Lanovara case became stone cold, and what few feeble leads we had fizzled.

Mid-week presented us with a nice, simple husband-wife killing followed by a drive-by shooting. Both cases were wrapped up with little effort, and I still managed time to get through enough paperwork so as to see portions of the top of my desk.

It was nice to have the breath-catching time. However, the relative peace and quiet would soon come to an end. Our killer was about to deal another card...and raise the ante.

CHAPTER SIX

A QUEEN OF SORTS

It was the time of year I hated most. Even after four months of cold and snow, winter was still hanging on, and offering little promise of spring. Football season was over, and basketball doesn't really wind my clock although it does help pass the dismal season. When the phone woke me up Sunday morning, the jack hammer working on my brain, just behind my forehead, reminded me I had been doing too much drinking lately. The phone gave up before I got to it, so I stopped by the refrigerator and pulled down two long swallows of orange juice directly out of the container, an act that would have thrown my mother and my ex-wife into a litany. The juice had just found my stomach when the phone cranked up again. This time I managed to get to it as the third ring was piercing my ear drum.

"Yeah," I answered in a tone that was meant to tell my caller I was not happy about them bothering me while I was in this state.

"Lieutenant Amato?" the female inquired.

"Right."

"This is Operator 616 from Communications. You got a body behind Headquarters. The press says it's a murder."

"The press?"

"Right, sir. It looks like they got a call that a body was back there, and they sent a reporter and a photographer over. After they found the body, they called us. The Sergeant at the scene told us to call you, and said you will probably want to call in at least one team."

"Really? What makes him say that?"

"He said there's a Queen of Spades on the body."

I had the operator notify Verno, Donovan, Mancini and Major Novitski.

I took three minutes to run myself through the shower, and 35 minutes later I pulled my car into the madness of the parking lot behind Headquarters. The triangular parking lot was still referred to as "Pine Alley" although the tiny street ceased to exist back in the late 1950's when the Public Safety building was built. For the last 40-odd years, the location was used as a parking lot for cop cars. On weekends, with most of the operations in headquarters shut down, the parking lot was void of people and the normal weekday activities. Our killer obviously was toned into that fact, and had taken advantage of it to stage his most recent endeavor.

I made my way past an assortment of television, newspaper, and radio reporters. Finally I got to the uniformed Lieutenant who had taken command of the scene.

"What have you got, Gene?" I asked as I looked at the body propped up against the left, rear tire of a police car.

"The scene's all messed up, Lute. These news animals got here before us."

"I heard. Don't sweat it. I'm sure your guys did all they could."

"From what we could piece together, this morning at about seven-thirty, a guy calls the Democrat and Chronicle and tells them he put a body back here. Shortly after calling our friends at the newspaper, he calls Channels 8, 10, 13, and at least two radio stations, and gives them the same information. It looks like Channel 8 and the D&C reporter got here about the same time. Naturally, they gather around like a herd of elephants before they finally call us down to the scene. As soon as we got here, we cleared them back about a hundred feet or so, but even so, Mike, there were foot prints, paper, film wrappers and all kinds of trash laying here by then."

"You got names for all these jerks? Names and who they work for?"

"I got two guys doing that. Verno is here already. I think he's with the first few news guys that got here."

Novitski tapped me on the shoulder, and I gave him a ten second re-cap of what Lieutenant Gene Shannon had given me.

"What about the victim?" the Major asked.

"I was just getting to that, sir," Shannon said with a nod. "Female, white, about 60 years maybe, as you can see. She's unidentified so far, but one of my guys, Officer Gonzalez, says she's a boozer from around Plymouth Avenue, up by what the guys call 'Wino Plaza.' I got Gonzalez in Records now, trying to see if he can dig up a photo or something. Oh, and the only wound I could see is the obvious one in the side of her head."

Charlie Novitski and I tried to pick a clean path to the victim, but gave up when we saw the amount of trampling that had already been done. Not bothering to try to locate a clean path - for there wasn't one - we went directly to the body. While the Major crouched down next to the body, I began to jot notes on my observations as well as the observations Novitski was making and calling out to me.

Our victim had accumulated some hard miles in her life. Now, in death, her five foot, one inch body looked relieved that life was over. Although it was only about twenty degrees outside, she was wearing slippers on her feet, and under her worn, old, brown, JC Penny's coat, she wore a simple nightgown. The killer had put his gun, probably the .9mm, well above her left temple and fired one shot that obviously went down, through the entire brain, and exited the right side of her neck.

One thing was very obvious - based on the lack of blood at the scene, and the fact that she was not dressed for the weather - the obvious conclusion was that she was killed somewhere else and then dumped here in the back lot of the Police Department. And, unlike our first two bodies, our Jane Doe's playing card was not concealed. It was pinned proudly to her coat.

"The scum ball took time to pin it on her," Novitski grunted as he raised himself up to a standing position.

While the technicians did their work, Novitski went over and handled the media people. With that out of the way for me, I went over to where Al Verno and Frank Donovan were consulting with the crime scene technician. I picked up what little information they had and told them I would meet them in the office when they were done.

"I told you this guy was gonna go public, Lute," Donovan said.

I nodded to him and sighed. Leaving the scene, I stopped by Sophie's Diner, exchanged some pleasantries with Andy, and got some donuts for the squad. Back in the office, I put on some coffee, and got ready for a long couple of days. Unlike our first two victims, we were going to have to do a lot of leg work on this one just to get her identified and locate the scene of the killing. Our whacko was not only getting more brazen, he was making us work harder. I was beginning to hate this mope!

A young cop I didn't recognize knocked on the frame of my doorway as I waited for the coffee pot to do it's thing. I looked up and waved him in.

"Lieutenant Amato? I'm Officer Gonzalez."

"Yeah, sure kid. Come on in."

"I told my boss, you know, Lt. Shannon, that I thought I knew the woman that got killed, and he told me to try to ID her."

"Right," I acknowledged. "So, what have you got?"

"Her name is Mary Ellen Williams, 52 years of age, last known address is 228 Clifton Street. She's got nineteen priors. They're mostly for prostitution, disorderly conduct, public intoxication, and one bust for possession of marijuana."

I took the piece of paper and mug shot he held out for me, and told him to pour himself some coffee.

"No thanks, Lieutenant," he said politely. "I don't drink it."

Damned new breed, I thought. These hair blowing, mousse-using, baby-faced, suburban-raised, kids don't even drink coffee! What the hell was the job coming to? I acknowledged his rejection with a smile, and asked, "Anything in her record about being called Queenie, or something of that nature?"

"Not that I noted, Lieutenant. But, I can go back and check."

"Yeah, do that," I said, trying not to sound annoyed. "And also go ahead and make a copy of her entire record, her rap sheet, and the front and back of the record folder. Also, get me a couple of more photos."

"Will do," Gonzalez said eagerly.

Before the neophyte cop could make it down the hallway, I went to the doorway and shouted to him, "And leave the folder out with a notation for the technicians to run off another fifteen, no, make it twenty more photos of her for us." God knows, I thought we would need them over the next couple of days while we went through trying to trace her last movements.

Less than a half hour later the no-coffee-drinking young copper returned and handed me six sheets of paper. "This is a copy of the victim's record folder, her rap sheet and her last booking report from two years ago."

"Do you have a first name, Officer Gonzalez?" I asked.

"Herminio, sir. Like Herman. But the guys on my platoon call me Deek."

"Deek?" I repeated.

"Deek, sir. It's kind of an inside joke, from back in the academy," Gonzalez explained with a little shrug that hinted of embarrassment.

"Well, nice job on this, Deek. I appreciate cops who know what's going on and who's hanging around on their beat. You're going to do all right on this job, kid."

After Gonzalez left the office, I freshened up my coffee and sat down at the desk to review the information he had delivered. Our victim, the late Ms. Williams, had a rap sheet that told the story of her life in short clips of arrest data. She took her first bust as a prostitute, when she was eighteen. Over the next 34 years, she lived her life as a marginal citizen trying to get rich without working for it. In her later years, she probably just gave up on it, and merely tried to survive in rooming house after rooming house.

On the second sheet of paper I found what I had been looking for. Like most street people, Mary Williams had acquired a list of names she preferred more so than the one given her by her parents. Added to the list were the nicknames thrown on her by pimps and friends who would later become her enemies. Under a column saved for alias names, Mary Williams had accumulated an impressive list of pseudonyms that were assumed for a time and later cast off. Mary Alan...Mary Allan....Queen Mary....Queen Mary Williams....Queenie Williams...Mary Queen...Queen Mary Allan...Queenie Allan.

So here we have a woman, a reject of society, dressed in what probably amounted to half of her entire wardrobe, laying dead in the freezing cold of our parking lot, killed simply because she selected, or was given, an alias that fit into some crazy person's private war. Even in death, life had dealt her a lousy hand. I suppose it was just the luck of the draw.

Before I could muse more about the sick world in which I lived, Novitski came into the office, followed by Al Verno, and Frank Donovan. The Major authorized calling in another crew member, so Mancini put a call into Bobby St. John. We went through a few more cups of coffee, as we laid out the day. The first order of business was to search for the original crime scene. From there we may be led to our killer.

Four hours later we had trailed Mary Williams' series of moves from Clifton Street, to a filthy little hotel that had long out lived its usefulness, to another rooming house, and finally, to a small studio apartment next to a sporting goods store on Genesee Street. It was there in the cramped, tidy apartment that we found Mary's brains, blood, and bone fragments spread across her kitchen wall and floor.

The scene depicted a picture of the victim seated at one end of the small, round, wooden kitchen table as her killer stood at her side and propelled a bullet into her head. The bullet made its way through the frail woman and exited, pushing the substances of life out of her and spreading it along the wall next to where her body had been seated.

Our best guess was that Queen Mary Williams knew her killer, and had welcomed the predator into her home. Two mismatched glasses sat on the table, along with four empty beer cans. The apartment showed no signs of a break-in and the killer even took the time to lock the door behind him when leaving. Williams had apparently been carried from the scene, loaded into a car, and then neatly deposited at our door step before the killer made his calls to the media people.

The evidence at the scene told its own story, but not everything. It did not tell us how the killer had smiled when he pulled the trigger. The brains and the blood could not tell us that Mary Williams had been happy to meet the man that would be her killer, that she looked forward to his visit and that she felt safe and comfortable with him. The four empty beer cans would not hold fingerprints for us to examine and they did not tell us the details of the killer being proud that he had scammed the woman to meet with him and let him into her little corner of the world so that he could kill her. The mismatched glasses told a little about the victim's poverty but they could not let us know they had been clicked together in a toast to the man's "new venture," which, it so happened, included her murder. The three-room apartment did not speak a word of how the killer had dressed Mary Williams in her coat and how he joked with the body about dressing her for public display as he pinned the Queen of Spades on her well worn coat.

Later, when we viewed the videos taken by the news people, we would angrily comment that Queenie Williams' legs had been spread wide apart when the killer positioned her, so that in death she would be humiliated by her killer just in case life had spared her any tiny bit of embarrassment.

While the technicians methodically went about their tasks, Verno and Donovan sat down with the landlady. Esther Foster was a gentle, soft-spoken Black woman who often called her God to bear witness to her shock and grief over the loss of her new found friend and tenant.

"Praise Jesus," she proclaimed. "Miss Williams was a kind, Christian woman. She moved in here back four months ago and her and me, well, Lord Almighty, we just took to each other. She was quiet. Kept to herself mostly, but, Praise Jesus, she give you a big smile and warm, 'Hello' every time she see you. Paid her rent on time, even ahead of time some months. Lord God Almighty! Why in God's green earth would somebody do this to her?"

I didn't have an answer for Miss Foster. The same question had plagued me for years, and no matter where I looked for the answer, it was not forthcoming. I had given up on God providing answers to my questions. Consequently, I also gave up asking the question and concentrated my efforts on finding the ones who committed the deeds. Time, the great teacher, had educated me to the fact that many times not even the killer had the answer.

I left the two detectives with Foster and went back up to oversee the technicians processing the scene. Without any hint of indulgence, I instructed them, "Coat this place with fingerprint powder. If you don't have enough, go back and get more. If the city doesn't have enough, get the distributor to send in more. This place is the only frigging lead we have, and I don't want anything missed!"

Twenty minutes later, while the technicians were discovering everything they were dusting was showing signs it had been wiped down carefully, the dispatcher had me return to the office to meet with the Major. Once back at headquarters, I learned that Novitski had briefed Westfield. Our beloved Chief had given the go ahead to hold a press conference. Normally Ben Westfield would have been more than happy to put his pretty face and custom-made suit in front of the cameras, but sensing the potential explosive nature of this press meeting, he had ordered me to be the one to confront the mob of arrogant, self-righteous, reporters. If there was going to be hell to pay for this latest development, Westfield wanted a whipping boy out there to blame, and, who better to fill that position than little old me!

       I walked into the Chief's Conference Room. The table top was strung with wires that came up from three sides of the table and led to a bank of microphones at the head of the table. Before I could adjust my eyes to the blinding lights provided by all three television stations, questions were shouted from around the room. I waited until I was seated before I made my opening remarks.

       "Ladies and gentleman," I began and then cleared my throat. "I will give you a statement about the investigation that is under way, and then I will have time for only a few questions." I didn't wait for the commotion to begin again, before telling them the department was investigating, "...the recent murder of Mary Ellen Williams, a 52 year-old woman whose body was found in the rear parking lot of Police Headquarters this morning." I muttered something about several leads that were being pursued. Gratuitously I threw in that Chief Westfield was supporting the investigation with the entire resources of the Department.

       My inquiry, "Questions?" drew a chaotic mass of yelling and shoving as each media animal tried to get past his or her colleagues and demand an answer to an individual question that was believed to be more insightful than the others. I waited for the roar to settle down.

       Finally, after the commotion subsided, a young reporter from Channel 8, who had been relegated the lowly assignment of weekend coverage and now saw this story as her way out of the weekends and into evening news, asked above the rest, "Are you now ready to admit, now that we have heard it from the killer's....ah, *alleged* killer's mouth, that this murder and the murders of Misters Lanovara and Landers, are all connected."

       "We have seen the possibility of that connection all along and have been pursuing that possibility ever since the finding of Jack Landers' body."

       "The caller said he has left calling cards for you with each of the bodies," a school boy looking reporter from the Democrat and Chronicle said. Embarrassed to find himself half standing as he made his comment, he looked around, sat down, and asked, "Will you comment on those 'calling cards'? Are they playing cards such as we saw on today's victim?"

"I'm sorry, but I will not comment on any evidence that may or may not have been left at any of the scenes."

"Do you expect more killings of this nature, this string that now has been started?" an anonymous voice asked from somewhere on the far side of the table.

"We are concerned we are dealing with a person who may be very distraught. Due to the fact that he is in this mental situation, we are of course concerned, as we always are, that more citizens of the community may be in danger."

"Lieutenant?" the school boy from the D&C asked in an almost plea, "Are you going to admit to us, what we already know, and that is, that the killer is leaving you a playing card on each of his victims?"

"Like I said, I am not going to comment..."

"Starting with the Ten of Spades on Mister Frankie Ten Times Lanovara," he continued over my voice. "To the Jack of Spades on the Jack of All Trades, Jack Landers, and now the Queen of Spades, the very Queen of Spades all of us personally saw this morning, on Miss Williams' coat?'

"What I am saying young man," I said as I leaned forward and pointed my finger at him. "Is that it is dangerous and fool hearty to go off on some wild theory, such as your newspaper did with this L-A-N thing, just a few days ago. Other than that, I will not comment on anything that may be of an evidentiary nature." I looked around the room, rather proud of myself for embarrassing the little puppy reporter.

Leonard Gressin, a tall, lean reporter with Channel 13, raised his hand politely and asked, "Lieutenant?"

Happy to see one familiar, old-time face out of all the part time, weekend weenies of the press, I nodded to him and asked, "Leonard?"

"When my colleague from the print media asked about the caller telling us that he is leaving *you* calling cards, are you fully aware of what he means by 'you'?"

"I suppose the reference is to the Department, or perhaps more to the investigators on this case. Why? What's your point?"

"My point is this, Lieutenant Amato, the caller told us he is challenging you, you personally. He told us, and I quote here, 'I have been leaving Detective Amato my calling card, and he is too stupid to get me. You tell him I can get to anyone, anyone at all, even him, and he can't stop me!'"

It took me a second to respond, so I cleared my throat, and then managed a smile. "Well Len, I would say the caller wants to make this personal, and I refuse to lower myself to his level. However, with a quote as exact as that, I would guess you have a tape of the call, and naturally, I suppose a professional news agency such as yours would see it as its civic duty to make the tape available to the police." My voice made the statement, but my raised eyebrows asked the question.

"We would be happy to, Lieutenant," Gressin said with a smile and a tip of the head.

The news conference went on for another ten minutes. As always, I tried to say a lot without giving up any specific information. With very few exceptions, the same questions were asked repeatedly. If a reporter from one media asked a particularly insightful question, each of the TV and radio reporters would repeat it in some fashion. Later in the day their particular station would broadcast their outstanding reporter asking the probing question.

The event ended when Donovan, as arranged prior to the media feeding frenzy, paged me exactly on time, providing me with an excuse to leave the reporters without getting to all of their questions.

It was about one o'clock in the morning when I finally made it to the relative comfort of my bed. In the twilight zone that lingers between sleep and waking, I had to admit there wasn't much to think about. With the exception of finding the crime scene, the entire eighteen hour work day had added up to a big zero. Zip. *Niente.* No runs. No hits. And, as far as I knew at this point, no errors.

The crime scene had given us little with which to work. The entire apartment yielded less than two dozen finger prints, and all of those belonged to our victim or to her landlady, Esther Foster. The guys had been able to interview just about all of the tenants in the other four apartment units. That also led nowhere. As far as anyone knew, Queenie Williams had no male callers, and she lived a quiet life. As near as her few friends and neighbors could tell, her only source of income was some type of government subsistence and some spare change she made playing the numbers.

The Channel 13 lead also went no place. None of the other stations, nor the newspaper clowns, had a recording of the caller. We picked up a copy of the tape from Leonard Gressin and listened repeatedly to the caller's short-clipped words. It was obvious he had disguised his voice and tried - with some degree of success - to give himself a mechanical, almost robotic speech. I couldn't help becoming angry at his subtle joy in breaking our chops.

Our big accomplishment of the day was being able to fix the last time Mary Williams was seen alive. That did us a little good, but it was nothing to get excited over. Paula and Wayne Crosby, Williams' upstairs neighbors, saw her at about 7:00 P.M., Saturday night, as they were leaving and Mary was coming home. They spoke only long enough to exchange greetings, and for our most recent victim to inquire about the time. The Crosby's said Mary said something to the effect that she was glad it was earlier than she had expected, because she had to, "neaten up" her place for some company. Naturally, the Crosby's, nor any other living creature that we knew of, had seen the company that Mary Williams awaited.

The sum total of the entire day was that we were now 90 percent sure our killer was a male...and, of course, that he really enjoyed making asses of the cops, especially this cop! My mind drifted back to my conversation with Frank Donovan. How had he put it? Chewing on the hamburger a few days ago, while we had a few beers, he had said something like, "I wouldn't be surprised if the killer goes to the press." Had he simply sensed what our whacko killer had very well confirmed for us now? Was he really that intuitive?

On top of my wondering about my good friend and reliable detective was the gnawing mental taunting that these killings were somehow about me.

In the darkness I found myself becoming angry. This bastard! How could he do this? How could he make me suspect my friends while he killed the innocents. I was here to protect these people, and this mad man, this crazy animal, was out there killing them because of me, because of something I did, or knew, or said, or was. The irony of it went to my gut. Was it truly possible that people were getting killed because I, the one who was supposed to protect them, had done something to set off this mental defect? If he wants me, why not come and get me? Why does he have to use these other people in order to get to me? Was that the scheme? Was his grand plan to humiliate me first, make me suffer through all these other deaths before causing mine?

In the darkness of the night I thought about calling Diane, but dismissed the thought. It had been six, maybe seven weeks since we talked, and by calling her now I would simply let on how much I needed her.

Instead of making the call, I got up and rummaged through the bathroom. Finally I found the roll of antacids. I chewed a couple of them and washed them down with some left over vodka and melted ice cubes I had left on the living room coffee table. Going out on to the balcony, I lit a cigarette and gazed out at suburbia. As my stomach settled down to a mumbled churning, I said to the night air, "Ah! Coffee, booze, antacids and cigarettes. The only true friends a busted down cop has to keep him company."

CHAPTER SEVEN

OPENING OLD WOUNDS

I won't bother you with the details of what didn't happen over the next couple of days. Let it suffice to say we didn't get too far with Mary Williams' homicide. Every corner we turned became a dead end. Every lead led us nowhere. It was kind of like the old joke - we were lost, but we were making great time! The only good thing to come out of the Williams homicide - if there is ever a good thing to come out of a homicide - is that Bolson's L-A-N theory went down the toilet.

The news people were killing us. They seemed only too anxious to promote the feeling of fear in the streets as a killer cloaked in anonymity selected his victims based on a criteria known only to him. And, of course, they were equally thrilled to rhetorically ask what the police were doing to catch the killer.

Whatever time spent on the investigation was matched and exceeded by the time we spent on the phone reassuring every person named King, associated with anything connected to King, or paranoid about any other damn thing in their lives, that they were not the next victim. In reality, we had no idea who our nut had targeted to have the King of Spades placed on his or her lifeless body. We had failed to predict who might be the Queen victim. Mary Williams wasn't even on our list of Queen candidates. Now we were in the process of compiling a list of over five hundred names who might become the recipient of the fourth card.

Even though there was little to report, my dreaded daily treks to the Chief's Office continued. Maybe I was becoming desensitized to our over-bearing leader, but it seemed that he was becoming more of a normal human being. He was easier to deal with, but I still didn't like or trust him. Westfield began to listen to my briefings, and then asked relevant questions about the investigation, never once attempting to revive his earlier mob-connection theory. At the same time, Novitski suggested a couple of more times that I talk to Westfield. Each time I gave kind of a half-hearted acknowledgment, but stayed away from any lay-the-cards-on-the-table chats with the Chief. He was the Chief and I was a half way up the ladder flunky. The percentages of me coming out a winner in such a supposed man-to-man chat were not in my favor. If there was no way I could win the game, then there was no sense in playing.

It was a Tuesday morning when I sensed a new change in Benjamin Westfield. Besides seeming to be more quiet, the Chief jotted down a few notes. When I was done, he put his pen down, closed the pad and pushed himself away from his desk. I had seen, and used, this close-the-notebook trick too often. Reporters loved to use the technique with cops. The closing of the notebook indicated the remainder of the conversation was going to be confidential, and consequently, the person being interviewed was suppose to relax. It was also effective in my job, when interrogating some mope from the streets. I prepared myself for Westfield's next move. It was sure to be a question introduced by the phrase, "Off the record now..."

However, instead of what I expected, the Chief asked, "How are your people holding up under all of this, Lieutenant?"

"Sir?" was the only response I could manage.

"The investigators down there in Violent Crimes, how are they doing?"

My mind tried to process the question. Why was it being asked? What was he after? How was whatever I answered going to be turned around and used against me?

I knew the guys were dragging. They were tired and they were frustrated. Besides the normal work load of assorted fresh cases of armed robberies, rapes, murders, and near-murders that came in nightly, they had their old cases to carry. This new case, this serial thing, was burying them. They were working long hours and their home lives were suffering. Sooner or later the arguments at home would become worse and their attitudes toward the job and each other would pay the price. Things were not good "down there in Violent Crimes" but that wasn't something I wanted to share with Ben Westfield.

"Everything's okay, Chief. They're putting in a lot of hours, but there aren't any serious problems." Then I couldn't help but ask, "Why?"

"I was wondering, that's all," he answered. Then, as he looked up to the ceiling, swiveled back and forth in his chair, he took a deep breath and blew it out with a sigh. Westfield then turned back toward me. "These types of cases impact people. Many times one might not even sense it, but they do, and when they do manifest themselves, it can be tragic."

There was one of those pregnant pauses after his philosophical observation. I knew all too well what he was talking about because I had lost one of my investigators to a nervous breakdown, two were in or just completing the divorce process, and one of my former Detectives had ended up attempting suicide before he finally left the squad. My own divorce could be chalked up to "things down there in Violent Crimes" but that also was none of the Chief's business.

Sensing the conversation was over, I got up to leave, but Westfield asked me to hang on for a minute.

"Problem?" I asked.

"Your Major suggested that you and I talk. He, ah, said that some things between you and I need to be cleared up, to kind of, you know, maybe to clear the air, so to speak." The man was obviously uncomfortable with the subject. I was irritated that Novitski had pushed the issue with the Chief, but decided to play this scene straight, and ease Ben Westfield's uneasiness. The lean, neat, man's voice was calm, but his eyes gave away a certain something, something I couldn't identify. He was speaking with his lips, but his eyes were studying me, as if analyzing my inner being.

"The only thing we need to clear the air on, Chief," I said in the most benevolent tone I could develop. "Is that we always seem to be at odds, and, well, to be perfectly frank, I'm concerned it's something personal between you and I."

"Go on," he said with a sincere voice.

Go on? Go on? You started this conversation and now you want to pass the ball to me, I thought to myself. Serves me right for dropping my guard. Sensing I was being trapped into spilling my guts while he stood silent, I suggested, "Well, if I'm off base, and there is nothing wrong between us, then just tell me, and I will take you at your word. On the other hand, if it is something personal, and you have the time, I hope we can make it right."

Again, silence roared.

Finally, a half minute later he said, "There's no denying it, Lieutenant, our relationship is not the best. I guess I haven't kept my feelings toward you in check, and those, ah, those feelings, do seem to spill over in our day-to-day dealings." The Chief paused for a full ten seconds, and I felt he was not waiting for me to jump in, but rather, he was trying to mentally develop his next point. Finally the vacuum of silence was violated, and he said, "You know it goes back to William, I suppose."

There it was! With a loud thud, the subject was on the table. Having opened the wound, Ben Westfield then looked at me with just the faintest trace of a smile...or malice.

"Chief, I was just doing my job. It was nothing personal."

"Come on, Lieutenant!" he said in a voice that was not anger, but almost a plea. "There's doing the job, and then there's *doing the job*!" He waited for a response, and not getting one, he continued. "I'll concede that you may have seen the incident as simply doing your job, but it was a minor thing, a neighborhood thing among kids. It could have been handled differently. We could have kept it in-house."

"Chief," I said softly. "It was a rape."

"*Technically*, it was rape," he said, as if correcting my grammar. "It was statutory, sure, but it was hardly rape. Damn it, Lieutenant, you ruined the boy's life." I wondered if I should even continue the conversation, but I knew there was no way out of it now. Besides, the gate was opened, so, what the hell? Hadn't I been waiting years to get this thing cleaned up and out of the way? We might as well go through with the thing now, and get it out in the open, and maybe resolved.

I should have thought about the percentages once again, but I didn't. "The girl was fifteen-years-old," my voice said in a voice that almost squeaked. "Your son was seventeen. And," I paused for effect, "there were clear signs of force. What was I supposed to have done?"

"You could have used some common sense, Lieutenant," Westfield said in soft but sardonic sort of way. "For God's sake, she was the neighborhood slut. She was screwing half the damn neighborhood, and you knew that, Mike. You knew that!"

"You know what? You guys make me laugh. You bosses with that 'you should have used some common sense' line. Every time something doesn't go your way, you drag out the common sense bull." My voice remained calm. Unfortunately, my choice of words indicated the anger brewing in my guts.

"It's basic common sense not to make a mountain out of a mole hill, Lieutenant!" Westfield said with some emphasis and a little anger of his own.

"It's not that simple, Chief. You have to put the damn thing is perspective," I reasoned. "Don't forget what was going on back then. The department had just been ripped apart with the O'Connor Commission Report. They had destroyed us over some of the games that were being played with fixed tickets, cases that were being buried, and all the other crap that was going on back then." I had been holding this thing in my gut for all these years, and now that he had opened the door, I knew exactly what needed to be said. I had said the words a couple of hundred times when I had argued with Westfield's shadow that emerged during some of my more notable drunken stupors.

"The girl's parents raised holy hell," I told the man asking for common sense. "They were screaming about going to the press, the District Attorney, the Governor, and everybody else in the world. I ran the entire thing past my boss and he said to charge your kid."

"We go back a long time, Lieutenant. We were in the Academy together. Right? We worked together back in the foot beat days. Did you forget all that? You should have talked to me first, Mike. That's all I'm saying." His forehead wrinkled and he sounded like he was beseeching me to understand his religious beliefs. "You should have had a sit down with me and given me the chance to meet with the girl's parents. You could have at least given me the chance to talk with the girl and her folks. We could have worked it out."

I thought he was near tears, but he took a breath, and it seemed, in that short second, regained his composure. With his composure he regained control of the dialogue. "You ruined the boy's life, Lieutenant. Billy was never the same after he took that rap. In your haste you turned him from a good kid to a...." he stammered as he searched for the right word. "A failure, a vagrant who wanders aimlessly from place to place just looking to get back some, some dignity in his life."

I wasn't buying this poor Billy crap. Life is choices and the kid had made his own choices. He crossed the line from right to wrong. It wasn't my doing and I wasn't taking the fall for it. I wanted to take this man and shake him, and talk to him about accountability, about Billy being responsible for his own acts, and the results of those acts. Instead, I took a gentle approach and let my judgments be silent judgments. This thing had to end and be done with.

"In hind sight, maybe I could have sought some other resolution, maybe I should have," I conceded the point. "But, then again, right then and there, I did what I could, and I did what I thought was right, Chief. I went to my Captain, and I got his advice. He said to charge your boy, so I charged him. He said he would square it with you, and for me to stay out of it. He was as paranoid as hell about being sure it didn't look like we were sweeping it all under the rug because it was a cop's kid. You remember what it was like? Everyone was paranoid about everything."

The conversation also brought to mind the agonizing I had done over the William Westfield arrest. I was sure most of the cops on the job would give me the cold shoulder after I arrested Captain Ben Westfield's kid. I truly expected to be ostracized by the members of the department. But, at that time and many times since then, I remembered my mentor's advice. I was broken in by an old time beat cop named Trapper Jokovich and it was Trapper who told me to always do the right thing regardless of the second guessing that was sure to come. Busting Bill Westfield had been the right thing. I could live with it. The Chief needed to learn to live with it.

Westfield looked at me as if he was etching each and every feature of my face into his memory. Finally he said, "You were wrong, Lieutenant. You were wrong then, and you're wrong now. Maybe you don't want to hear it, but I think you were doing then what you are doing right now." When I didn't respond and offer him an opening to explain what he meant by that last remark, he continued. "You were grandstanding, Lieutenant. Plain and simple, you were trying to make a reputation for yourself, a reputation for *Ace* Detective Mike Amato, the gallant crime fighter on the white horse." The Chief paused, probably just for effect, before he waved both hands in the air and said, "Oh no! Ace Amato was not going to be swayed by Captain Westfield!"

Now I no longer wanted to shake some sense into him. Now I wanted to punch him in the face! Billy and two of his friends had held the girl down and taken turns with her. Sure, I knew she was no virgin. After talking to people around the neighborhood, it was no secret she was the high school free piece of tail. But still, she was raped. It wasn't just statutory, it was rape! She had a right to say yes or no to whomever wanted to get into her pants. She had refused them access and they beat her. Pure, forced, against her will, rape! Billy Westfield and his two bully buddies were mad because the girl wouldn't put out to them. It was their pride, their inflated egos, their demanding for themselves what the girl gave freely to other guys, that got them into trouble. It wasn't my fault Bill Westfield ended up with a rap sheet, it was his own meanness that earned him a criminal record. I bit my lower lip and simply said, "I respect your opinion, Chief, but I don't think you are seeing the whole picture."

"You're right, Lieutenant, it is my opinion. And obviously, it is an opinion you do not share," he said as he continued to study me with narrowed eyes and a sliver of a grin.

This conversation was going nowhere good. Right then, right at that very point, the conversation changed directions. This was no longer a peace-making conversation. This was becoming an in-your-face argument. I wanted to get up, to just get up from the chair and leave, but I couldn't. It was as if a magnet was pulling my butt down into the seat. I should have gotten up and left right then, right there, that second. For better or for worse, I didn't.

For Ben Westfield, time had obliterated the facts of the case. I wanted him to remember those facts. "The girl suffered a black eye, bruised ribs, and a dislocated shoulder, Chief. Her panties were torn and her blouse had been ripped open. The marks on her wrists substantiated her story that she had been tied up to a ceiling beam in the garage. All that, along with the presence of sperm in her vagina and hair, sure made it sound like a rape to me." I paused before taking a cheap shot I just couldn't resist. "I don't think you have to be an *ace detective* to figure that one out."

Westfield examined the cuticles of his right hand as he commented, "You have your opinions and I have mine."

"And, I suppose you have other opinions too, Chief. You have some more opinions and we're going to get into those too, aren't we?"

Westfield smiled. It was a weak smile that started in the left corner of his mouth, began to spread across his lips, but stopped suddenly. It stopped and froze, and when it did, it became a sneer.

"Yes, Lieutenant. I have other opinions. I have the opinion that you're a renegade. You're the type of guy who always has to make waves, always has to do things his own way, always hears a different drummer. You, and those like you, see yourselves as the only true cops. You resent those of us who chose another career path. You resent those of us who came into the Department and saw another way to the top. You came on the job and you decided to be one of those, those, crime fighters as you like to think of yourselves. Street cops. Real cops. That's what you like to be called, isn't it?"

I merely shrugged. This was his show now. I had my say, so I might as well let him have his say. I wasn't going back on the defensive by answering his rhetorical questions.

"I know what you and the other, 'street cops' call us," Westfield continued as he got out of his chair and stood, looking at a picture behind his desk with his back to me. "You call us the, 'Briefcase cops,' the 'Gunless.' Oh, it's all very cute. You look down your noses at us while you go out on your streets and play cops and robbers like a bunch of kids. That was the thing with your Captain back then, the oh so righteous Captain Thompson. He hated me too." Westfield turned to face me now. "He also resented me for accomplishing what he couldn't do. It infuriated him to no end that it took him twenty-some odd years to make Captain and I had made it in less than half that time. He used you, Amato. Thompson used you to get to me through my son! Well, let me tell you something, Lieutenant," he said very evenly, without raising his voice as he normally liked to do. "I paid my dues too! While you and Thompson, and the other grunt cops were out there grabbing

all the glory, I and some others were in here making this department run."
He paused again, and rotated slightly away from my direction. "The thing is
this," Westfield said as he turned back suddenly to face me and make his
point. "You and your type aren't running this department. You got left behind.
This is a new department with new ways, and you haven't kept up, Lieutenant.
You're a dinosaur! There is no place for you in this department, *my*
department! You see, while you were plotting your career as a crime fighter,
you didn't figure that some day Captain Westfield would be Chief Westfield!"
He was on a roll now and he wanted to get all this out. Like me, he had been
waiting years to say this, and now he was going to dump it all.

"So now you have to come up and report to me every day because I say
so, and you don't like that. His voice began to rise in volume and pitch.
"Well, that's too damn bad, Lieutenant! You talk about choices like some
pious saint. Well, you made your choices and I made mine. My choices got
me here, and your choices kept you there on your precious streets. You want
facts? Here's a fact for you. You resent me being here. You resent me being
able to order you around. You resent the fact that I, one of the 'gunless' that
you joke about, got to be your Chief of Police!"

"And *you* resent *me*, Chief." My retort was of schoolboy caliber, but I
was so mad I, it was the best I could do at the moment. I wasn't going to be
a whipping boy for this guy's inflated ego and his wounded pride. "Yeah, I
made choices...choices I'm glad I made. You say I'm a dinosaur, well, maybe
so. But the reality of it is, is that you need dinosaurs like me. You guys in the
vests and silk ties, you need me and the other street cops you ridicule. We're
the ones who make you look good. We're the ones who go out and lay our
dicks on the line so you can stand up next to the politicians and take credit
for the streets being safe."

"You can go now, Lieutenant," Westfield said without turning around
from the picture he was now straightening. He was a man who needed to be
in control and he wasn't going to allow me to wrestle that control from him.
He was an arrogant, self-centered, ego-maniac and wasn't about to give my
rantings the respect of a reply.

"I don't think so, Chief. You started this. You opened this conversation
with a nice level, man-to-man chat. I thought we were finally going to settle
this thing, but hell no! You had to take your shots at me, and now you want
to call a time out. Tough! Now you stand still while I take my shots. You
want to do your thing, then fine, do your thing. But you understand full well,
you acknowledge in your gut that you need me...need me and resent me as
much as I resent you."

"Get out, Lieutenant," he said calmly, waving the back of his hand at me.

The chair's seat finally released its grip on me, and I stood up, almost shouting, "You need me and you resent me, and do you know why you resent me? You resent me because I *don't* need you! You know that, and that just pisses you off to no end."

"This meeting is over, Lieutenant. Now get out of here!" Ben Westfield said to me flatly with just the slightest edge on his voice.

I left the office with the realization that the Chief was losing it. He had gone over the top of the hill. He was going nuts! The only confused emotion I had as I left the office was that I felt sorry for him.

A few days slipped by and nothing notable happened. I stopped reporting to the Chief's Office every morning, but nothing was said. Like everything else in the Department, an order only lived so long before it was killed or it died a natural death.

Novitski asked me about the conversation with Westfield, but I just passed it off with a comment that the entire thing ended up being pretty ugly. His thirty-two years on the job told him that the matter was something he was better off not knowing about.

I threw myself into the case. Putting Westfield, department politics and the petty jealousies aside, I dove into the reports, chasing leads and knocking on doors. Art Mancini, the temporary help from OCB, turned out to be a real pleasure with whom to work. He had a nose for leads, loved to interview people, and, his dead-pan sense of humor kept me in good spirits. Sergeant Mancini moved, talked and even dressed like the mob guys he normally investigated. And, like the wiseguys, he had developed a sense for reading people, for smelling their weaknesses, and exploiting those weaknesses. Time and again, I found him asking that one additional question, taking the one extra step with some street-smart mug, and pulling out that last little tidbit of information.

We were trying to run down a guy named Harold. It was the name of a man that one of Mary Williams' neighbors threw into the game. The elderly woman said Mary sometimes talked about Harold as if he was a close personal friend, or perhaps, a boyfriend, or even an ex-husband. Mancini and I talked to almost anyone with whom Queen Mary had ever had contact. We talked to her street friends, people she had called when she had been busted, friends of friends, shirt-tail relatives, and former neighbors. Still, there was no lead on this Harold guy.

Based on a half dozen little, almost meaningless, pieces of information, we were looking into the possibility of our subject living in the area of East Main and Gibbs Street. We ran Harold's and Mary's names and descriptions past fifteen, twenty people in the area. It was getting to be the end of a very long, boring day when we ran into Thelma Tindendale, a stout little woman living in a row house about halfway down a block of row houses.

"You saying 'Harold'," she said. "But you meaning Harrod!"

"I don't get you," Mancini said.

"Everyone think his name be Harold. All the time folks here be calling him Harold, but the man's name be Harrod, Harrod Jones. Him and Queenie Williams be long-time friends...if you get my meaning," she offered with a wink.

"You know where we can find him and talk to him?"

"*Talk* to him? No, I don't know where you can get to be to talk to him."

I was about to turn around and walk away, when Mancini smiled at the hefty woman and asked, "But, you do know where we can find him, right?"

"You can find him, but you can't talk to him no way," Thelma said with a husky laugh, enjoying her give and take with the two cops at her door.

"Meaning...?" Art asked with a return chuckle.

"He dead," she said with a laugh. "Harrod dead and buried. The man been dead maybe two, three years now!"

Back in the car, we headed toward Headquarters with Art Mancini laughing as the car swept a U-turn in the street.

"What the hell's so funny, Art?" I had to ask. "You and her have a thing going?"

"She was having the time of her life, Lute. We were the best entertainment she's had since Ed Sullivan was on television."

Two days work had just gone down the tubes and led nowhere, but Mancini was getting a kick out of it. We rode the rest of the way in silence, and as we did so I stole a couple of glances at my temporary partner. Like I said, I kind of liked the guy and the way he worked. Still, there was something about him, something that was wrong, or maybe something that was too right. Maybe it was the nagging clue we developed in the Landers homicide, the lead about the union leader having a meeting with a detective. I suggested to myself that I was too suspicious, too weary of good fortune, of things that gave a feeling that everything was okay. As we entered the underground parking of the Public Safety Building, my cautious side reminded me to be careful around anyone who may be in good favor with Ben Westfield.

On the way up to the Detective Bureau, we stopped at the Records Section. When we checked Mary Williams' record along with Harrod Jones' criminal history, we found the link. Several of them to be exact. The two had lived

together back in the early 1970's. On one occasion they had even been arrested
at the same drug house at the same time. Now, over twenty-five years later
they were united again. Harrod had died peacefully and naturally in the
Veteran's Hospital. Mary had died violently at the hands of a psycho.

The sun was down when I pushed myself away from the typewriter. I
was pissed that Bolson, with all of his computer programs, had missed the
Williams and Jones connection, but decided to put the matter aside. I pulled
my bottle of Sambuca out of the bottom drawer of the desk and poured a shot
in the coffee cup I needed to refill. The sweet, licorice-flavored liqueur did
little to hide the nastiness of burnt, stale, hours old coffee.

Three victims were in their graves, and we had nothing. Suspects? Oh,
yes! We had suspects. We had a whole list of *possible* suspects, but not one
single *probable* suspect. At this point we could all, even Westfield, eliminate
the Mafia crowd as being suspect. That was of little consolation when you
consider the list of suspects that had taken the mob's place. Some cop on the
department, or some other department, came into range as a possible suspect.
Every nut case walking the streets and afraid the Martians were sending
signals into his brain was a suspect. A couple of hundred of people who had
an ax to grind with me were possible suspects. Our guy could be some old
fan of mine who was fresh out of Attica and had decided to even the score
and make my life miserable for a while. If we took the time to sit down and
draw up the list, we would probably end up with one longer than the list of
potential next victims. Oh, yes sir, we had possible suspects up the kazoo...but
we only had one *probable* suspect. The mope who called the press on Sunday
morning a week and a half ago was the only probable suspect...and that took
us full circle, all the way back to square one. Every nut case, every one with
a score to settle with me, every person out there with a need for notoriety
could have been the caller.

That was the calling card of this whole damn case. It was a circle jerk.
Every avenue took us to a blind alley, leading onto a street to nowhere, bringing
us to a dead end.

I stacked the reports back into the accordion folder. The photos and the
tech sheets went toward the back, the reports in the middle and the lead
sheets to the front. Unfortunately, it was the latter that took up the least space.
I set Mary Williams' and Harrod Jones' criminal records in my, "To Be Filed"
basket and made a mental note to insure they were returned to the
Department's Records Section the next day.

Finally, for the first time since this case started, I had a bright idea. What
we had found out when we laid Jones' file next to Williams' file was very
interesting. What were we going to find to be very interesting when we

compared all three of our victim's files? Lanovara's, Landers', and Williams' records had to be laid side by side and compared line by line. Could it be the three of them connected in some way, just like we found the connection between Mary and Harrod? Could it be they used the same lawyer? The same bail bondsman perhaps? Maybe they all came from the same neighborhood. God in heaven, make it that simple, please do!

One call to Sergeant Jeff Bolson at home instantly broke my bubble. He had already done what I proposed.

"I did it, Lieutenant. I dumped it all into the data base and ran it every possible way. I included their criminal histories, the background information we had, even their high schools. Nothing! I came up with nothing. There is no link," he said with finality.

"I thought you might have, Sergeant," I lied. "But I want to do it again. Okay? Just go with me on this, all right? I want to take every possible factor, their lawyers, barbers, religion, and so forth. Everything!" I decided not to mention him missing the connection between Mary Williams and Harrod Jones, a connection that took us two full work days to run down!

I hung up the phone and considered the possibility of doing it myself, with my own eyes instead of through some computer. That way, done by a human, there's no error, no miscalculation, no wrong keys punched.

I stood at my desk and threw the stapler across the room. Here it was, well past quitting time, and I was sitting around an empty office, trying to create work. Diane was right. The job did consume me. The job, the cops, and the dead bodies were the only things to which I could commit myself. The day she left me she had told me I was weak, too weak to let go of the job. What I saw as strength, dedication, and responsibility, she had seen as weakness, stubbornness, and ego.

For the past few days I had toyed with the idea of making a call, and now, alone in the office, I did it. I danced my fingers over the buttons and took a deep breath as the call was connected. On the second ring I thought about hanging up the phone, but she answered on the third ring, and the choice was made for me.

"Hi," I said. "This is Mike."

"Well hello, Michael. It's been a while."

"So, how's it going with you?"

"Pretty good. I've been working hard with a couple of work projects."

My brain went dead as I now tried to make small talk and realized I should have thought this call out a little better. We exchanged a few more mindless sentences around a couple of safe subjects before she asked, "Is there any special reason for this call, Michael?"

"Can't a guy just call his ex-wife once in awhile to see how she is?" I asked and caught myself blushing.

"Sure he can, but he usually only calls when he doesn't have a dead body to keep him occupied, and he's totally intoxicated."

"Wow!" I said with feigned shock. "That hurt!"

"So why are you calling?" Diane asked. "From what I see in the papers you are up to your neck in bodies, and those are usually the times I don't hear from you...and didn't hear from you, even when we were married."

"I just had a couple of minutes and realized it's been a month or so since we last talked."

"Almost three months, Michael," she corrected.

"Yeah, well, I thought anyway that I should call and see if maybe we could have dinner or something." I said it and then cringed, not knowing if I had opened the door for more criticism.

Surprisingly, she said, "That would be nice. It's been quite a while since we sat and talked face to face. It might be nice to do that."

My blush had blossomed into a smile as we made arrangements, being ever so careful to leave the door open to the possibility of last minute changes, "...if something comes up."

"Something will come up, Michael," she said lightly. "It always does. It always did. You have my pager number, so give me a call when you can't make it because of *the job*."

I left the office and drove directly home. I changed into some sweats and, after a couple of belts of Southern Comfort, made some pasta. Scanning television channels with the remote, I finally found a boxing match on cable. A half dozen more shots of liquor found their way to my gut before I finally turned in. I spent the majority of my hours in the sack tossing, turning and thinking, but not sleeping. The booze had done little to numb my brain.

I replayed my conversation with Ben Westfield a couple of dozen times. What the hell was all that about? It looked like he began with an attempt to bury the hatchet we had been tossing around for a decade, but it sure as hell didn't end up that way. I was fairly comfortable with the feeling that I wasn't responsible for turning the conversation around, but, on the other hand, I couldn't be positive. People say I tend to be abrasive. Maybe my abrasivness kicked in automatically. My best guess was that he just had the entire thing on his chest for so long. He had to dump it sooner or later, and today was the day. Remembering how he had looked at me, absorbing me, and, maybe in doing so he observed something in me, some weakness that made him think it was the right time to attack. Regardless of what had changed his attempt at truce into an attack, it was clear he carried a ton of baggage over me busting his kid. Maybe if the tables were turned, maybe I would want to make each waking day of his life as miserable as he tried to make mine.

My conscience was clear about Westfield's kid. He did the crime and he had to take his licks. But, if my conscience was so clear, then why wasn't I sleeping? I thought about what Trapper Jokovich had taught me half a lifetime earlier. I had done the right thing with Westfield's kid, and, I had done the thing right. So, the hell with it!

I probably drifted off for an hour or so, and then my mind nudged me awake again. The murders. Three dead people. Three people who would no longer move around with the rest of us. Frankie Ten Times was no loss to the world, but he was a victim, my victim. I was responsible for him, for seeking his revenge, for seeing that his killer was removed from the general population. Even forgetting the fat bastard, there was Jack Landers. Landers probably had his share of Ben Westfields buried in his past, people who hated him for the rights he had done that were perceived as wrongs by the company owners who had to pay their people more money and grant them better benefits. Still, the guy was no threat to anyone. He was a father and a grandfather, a senior citizen who targeted no one for pain, and should have not been anyone's target for a bullet.

I flipped over on my stomach, punched my pillow into a mound and buried my head into it, as if doing so would push me into a sleep. Instead of sleep I saw Mary Williams propped up against the wheel of a car in the snow-covered parking lot. Lanovara was a predator. Jack Landers was a mover and a shaker. She had been neither. However, the killer had selected her all the same. Selected her why? Selected her because she had been unfortunate enough to have a nickname tagged on her twenty years ago?

And then there was us. Homicide. Detectives. The Police Department. A crime lab. The public looked at us and asked us why, and we had to tell them we had no idea why. Three bodies. Three crime scenes. Five bullets. Zero leads. Nothing to go on. No ideas. No suspects. And, to make matters worse, while we were supposed to be the salvation, maybe one of us was the killer.

Even if we had a suspect, what the hell would we do with him? There were no witnesses, so there was no promise of a solution in a line up. Without the gun and a confession, we had nothing. I had never felt so damned useless!

Standing in front of the toilet, urinating, at three forty-five in the morning, a scary thought struck me. A line up! What if our killer was, in essence, doing a line up? What if this thing about me and him was a scam? What if the Ace was not the card he needed to make his hand? We're looking at the end, but maybe we should be looking at the beginning or the middle. If he already hit his target, then we're being diverted to look for something that isn't going to matter.

Then, leaving the toilet I laughed at myself. We already had more than enough theories, and here I was, in the middle of the night, taking a leak and searching for new theories.

That night I prayed for a break in the case. The terrible thing about prayers is that they are sometimes answered.

CHAPTER EIGHT

A LEAD

It was 5:10 A.M. when I walked into Sophie's, dropped some change in the cup by the front door and picked up a morning paper to read with my breakfast.

"Good God, Lieutenant!" Andy exclaimed as he pressed his finger tips to his chest. "Aren't you the early bird?"

"Couldn't sleep," I said as if apologizing for my earlier than usual arrival.

"And, you look it, dear boy. You look like shit!"

"Thanks for sharing that with me, Andy, but bring me the usual and keep the coffee cup filled at all times."

The paper had another story about the homicides....along with another shot at us for having done nothing. I flipped to the sports section and read the account of the boxing match I had watched on cable eight hours earlier. The account sounded similar to the fight I had seen, but the reporter obviously liked the champ a lot more than I did, and made the bout sound like a crusade, rather than the boring dance it really was.

I tried to keep my focus on the paper, but my mind kept wandering to the office. Finally I gave up on the paper. A half hour later, I walked into the office and started a pot of coffee. Fifteen minutes later I was surprised to see Frank Donovan pouring his first cup of the morning.

"Hey, Lieutenant," he said with a smile. "I was wondering who was the good fairy that started the coffee."

"Is that a fag joke, Frank?" I asked with a crooked grin as I let him fill my

95

cup.

"If the shoe fits..." he said with a mirror of my grin.

We added cream and sugar to our coffees as I asked, "What brings you in so early?"

"Verno and me are behind a day and a half on reports, so I thought I would get a jump on some of them before the herd arrives. What brings you in?"

"I got a hair-brain idea that kept me up half the night, and besides, I wanted to sit down and go through the rap sheets and the reports covering the personal histories on our three stiffs."

I told Frank Donovan about my idea that maybe, just an outside chance, the three victims had something in common, some thread that tied them all together. He listened with an occasional nod and then suggested that he and Al Verno do it with Mancini and I, so that we had four minds absorbing it all.

"So, what's the hair-brain idea?" he asked.

"What if our guy isn't targeting an Ace for his premier hit? What if he already got the one he wanted?"

"I don't follow you," he said with a wrinkled forehead.

"When we do a six-man line up, we don't put the suspect at the head or the end of the line, do we? No! We put him in the middle, in position, two, three, or four. Right?"

"Right," Donovan acknowledged. "So?"

"So," I continued. "So maybe our guy wanted to get to Landers, or maybe even Williams for some reason. He hits the one he wants, and he creates the illusion there will be more. We busy ourselves with who is coming, but he has already nailed the one he *really* wanted!" I looked at Donovan for some reaction, some confirmation that I was onto something.

"Could be," he said with a shrug. "Who the hell knows."

"But, you don't think so, do you?"

"Mike, I don't know. All I'm saying is that I don't know." Donovan took a full swallow of coffee, and continued. "There was a time when a murder had some logic, some reason, some sense to it. Even the screwy ones, and they were few and far between, had some, some kind of, you know, some normalcy in some weird way. You know what I mean? But now, who the hell knows what makes these animals tick."

"If he already hit his target, then we're spinning our wheels. See what I mean? We may never get a shot at this guy."

"So we find ourselves in a problem no matter what way it goes," Donovan acknowledged. "If he doesn't go forward with the two remaining, potential victims, we're screwed out of the chance to develop any leads. Then again, if he does continue, we got one, maybe two more bodies to handle."

"Right! We find ourselves hoping this is it, but, on the other hand, if we ever want to get our hands on the killer, we have to pull for him to do it again. It's a hell of spot to be in, but, then again, it's the only decent shot we got."

Donovan shrugged again and moved across the room to pull some blank reports out of the supply cabinet. I watched as he went to his typewriter, perhaps wondering if I was losing all signs of sensibility. As I made my way to the Records Section, I knew my conversation sounded stupid, and I was a little embarrassed by it. At four o'clock in the morning, standing over the toilet bowl, it seemed like some type of revelation. Now, in the squad room, under the light of day, it sounded like babbling.

Down in records, I turned my attention to something that seemed more real, more tangible. I pulled everything I could think of that might apply to our three bodies. I got a clerk to help me on the computers and together we searched motor vehicle records, criminal histories, field contacts, victim histories, traffic tickets, and anything else we could get into. By the time 7:30 A.M. rolled around we had accumulated a pile of paper a couple of inches thick.

Back in the squad room, I handed the stack of paper to Sergeant Bolson and instructed him to enter every bit of data from the sheets into the computerized case file. Bolson reminded me that he had already been through the routine. With little patience, I told him to do it again. Before I could set up a squad meeting for later in the day, when all of us could sit down and comb through everything, Al Verno called out to me to pick up line one.

"Lieutenant Amato," I said into the phone as I reached for the coffee cup with my free hand.

"Are you the detective handling these murders where the guy is leaving cards on the bodies?" the youthful male voice asked.

"That's right."

"I think I know who may be doing those killings." There was a long second of silence before he asked, "Can I talk to you about it?"

Can you talk to me, I thought to myself. Can you talk to me? I'll kiss your sweet ass on the corner Main and State Streets if you'll talk to me!

"You sure can," I said in what I thought was a calm voice. At the same time I snapped my fingers toward the guys in the squad room. Mancini caught my cue and picked up the extension as he pulled out a pen and clicked it into the ready position. "So what is it you know?"

"I think my buddy, a guy I kind of know from around here, is doing the murders," he said haltingly as Mancini scribbled notes and left me free to think and talk.

"Who am I talking to?" I asked.

"I don't know if I should give you my name. This guy's a little crazy. I don't want him coming back at me if he finds out I turned him in."

"He don't have to know your name," I said casually. "It's just that I like to know who I'm talking to."

"But I'm, I'm not sure I want to do that now, Detective. Can we just talk for now?"

"Sure," I answered. The guy sounded like he needed to be handled gently. For the time being I was going to let him play it his way. "What is it you want to talk to me about?"

"This guy, the one who is killing these people, he's bragging about it," the voice continued.

"Bragging? What do you mean? Bragging about what?" I stalled as Mancini got Verno's attention and Al Verno began to set the wheels in motion to try for a trace on the line.

"He's saying that he's got all the cops tied up on these murders so he can go ahead and deal drugs without being hassled."

In reality, the tactic was stupid, but in the mind of some whacked-out junkie it might make sense. The Narc guys were rolling along doing their thing in spite of these murders. That aside, who knows what was going on in the killer's mind.

"What's your friend's name?" I asked, hoping I wasn't pushing too far, too fast.

"He's not a friend. I just, you know, kind of know him, that's all."

"Oh, okay, right," I mumbled as I made a mental note not to make that mistake again. "This guy you know, this acquaintance of yours, what's his name?"

"Are you tracing this," the voice asked in a panic as if the thought had suddenly popped into his mind.

"I couldn't do that even if I wanted to. I can't talk to you and trace at the same time."

"You recording this?"

"Look, son," I offered in a consoling tone. "My recorder's batteries have been dead for a month. Besides, the City of Rochester is rather tight-fisted with their money when it comes to the cops, so we aren't even set up to record you if I wanted to." Both points were the God's honest truth! "I understand you're nervous about this, but I don't want you to be scared. This is important to me, this information you want to give me is important, and I don't want you to be concerned about me tracing or recording it."

"I'm gonna hang up!" he announced.

I had to reach down deep to pull the next line out of the bag of tricks.

"Okay," I said trying to sound understanding. "Okay, I understand you're afraid I might try to trace the call. But, if you do hang up, just call me back. Okay? Call me back? Anytime you want, you call me back. You can call me back and just talk for ten seconds. Okay? Just call me back and take ten seconds to tell me the guy's name. Okay?"

There was silence on the phone. I looked at the mouthpiece as if looking into it would bring the caller back. Suddenly, just as I reconciled myself to the fact the caller had hung up, the voice said, "Teddy. Teddy Roberts."

"That's his or your name?" I asked. Stalling for time, I mispronounced the last name. "Robertson? Teddy Robertson?"

"Roberts," he said with a sound of impatience. "R-O-B-E-R-T-S! That's his name."

"Roberts. Right, Roberts," I repeated. "But what makes you think..."

"Jessie."

"What? Who's Jessie? Is his name Jessie or Teddy," I asked in obvious confusion.

"Me," he said in exasperation. "You can call me Jessie, like Jessie James."

"Okay, Jessie. Thanks, I appreciate that. But, how do you....?"

The phone went dead. The click was loud and clear, but still I repeated, "Hello? Hello?" My searching words did nothing to change the fact the caller had left me hanging.

For the first time in weeks, the detectives in the squad room came to life. Like lions who had just been thrown a raw piece of meat, they lunged at the information. Finally, they had something of substance, something to sink their teeth into, something to rip apart. Verno and Donovan headed for the Records Section. Mancini called over his shoulder that he was on his way down to Vice to see if they had a Teddy Roberts on their hit parade. Bobby St. John and Jimmy Paskell pulled out the phone book and city directory, and began flipping through pages. Even Sergeant Jeff Bolson came to life, clicking away at his computer's key board.

I went down the hall and gave Major Novitski the news. He gave me a broad smile and then sent me up to see the Chief. When I gave Westfield the information he seemed relieved, and even allowed his usually erect body to noticeably relax.

"It may be nothing, you know," he cautioned. "Don't forget, there's a lot of people out there who like to give police false leads. Don't get too carried away by it, but do what you can...just do it as a department, without any grandstanding."

The guy never missed an opportunity to a take a cheap shot! Ignoring the remark I simply said, "Right, Chief," and left the room.

The elevator couldn't get back to the DB floor fast enough for me. I wanted to get back there and jump into this thing. I wanted to dive into it and feel the rush of being successful again.

Within a half hour, we had a list of six names to work off. Three of the names had criminal records, and three did not. Theodore Andrew Roberts, 26 years of age, was a drug user with three priors for drug possession and grand larceny. Ted Edward "Ted-E" Roberts, 44 years old, had fourteen arrests for robberies, burglaries and assault. Theodore Scott Roberts, 19 years of age, had one arrest for DWI. The three virgins on our list were 25, 29 and 66 years of age. The oldest one was also a Reverend, but based on everything else in this screwy case, he wasn't eliminated just because he wore a stiff collar.

We split the six names up evenly among the three teams. The order of the day was to get background, dig up photos, get into the person's history, but, under no circumstances rattle his cage. This phase of the investigation had to be as quiet as possible. Every precaution was to be taken so as to not give the suspect any idea we were narrowing in on him.

"If the papers get one word about this, I am going to own someone's shield, and their butt," I announced as we threw on our coats.

Halfway through the day I remembered to say a prayer of thanks to St. Michael, the Patron Saint of Police, that the new lead had taken a couple of hundred people off of my mental list of suspects. Even though I was grateful for the development, experience told me that many leads such as this turn out to be nothing. More often than not they come from a jerk who wants to get even with the guy who stole his girl, or to bust the chops of the guy next door with the barking dog.

It was after three o'clock in the afternoon when the last of the investigators made it back to the office. We took over the Detective Bureau Conference Room and began to hash over what we had picked up in the last five hours. Although we couldn't eliminate anyone of our "possibles," we worked to develop which one of our six Teddy Roberts was the "probable" suspect. One by one, we went through what each of the teams had discovered during the course of the day. For one reason or another, we eliminated each of the Teddy Roberts that was without a criminal record. The 44-year-old Teddy Roberts had been serving a one-year sentence for drug possession during the first two killings, and was subsequently removed from our list of probables.

We were just into a discussion on our last two "possibles", when Jeannie Simms, the Detective Bureau receptionist, came in and told us a man named

Jessie had called and said he would call back in ten minutes.

We moved the meeting back into the squad room, where Art Mancini prepared to record the expected call. Frank Donovan worked with the phone company on getting a trap set up on the in-coming lines. With a little bit of luck, and enough verbiage to keep Jessie on the line, we would be able to trap the line and at least determine the location from which the call came. We all suspected the call would come from a pay phone, but what the heck, at this point of the investigation a little piece of something would be much better than the whole lot of nothing we were presently holding.

Ten minutes went by. Fifteen minutes. Twenty minutes. Suddenly one line came to life. Then a second line lit up, followed immediately by a third line. We took all three calls but none of the callers was our elusive Jessie. Thirteen minutes and two more phone calls later, Jessie finally called.

As planned, Bobby St. John answered the phone and then asked loud enough for the caller to overhear, "Is the Lieutenant around?"

"He's in the can," Paskell answered loud enough to be heard by the caller.

"I got a call for him here. See if he can take it."

Ten seconds later, Paskell said loudly, "He's coming now."

The charade had bought us about seventeen seconds of time when I finally picked up the line, and said casually, "Amato here."

"This is Jessie," the voice said. Before I could say anything, he added, "I'll call you back."

I hung up the phone and looked up to see six sets of eyes looking at me with question marks. "He'll call back," I said lamely.

The ploy had gotten us no where. No trace was possible in the short time Jessie had been on the line.

For the next ten minutes we speculated about the call. Had Jessie been spooked because I delayed in taking his call, or was he simply toying with us? Was he the killer, and was he just stringing us along? Hadn't our suspect told the reporters he was challenging us to catch him? Was this part of the challenge? Was he simply a witness or holding some knowledge about the crime or the suspect? Was he simply afraid we would blow his anonymity? Maybe he was just overly cautious. Maybe somebody walked into wherever he was calling from and he didn't want to talk in front of the visitor.

The squad room finally fell to silence. Each detective busied himself with some charade of a task, but each remained at his desk. There was a certain tension to be felt in the room but it was masked with calmness. The large, silent squad room felt as if it was becoming warmer and stifling. From time to time one of the guys exchanged a glance with one of the others. The look was capped with a smile, a flick of the eyebrows, or a frown. Waiting was becoming a toil.

Fifteen minutes later the phone rang again. After the second ring, I picked up the phone and mumbled, "Amato."

"This is Jessie," the caller said.

"Hey, Jessie," I said cheerfully. "What happened man?"

"I thought you were stalling."

"Stalling? Jessie, I was waiting for a half hour for you to call. I had to go to the john."

"Did you find him?" he asked, not bothering to chit-chat with me.

"We found six, Jessie. Believe it or not, there are at least six Teddy Roberts in the city. We've been out all day trying to..."

"He's the one who lives on the 600 block of Monroe Avenue. He's about twenty-four, maybe twenty-five years old."

"Okay, okay. Good. Twenty-four, or twenty-five, right?"

"Look, Lieutenant," Jessie said in more of a request than an admonishment. "Don't screw me around. If you're trying to keep me on the line, it won't do any good. I'm on a phone with about five, six hundred people around me. Even if you get a cop here in one minute, I'll just be a face in the crowd."

"Jessie," I said in a tone to let him know I was a little offended by his insinuation. "I'm not about to jerk you around. This is important to me. Okay? I want to make sure I get this information down right. Okay? You mind that?"

"Keep cool, Detective Amato. I just have to be careful here. It's my ass hanging out on the line. If Teddy thinks I'm the one ratting him off, I'm dead meat."

"I'm cool, Jessie," I said matter-of-factly. "And, I'm not interested in identifying you. I don't even want to know who you are. You probably have a rap sheet yourself, and therefore, you would make a lousy witness on the stand. To tell you the absolute truth, I'm more than likely better off just having an anonymous source on this rather than a real, live witness that I would have to produce to a defense attorney for cross-examination."

What I was saying wasn't a total lie, and he seemed to mull it over before he continued the conversation. "When you do find him, don't mess with him too soon, okay?"

"Why's that?" I asked as Donovan gave me a thumbs-up sign, and instantly called the dispatcher to get a car to Jessie's location. At the very same second, Paskell and St. John looked at a notation Donovan had scribbled, grabbed their coats and ran to the elevators.

"He's still got the gun, but I think he has it hidden somewhere away from his place. When I know he's got it with him, I'll call you and let you know. Till then..."

"Hang on, Jessie," I almost yelled. "What apartment?"

"What do you mean, 'what apartment?'" the befuddled voice asked.

"I know this city pretty well, Jessie, and I think that area of Monroe Avenue is pretty much all apartments. Right? Am I right?"

"Yeah, yeah," Jessie acknowledged. "It is an apartment. "You're pretty sharp, Detective. Pretty sharp!" I could almost hear his smile.

"So, what apartment is Roberts in? That is, if you don't mind me asking?" I added.

"Now you're breaking *my* balls, Lieutenant," Jessie said with a little laugh.

"No, I'm not, Jessie. I'm just saying...."

"D. Apartment D. At least I'm pretty sure it's D. It's on the second floor, on the right."

"That helps a lot. It really does. I appreciate...."

Again he cut me off in mid-sentence. "Just don't go there, yet. Don't go there!" he emphasized almost angrily. "Bye for now, Lieutenant. I've got to go now. Your boys just showed up."

The call had originated from a telephone kiosk on the upper level of Midtown Plaza right in the center of downtown. Just as Jessie had said, there had to be a couple of hundred, maybe a thousand people criss-crossing through the plaza as shoppers moved from store to store and office workers made their way to buses, parking lots and early evening appointments. The uniformed officers had entered through the south doors and, unfortunately, the phone Jessie had used was on the plaza level, near the north side of the mall. By time the uniforms found the right phone, the bank of four pay phones was void of any caller. Jimmy Paskell had a technician process the phones, but the one that had been the source of the call was clean. Jessie was obviously a very cautious informant .

Before calling it a night, we had a discussion about setting up a surveillance on Teddy Roberts. It was decided, based on the little information we had so far, the risk of getting made on a surveillance - when we really didn't know what we were looking for - was too big. I called the shot and sent everyone home. Tomorrow would be a new day with new opportunities.

Thankfully, the Chief was gone for the evening by time we got down to printing the phone, so I briefed the Major on the net results of the day and then he called Westfield's office and left a message on his voice mail. With the Detective Bureau fairly quiet by then, I retired to my office with a mug of Sambuca-laced coffee. I closed my eyes, leaned back in the chair with my feet propped up on the desk and popped a couple of antacids as I listened to the tape recording of Jessie's call. I played it through once and then once again. The office was quiet and peaceful after the tape recorder clicked off. With my eyes still closed, I reached out for my cigarette pack, withdrew one and lit it. I blew the first drag out in a long, slow, exhale and was about to take a second lung-full of smoke when my eyes opened wide and I slammed my feet to the floor.

"What the...?" I asked of the quiet, dark, room, as I grabbed the recorder and hit the rewind button. I let the tape play through to the one part, the one, singular phrase I sought. I rewound it again and then again. What was it that was being said, not necessarily said in the words, but in the inflection, the tone?

I played it once more.

"Now, you're breaking *my* balls, Lieutenant!" the tape echoed in my empty office.

What did he mean by that? Maybe he meant it as an off-the-cuff remark, but it hinted at something, some hidden meaning. I took that little inflection, the slight emphasis on the word, "my" as meaning he was intent on breaking my balls, and then, when I asked the question about Teddy's apartment, my little stooge thought I was breaking his balls. Was that his game? Was this all a set up to lead us down another blind alley to nowhere? Was Jessie serious, or, as Ben Westfield had theorized, was he just another street guy who enjoyed messing with the cops? I had learned years ago that words were just sounds. The very important thing was *how* the word was said and used that carried the true meaning. Mister Jessie X had said his words in just a simple phrase, a smart side comment, but the little emphasis on one word was telling us a lot more than he intended to say. I played the recording a few more times, and got to know his voice, the rhythm of his words, his tone and cadence. Still, each time I listened, I heard the slight emphasis. It was very probable, based on the tape recorded voice, Jessie thought I was making a fool of him, when it was he who was attempting to make a fool of the cops.

I left the office and headed for a little bar out in the suburbs, near my apartment. This was not a night to get drunk. There was going to be a lot of work to get done tomorrow and I needed to be on top of my game. I just needed a drink or two to take the edge off the day. Alone in the crowd, I toasted Jessie and Teddy Roberts and, in my silent tribute to them, I smiled for the first time in months. Somewhere between the third and the fifth Southern Comfort my smile went away, and in the mirror I saw the face I knew, the face of doubt. I needed to bring my happiness in check and not get too carried away over one unproved informant...or whatever the hell Jessie truly was in this game we had been playing. By the sixth shot I found myself wondering if Jessie's, "Now you're breaking *my* balls," comment really meant anything at all. Maybe I was reading something that just wasn't there. The kid probably made the comment just off the cuff, without even thinking about it. Doubt overtook optimism.

There was a time when I trusted my judgment, my hunch, my feeling about something. The case was ruining me mentally and physically. I trusted no one and nothing, not cops, my bosses, or, for that matter, even myself.

Someone, sometime, someplace wrote, "No man is an island." I doubted the accuracy of that statement. In the bar, with fifty or sixty people around me engaged in conversations and relationships, I felt like an island. At one time I enjoyed being alone, but now I was feeling lonely. There's a difference. There's a big difference.

I wanted the comfort of Diane being with me, next to me, across from me. For years I had shuffled her off to the side. Now I missed her. I missed the relationship. Even an island has the comfort of being surrounded and touched by the ocean. I had nothing. There were no friends, no buddies with whom I was close. Oh sure, the cops were confidants. However, as the boss of the squad, I had purposely kept them all, even Donovan, at a distance. The job required me to make decisions that had to be based on the needs of the case, not on friendships. The job demanded it. The job demanded a lot. The job.

Alone in the crowded bar, my thoughts were filled with Diane. I wanted the scent of White Shoulders perfume in my nose. My eyes craved the sight of her casual beauty. My ears demanded to hear her voice. More than my senses, my inner soul longed for the life we once enjoyed. Age does strange things to a body and a mind. Now, in my late forties, I craved what I had so abundantly ten years earlier. I yearned for what I had had...and what I had ignored.

Love ignored can not endure. Therefore, what had endured what was what I loved. The job. Diane, as usual, had been right. I could not keep what we had if I loved the job more than I loved her. She couldn't understand the job was a duty, a responsibility. I couldn't understand she was right. I once loved the job more than I loved and cared for her. Now I had the job, but had lost her. In order to get her back I would have to turn my back on the job. I knew that's what it would take. Somewhere way past being drunk, I made a decision.

I called for a cab and on the way to my apartment I made the less than silent vow to give up the job. Alone, in my melancholy stupor, I found my love for the job decaying. What had endured was my love—and need—for Diane. Diane was more important than the cases. She was central to my life.

All the rest was meaningless. I would have to leave the job way behind and make Diane the meaning in my life. I would quit the job. At least I would cut way back on the number of hours I put into it. That's what I would do...right after this case.

Before noon the next day we knew as much about Theodore Andrew Roberts as one could possibly have known without having met him. The investigative teams had gone through each of the packages on his three arrests and the Narcs gave us what little they had on him. The Department of Motor Vehicles filled in the blanks on his car and driving record. I called in a few IOU's from friends in the Credit Bureau and the Department of Social Services. Their records were supposed to be confidential, but favors and debts owed easily overcome the need for confidentiality

It all summed up to this, Teddy Roberts was a loser! Like a character out of a Dickens' novel, our suspect was a product of the streets. His father was unknown and his mother was someone he contacted only when he was arrested and needed the bail money none of his so-called friends were willing, or able, to supply. He was what Narcs call a "Merchant", a seller of dope one day, and a buyer the next. Teddy had tried several times to become a dope dealer. He tried, but he even failed at that venture. The guy was a loser on all counts. Even his arrest record was unimpressive. He had taken two hits for possession of cocaine and one for a Grand Larceny. Both drug possessions were pled down to misdemeanors, and the GL was the result of an aborted shoplifting deal. The DMV had him as the recipient of four traffic tickets while driving an eight-year-old white Pontiac that was registered in his mother's name.

At 10:00 A.M., Donovan and Verno went into Teddy's neighborhood on the pretense of showing photos of some wanted guy from a shooting that was several years old. Working the scam, they knocked on the door of Apartment D at 640 Monroe Avenue and were greeted by a smiling Teddy. The smile turned to fear when he realized he had opened his door to two cops. Once he found they presented no threat to him personally, he let the door swing open. As he looked thoughtfully at the mug shot, our guys did a quick look-see around the depressing apartment. Teddy Roberts' living room, if one could call it that, contained a sofa, one sad looking end table and an over-stuffed chair. Best of all, the run-down joint faced the street. Because that area of Monroe Avenue contained a fair number of small businesses and assorted stores that created a lot of pedestrian and vehicular traffic, our surveillance of the apartment would be relatively easy.

Verno tried to dance his way into the apartment with a request to use Roberts' phone. That failed when Teddy simply offered, "Don't got one."

We divided up the surveillance into two shifts, with Donovan and Verno taking the first shift until about 8:00 P.M., and then Mancini and me taking over for the next twelve hours. The plan was to get a confession out of Roberts whenever we did pick him up, and in order to do that we needed an idea of how Teddy lived, who he saw, where he went and who came to visit him.

With the office finally void of any distractions, I turned my attention to the pile of reports and administrative paperwork that had been assembling on my desk while I had been diverted on to the Spades case, as we had begun to call it. I reviewed over fifty pages of reports on the other rapes, robberies, and homicides the teams were still juggling. Finally, when I took a break, I toyed with the idea of leaving the office early and grabbing a little shut-eye before the night's surveillance. Major Novitski had already been briefed, and I had been relieved to learn the Chief was out of town for a few days attending a conference of some sort. How nice it would be, my mind told me, to have this whole thing wrapped up by time he was back on the scene.

The phone broke my wishful thinking. "Lieutenant Amato," I answered.

"This is Jessie, Lieutenant. Did you find Teddy yet."

"Yeah, we found him, Jessie. Right now everything is on hold until you tell us he's got the gun on him." I paused a half second and asked, "So, does he?"

"No, not yet, but maybe tonight. Just be patient, Lieutenant. I'm gonna wrap this whole thing up for you."

"Then what?" I asked.

"What do you mean, 'Then what'?"

"What do you want out of this after you wrap it up for us?"

"I just want to see this guy put away is all. Believe me, I have my reasons!"

What reasons, I wondered. A girl problem? You want to cut in on his action with a broad? Some personal vendetta, maybe? Was there bad blood over a drug deal?

"Okay, I can buy that," I said. "But tell me one thing, will you, Jessie?"

"What do you wanna know?"

"How is it you know for sure when he has the gun, and when he doesn't?"

"I just know, that's all. I know this guy, and he trusts me. He tells me everything. I guess you're just gonna have to trust me, Lieutenant."

"Look, Jessie, just in case, when he does have the gun, and you call and I'm not here, I want you to call 9-1-1 and just tell them to get in contact with me and tell me the man has the package. Okay? You got that?"

"'The man has the package?' Detective Amato, that sounds like spy bullshit, like something out of the CIA," he said with a chuckle.

I had to smile at myself when he said it, and answered back, "Yeah, well, it's the best I can do right now."

"I'll be talking to you, Lute. Bye!"

I was still smiling when I set the phone back down in the cradle. Could it be I was taking a liking to this kid? He sure as hell was as savvy as can be, and seemed to have a bit of a sense of humor. But my smile was short lived as I began to question his reference to me as 'Lute.' The abbreviated term for Lieutenant was not necessarily police jargon, but it was kind of unusual for a young guy to use. We had used it back in Viet Nam and I'm sure it was around back in Korea and even World War Two. Could it be our snitch was a military vet? I made a mental note to have Sergeant Bolson do a computer search for any past arrests the department had where the person had the first name of Jessie - if that was really his first name - along with a military history. I didn't want Jessie involved in our court case if at all possible, but I sure wanted to know who he was. I didn't like having to trust people, especially people I didn't know. Jessie may have been amusing to talk to, but not knowing him was dangerous!

CHAPTER NINE

MAKING THE GRAB

By eight that night, Art Mancini and I were on Teddy Roberts' surveillance. Verno and Donovan had seen him leave the apartment twice during the day. One time he went to the store to buy some cigarettes, and the other time he walked north a couple of blocks to hang out with some other losers at a local, dingy, pool hall. My guys managed to snap two-dozen photographs of people entering and leaving 640 Monroe Avenue, but it was impossible to determine how many of those people ended up visiting Roberts.

While Art, looking very much like a bum, curled up in the doorway of a shop directly across from Roberts' place, I took up a position in the car about a half block down the street. I had done my share of surveillances under porches, on roof tops, and behind bushes on too many cold and windy nights. So, rank having its privileges, I took the car post while a much younger Sergeant Mancini pulled his well-worn fatigue jacket around him and nipped hot coffee out of a bottle that originally had been the home of some cheap wine.

The time of night, along with the distance I had to maintain from the apartment, did not allow the opportunity to photograph the few people who entered and left from the apartment's entrance. I counted seven people entering the address and four leaving it. Mancini, over the portable radio, gave each one of the comers and go-ers nicknames. I was just about to tell my partner I was going to move down to the greasy spoon a block away and grab us some fresh coffee when the dispatcher called and told me to go to a secure frequency.

"Lieutenant." the young voice said over the Tactical Channel. "We just got a call from a male telling us to have you call him right away. He said he was Jessie and the call is about your package, whatever that means, and that you had one minute to call him."

"How long ago did he call?"

"According to the time stamp on the card, about forty seconds ago."

I put the car in gear as I got the phone number from the 9-1-1 operator. Skidding to a stop at a phone booth a block away, I told Mancini what was going on. I dialed the number I had written on the palm of my hand and heard the phone ring four times before I heard Jessie's voice.

"That was close, Lieutenant," he said with that little hint of cockiness. "I was just getting ready to leave."

"You sure as hell didn't give me a lot of time, Jessie."

"I didn't want to, Amato. If I gave you time you would've checked to see where the number is, and you would have cops all over here by now...just like what happened at Midtown Mall the other day when you said you weren't tracing the call."

"Just the same, I..."

"Look, Detective, save the wind. I'm only gonna say this once, so pay attention. He's got the gun now. It's tucked in the cushion of the chair that faces the window."

"You sure? How do you know?" I asked quickly.

"I saw it there, that's how I know. The guy's a maniac. He was showing it off and saying how the cops ain't never gonna take him alive and shit like that."

"When did you...?"

"I'll save you some work, Lute. I'm calling from a pay phone across from the Liberty Pole on Main Street."

"Are you sure? Are you one-hundred percent sure?"

"I'm so sure that I'm gonna tell you to be careful. The guys is nuts. He'll take a shot at you if he knows you're coming. I hope you're wearing your bullet proof vest or that you get in the first shot." His voice wasn't urgent, but it was emphatic.

I felt for my absent body armor and tried to get in one last question. "Jessie, I need to know when..." I said into a phone that had already gone dead.

Knowing full well it was a waste of time, I sent a cop and a technician to the phone booth that Jessie had mentioned. Heading back to Monroe Avenue,

I joined up with Mancini and filled him in. Parked in a gas station, we laid out a plan. It wasn't much of a plan, but still, it was a plan. Due to the lack of a search warrant, the gun would have to be in plain view when we entered the apartment. Not wanting to strap Art with the perjury, I volunteered to be the one who spotted the gun.

Ten minutes later we were in Teddy's apartment, explaining to him that his name had come up on a recent burglary. Our approach had been careful and Mancini and I took the precaution of un-holstering our weapons and concealing them along our sides as we knocked on the door, announcing there was a gas leak in the building. If Jessie's information was correct, I didn't want to alert Roberts and let him get in the first shot. Once Teddy opened the door and we were sure he wasn't armed, we went into the burglary suspect ruse. While the skinny kid engaged Sergeant Mancini in a conversation about the United States Constitution and all of its protections, I went over to the ugly green chair with the busted leg and ran my hand around the cushion. On the left side of the tattered cushion I struck gold.

"What's this, Teddy?" I asked as I held the grip of the weapon between my thumb and forefinger.

"Where the hell did that come from?" he cried as he held his hands to his chest.

"Right here, in plain view, sticking out of the chair, right where you put it," I answered with a straight face.

"You planted it! You planted it!" Roberts protested.

Thirty minutes later, after having an evidence technician photograph and take possession of the gun, we were on our way to the Public Safety Building with our catch. Mancini arranged to have a Highland Section officer sit on Roberts' car until we could get a search warrant for it. During the ten-minute drive Teddy ran through his best presentations of outrage, anger, crying and pleading, not even bothering to shut up until we placed him in an interview room. While letting him stew for a few minutes, we put on a pot of coffee and arranged to have St. John and Paskell come in to start on the search warrant for the rest of Teddy's apartment and his white Pontiac. A closer examination of the weapon showed it to be the same make and caliber of the triple murder gun...and also revealed the serial number had been completely obliterated by means of a file. It was going to a be a very long night.

I took a minute to observe our suspect before I entered the interrogation room. I didn't like what I saw. The kid was pacing the floor and involved in a very animated conversation with himself. The second I opened the door, Roberts began to argue his innocence. It took a couple of more minutes to calm him down enough so that he would sip the coffee I had brought him.

For the next quarter of an hour we talked about his short, twenty-five year life, and then it was time to pop the subject to him.

"Teddy," I said as I looked him in the eye. "The reason you're down here is that the word is all over the street about you having shot a couple of people."

"Bullshit!" he bellowed.

I silenced him with a finger to my lips and cautioned him to listen to me before he started yelling and crying again.

"Hear me out, Teddy. You learn a lot more by listening than by talking. I'm going to be honest and up front with you and I want you to be honest with me. Okay? You ready to listen to me now?" At this point I didn't want him to talk, so I simply continued with my patter. "Now there are some people out on the streets saying some pretty nasty things about you. I know some of them are true, and maybe some of them are not so true. Okay? So now what we're going to do is talk to each other like men and we're going to separate the lies from the truth. Okay? You ready to deal with this like a man and help yourself out?"

"I'm a junkie, Detective, just a junkie. I ain't doing no shooting of anybody. You gotta believe me," he begged with tears in his eyes.

Again, I explained that only he could get himself out of this jam that other people were laying on him. Then I advised him of his rights. With that out of the way, I told the kid to call me by my first name. Then I asked, "So just tell me this, Teddy, where did you get the gun?"

"I didn't have no gun, Detective. That's what I'm saying. I ain't never had a gun in my whole life."

"Mike," I reminded him. "Call me Mike, okay?"

He ran the back of his hand and forearm under his nose as he sniffed in a bubble of snot that had been distracting me, and then he repeated himself. "I never had a gun, Mike. You gotta believe me. I swear to God, I never owned a gun."

"Teddy, like I said, I'm going to be real honest and up front with you, and I want you to do the same with me. Okay?"

"I am."

"Let me tell you something, and I want you to listen real good to what I say. Okay?" I bent low in my chair to look up at his face and once I got a nod from him, I continued. "We're going to check this weapon out, Teddy. We're going to run ballistics on it and I'll tell you right now, God forbid that gun comes up as being used in some shooting, some killing, and I'm pretty damn sure it will, you're going to be left holding the bag for it. You understand that?"

"I understand, but that ain't my gun, detect...Mike. I never saw it before you pulled it out of the chair."

"I didn't even have to pull it out, Teddy. The thing was sticking out like a cannon." That was a lie, but it was a lie I had to stick with for the rest of this case if I was ever going to get the weapon admitted into evidence. "That's the only way I knew it was there. I saw the thing! Plain as day. I almost jumped back when I saw it. Now, how could it be that I saw it, and you, you who lives there, you never saw it?"

"Because it wasn't there. I didn't have no gun. I'm telling you that!"

"You know what, Teddy? I'm gonna tell you something," I said, trying to model his speech, so he wouldn't think I was too, 'uptown' for him. "Like you said, you're just a junkie, and you and I both know that a junkie has to make a living. You get up in the morning and you gotta hit the floor thinking about how you're gonna get two, three hundred bucks today. Now this gun that you had there in your place, maybe you stole it from someone. I don't know! Maybe got it out of a car you broke into or maybe out of a house you burglarized. You see what I'm saying? If you stole it and you were gonna sell it to make some cash, well, that's minor stuff and I can handle that for you. But, if you sit here telling me this line of bull about never having seen the gun, and later it comes back that the gun was used in a shooting, then you're gonna have to eat the gun and face some heavy charges. Understand? You can't tell me now you never saw it, and then later, when ballistics comes in and tells us it was used in a shooting, tell me you just stole it out of some house."

"It's not my gun!" he shouted and then covered his head, expecting a slap in the chops for his tone of voice.

"Okay," I said calmly. "Then, whose gun is it?"

"I don't know whose gun it is. I never saw it! I never saw it! I never, never, ever, saw it!"

It was time for a new angle. "Look, Teddy," I said as I placed my right hand on his left shoulder. "I know you have to make ends meet. I know that sometimes you have to deal drugs in order to make those ends meet. Okay? I know that! I saw your rap sheet and I've talked to over twenty people about you. I know, from time to time, in order to make enough dough to get by, that you sell drugs. Did someone cop some drugs from you and paid you with the gun because they didn't have the cash?"

"No! No one paid me with a gun. I didn't steal the gun. It's not my gun! It's not my gun!"

We went on that way for well over an hour but I couldn't get him to budge. I went into a line of crap about my own brother being a junkie and about how I understood that a guy had to do things to survive, just as my assumed brother had to do. Still he didn't budge out of his denials. Switching subjects, I asked him why it would be all over the streets that he was the guy who had shot Mary Williams.

"Who?" he asked with his face wrinkled in a question mark.

"Mary Williams," I repeated.

"I never even heard of her, Mike," he said with a dead pan face.

I was pleased he was using my first name more easily now and so I pushed him a little farther.

"You ever tell anyone, you know, just fooling around, kind of just shucking and jiving, that you were the guy who was shooting those people that we're finding with the Queen of Spades and so on?"

He needed time to process that one. I couldn't tell if he didn't understand what I was asking, or if he was trying to stall. Finally the light bulb went on and he asked, "Those poker murders on the news?"

"Those are the ones, Teddy."

"No way, Mike! Come on. No way! Why the hell would I say that?"

I shrugged my shoulders and said, "Maybe, like I said, you were just talking, trying to impress some broad or something. I don't know why you would say it, but I do know that a number of people heard you say it."

The new subject brought the same response. Teddy Roberts swore up and down he was being framed, that he never said those words, never possessed a gun, and never would have the courage to shoot anyone. The trouble was, I was starting to believe him.

After almost two hours of questioning, I took a break from the room with the excuse of getting us some more coffee. Out in the hallway I was greeted by Bobby St. John.

"I've been listening," he said. "The kid's good."

"Yeah, too damn good," I replied. "What's been going on out here?"

"Like we expected, the phone booth on East Main Street was clean," St. John reported as we walked into the squad room. "No prints. We got the search warrant application almost finished, but it's kind of weak. We had a technician look at the gun. He confirms what we saw, it's the same make and model that put out the slugs on our homicides. We got a ballistics guy coming in to do a test fire and compare rounds from it to the three murders."

I filled my coffee cup and drank it down as we talked and decided to wait for a ballistics comparison on the gun. If it matched, then we would throw that into the search warrant application to strengthen it. In the mean time, I would press on with our suspect.

"Right now, I'm buying this kid," I told the detectives. "He's too strong in sticking to his story. Maybe he did get planted. Maybe our little snitch

Jessie planted him. The truth is, right now I don't know what to believe."

I flipped Paskell off with my middle finger when he asked, "Hey, Ace. Do you need a deck of cards in the interrogation room?"

I let the remark slide and went to the window. Looking out at the city, I ran things through my mind one last time before I went back to Teddy Roberts. If he didn't do the murders and if he was right about being planted with the gun, then the natural question was who had planted him. Whoever put that gun there would be the killer...and I was developing a nasty suspicion that the planter and the killer was my telephone buddy, the mysterious Jessie.

I filled two more cups with coffee. His had the sugar and cream. Mine had the Southern Comfort. Taking a deep breath, I headed back to the interrogation room.

Teddy Roberts was pacing the floor when I returned to him. I had him sit down before asking him who had been in his apartment over the past day or so. It took him almost a half-hour to recall everyone and approximately when they visited. I jotted down the names for future reference, but none of them fit into anything we had developed. When I asked which one of those people might have left the gun behind, he just shook his head and said he didn't think any of them would do that.

"This is important, Teddy."

"I know, Mike, but I really don't think any of them would carry a gun, and even if they would, why would they leave it at my place?"

"Why do you have so many friends coming and going so much, Teddy?"

"Truth?"

"That's the only thing I want to hear."

"I had a little smoke I got from some guy. I painted a lady's apartment and when she paid me I bought some reefer. I was selling off a joint or a couple of joints at a time." He looked at me and threw up his hands. "If you want to bust me for that, go ahead, but I still don't know shit about that gun or those killings."

I studied the kid for a few seconds and then decided to try something. "I'm gonna read you a list of names and I want you to tell me if you recognize any of them. Okay?"

"Okay. Go ahead. I'll tell you anything I know."

I picked up my pad, flipped over a couple of pages, and pretended to read names that weren't there. "Harold, or Harry St. John?"

"Never heard of him."

"A guy called Tommy the Tape?"

"Nope!"

"How about Freddie Thomas?" I asked and looked up at him.

"No."

"A dude named Jessie?"

"No."

"A girl named Rebecca?"

"Don't know her."

We talked another hour, but the sum total was a big fat zero. It was almost daylight when I took a break from the interrogation and made arrangements for Bobby St. John to take over for me. With Teddy Roberts' record we had no trouble throwing a weapons charge on the kid and that would be good enough to hold him for a few days until we got everything sorted out. The next few items on the agenda were to get the ballistics done, finish up the last paragraph of the search warrant for our suspect's car and then go through the entire vehicle with a fine tooth comb. If Teddy was our man, there hopefully would be some traces of Mary Williams in his car, that is if he was careless enough to use his own car when he moved her body from her apartment to the police parking lot on Pine Alley.

It was going to be a long day. Maybe it would even be a good day.

By the time Major Novitski came through the door at 8:45 in the morning the case was coming together and all of us were feeling rather good about ourselves. Over the next few hours, Lou Granger, our ballistics expert, matched a round fired from Roberts' gun - or, at least the gun we had found in his apartment - to each of the three killings. In going through the suspect's car, the technicians were able to come up with at least three spots of blood. It was later learned the blood was the same type and RH factor as the fluid that had once pumped life through Queen Mary Williams. The icing on the cake was finding several long strands of hair in the trunk area of the car. With some luck the forensic people might be able to tell us it was the same as Mary Williams' hair. The entire case was coming together very neatly. Thank you Saint Michael!

"Almost too neatly," I told Novitski as we moved into his office with full cups of coffee. Regardless of my thanks to the saints, I was still very much a skeptic about good luck.

"Sounds like you're looking the gift horse right in the mouth, clear to his ass, Lieutenant," the Major said. "Why?"

"This is going to sound weird, boss," I admitted. "But the kid is just too truthful. I've talked to him for over five hours and Bobby has been with him another three. We both read the same thing...he appears to be telling the truth."

"About what?"

"About not knowing the gun was there. About not shooting Williams or anyone else. About not hauling the body around." I held up a hand to stay off his next question, and said, "I know, I know, all the evidence is there. The gun is *the* gun. The blood in the car matches. There's no doubt in my mind that when we get the DNA back, whenever that is, it will be Williams' DNA. Everything says it's him, but damn it, I believe the kid."

"What are the other possibilities?" Novitski asked as he held his cup with both hands and raised his eyebrows as he moved the cup to his lips.

"He got planted by one of his friends. He's got nothing but jerks and crooks for buddies and he says he lets them all borrow his car when they need it. We saw it when we were staked out on him. There's a parade of people in and out of his apartment."

"So, what are you going to do about it, Lieutenant?"

"I say we charge him with the weapons possession, and while he's salted away, we use the time to run down his friends. I put a rush on the surveillance photos we have and when they're printed up I'm going to have him identify everyone he can. Bobby's got him writing up a list of all of his friends, acquaintances, and drug pals. Once we have them all identified, we begin to background them and pull in the ones that look good."

"What's he say about our boy Jessie?"

"Says he doesn't know a guy named Jessie."

"And you believe him?"

"I'm not betting the farm on it, but yeah, I do believe the kid."

"Okay," Novitski said as he pursed his lips together and nodded. "Handle it according to your plans and keep me advised."

I nodded and got up to leave when he told me the Chief was due back in town that afternoon.

"Get back to me about three-thirty or so," Novitski instructed. "I'll need to update the boss on what's the latest information. Until then, you keep a lid on this thing! Westfield isn't going to be too keen on us having this kid, the gun, the car, and still not charging him with the murders. He's got the media beating down his door. He wants to be able to put this case to bed."

We had a quick squad meeting to catch up on everything and make assignments. When everyone was gone, I grabbed Sergeant Jeff Bolson and inquired about his computer analysis. He pulled out a couple of reams of paper and showed them off like they were his refrigerator art from third grade. I nodded, grunted, and shook my head at all the right places. When he was done I asked him who saw his analytical handiwork besides me and the squad.

"No one, Lieutenant. Why?"

"Keep it that way!" I said. Then using Novitski's words, added, "I want a lid kept on this thing. It doesn't leave the squad. Understand?" Getting an affirmative nod, I returned to the interview room and a sleeping Teddy Roberts.

Besides me believing him, I think he was starting to believe me and the fact that I did not plant the gun in his apartment. Teddy and I went through it step by step from the top. Nothing in his story changed. He was home most of the afternoon and night and never saw the gun before I found it. Yes, he let a number of his friends drive his car, and some of them even kept it over night, for a few days on some occasions, but no, he couldn't remember if anyone had it on the Saturday night, Sunday morning time period of Mary Williams' killing. Not only was he willing to take a polygraph, he was insistent about it. He also demanded I take his fingerprints and compare them to any fingerprints we had at the crime scenes.

Taking the arrest report that Mancini had drawn up earlier, I brought Roberts down to booking, telling him that he would have to get some sleep before we could put him on the polygraph. Although he was relieved about not being charged with murder, he was none too happy to have the gun charge lodged against him.

By four in the afternoon each of the teams had reported in with updates on which friends of Teddy's they had been able to locate. Of the fourteen friends and associates of Teddy Roberts that we could locate, none would admit to him ever having a gun, talking about killing people, or even having the guts to shoot a gun, much less shoot at someone. Donovan upped the ante when he announced that he had re-interviewed Mary Williams' landlady and neighbors.

"Remember the Crosbys, Lute? They're Williams' neighbors who she told she was expecting a guest and had to hurry so she would have time to clean up the apartment."

I nodded.

"Well, Mr. Crosby remembers seeing a white car, an older white car, parked in front of their apartment house after they saw Williams the last time. He can't say if it was a Chevy, Pontiac, or Ford, but he describes it similar to Teddy Roberts car. Not too shabby, huh?"

I took the information to Novitski, and he told me not to leave for the day until we got clearance from the Chief.

"I gave him the rough edges of what's been going on, and he wants a full briefing as soon as he's done with some other matters," the Major said. "So stand by and we'll go up to see him as soon as he calls down."

I had been up and moving for the past sixteen hours and hadn't slept at all in the past forty-something hours. I went back to my office with the idea of grabbing some snooze time until Uncle Ben Westfield cleared his social calendar. I wasn't too happy with the sarcastic note left on my desk by the Lieutenant in Records Section, demanding I return the criminal history folders of Lanovara and Williams. I grabbed the two worn file folders and stormed out of the office, heading for the plaza level of the building to give Lieutenant Arnold a piece of my mind. In my haste I caught my sleeve on the door knob and spilled the contents of both folders half way down the hall. I was right in the middle of stringing together some very nasty Italian words when I saw the back of Mary Williams' folder.

When I first saw the scribbled initials and date, it didn't register in my mind that was too busy preparing my lips for a fresh string of profanity. Only after I had poured the contents of the two folders back in the correct files, and had punched the elevator down arrow, did I get hit with a flash of lightning. Then I looked at the back of Williams' folder. I had seen the back folders of criminal files thousands, maybe tens of thousands of times and I knew what the heading said, but still I read the words out loud as the elevator arrived, opened its doors and closed them without me entering the conveyance. I stood motionless three feet from the mechanical cage.

"Reviewing Officer Initial and Date Folder Upon Review," the message read. Mary Williams' list of officers who had pulled her file consisted of about fifteen entries. Right above Officer Hermino Gonzalez' initials and date, when he pulled the record for me, the day her body was found, were the initials, "PPP," along with this year's date of January sixth...roughly about three months before she was killed!

I knew the initials well. I had seen them first when I was fresh out of the academy a quarter of a century ago. Through the years I had seen them scribbled across reports from the field. And, most recently, I had seen them on messages coming down from the sixth floor offices of Chief Benjamin Westfield. PPP was Sergeant Peter Paul Polson, Administrative Aid to the Chief of Police.

CHAPTER TEN

DILEMMAS

After making a copy of the back cover of Mary Williams' folder for posterity's sake, I dropped the two criminal history folders off to a clerk in the Records Section, and then called the Major to tell him I would be back in the office in a few minutes.

The Plaza Level of the Public Safety Building is a large, drab concrete area. Exiting the elevators on this showroom of the PSB, there are three sets of heavy, double glass doors off to the left and the Headquarters desk straight ahead, about fifty feet away. Breaking out of the confines of the elevator, I turned to the left, my heels making a loud clicking noise as they struck the gray, granite tiles. I pushed my way through the center door. The night air hit me hard as I stepped out on to the large, concrete Civic Center Plaza that joined the city's Public Safety Building and the Monroe County Hall of Justice, diagonally to the left. Lighting a cigarette, I looked up at the stars and absorbed the peacefulness of the night. Except for an occasional passing car, the night was silent. Slowly, I walked east, toward the Exchange Street side of the plaza, thinking about hurrying down to the Holiday Inn on Main Street and getting a quick drink. It was about then that it finally struck me that my collar and the back of my shirt were soaked in sweat. A shiver ran through me that made me jerk my shoulders up in reaction to a quiver that rattled my upper body. I really don't know if the chill that spread through me was from the coldness of late winter in Rochester, or if it generated from the realization of what I had just discovered.

Having worked midnights a good portion of my career, I loved the night time. Midnight, and the early morning hours following, was a good time for cops. There were fewer bosses and a lot less traffic to contend with during those late hours. Besides, the people on the streets after midnight tended to be criminals, so it wasn't as difficult to sort out the good citizens from the bad ones after the clock got into the early morning hours. Even when I worked the 4 PM to Midnight shift, I would still get into my car late at night after the shift and drive around the city, thinking, wondering, and hoping. This night, as I looked up at the mostly clear sky, my thoughts drifted to Diane and the nights we would walk around the reservoir up on Cobbs Hill and plan our fifty years together...plans that fell about forty years shy.

My mind came back to the present as I looked up at the outside wall of the PSB and saw the lights on in the Chief's sixth floor office. I wanted to shake off the reality of Pete Polsen's initials on Mary Williams' criminal history folder and chalk it up to a matter of coincidence. However, too many years in this business had taught me that when you find a coincidence, it usually isn't one. Not one cop had checked Queen Mary's folder in seven years, and then, out of the blue, three months and a couple of weeks before she was killed, Polson gets the urge to look at her file. No way! It didn't make sense. It couldn't be written off as a quirk or just one of those crazy things that happen in the universe of time and space. Perhaps it was Polson who was the mysterious Detective that was to meet with Landers the night he became our second murder victim.

I lit a second cigarette from the first one and walked toward the Hall of Justice. Maybe I was subconsciously hoping to find justice lurking there behind the glass walls of the building. Maybe I was just plain reluctant to go back into the Public Safety Building and tell the Chief I had stumbled on the killer and that the killer was his Administrative Aide. With the cigarette stuck in the corner of my mouth and my hands shoved deep in my pockets, I walked back to the glass doors guarding the entrance to the PSB, already knowing I would not mention my suspicions to my Chief. No, I would sit on this piece of data for a day or so until the information settled in my own mind and I could sort it out in my own way. Taking one last drag on the butt before flipping it into the air, I saw Polson's sad, long face in a cloud of my own breath.

How did he figure into this thing? What motive did he have for killing three people? If this thing was about me, what was his problem with me? We had always been friendly, if not friends. I had no ax to grind with him. Did he have one to grind with me? Was he behind the killings, or was he behind the man doing the killings? If Teddy Roberts, or even the elusive

Jessie, was responsible for the deaths of Lanovara, Landers, and Williams, then how did Polson fit into this thing? Was he a connection for the killers? All three of the victims had criminal records. Did Pete Polson fit in there somehow? The computer had already run the records of all three victims and didn't find any common people, places, or cops that connected the three. Could it be Polson arrested all three and carried a long-time grudge against them? I would have to check that out personally. Still, all things considered, I couldn't see the mild, unruffled Sergeant Polson killing anyone. If he was involved in this thing, he was merely a conduit for the killer. The logical step was to get to Polson in order to get to the killer.

Novitski noted I looked strange when I returned to the fourth floor, and I blew it off to the cold air that had chilled me when I went out for a smoke. We kicked around small talk for another ten minutes before the Major's intercom lit up and the Chief beckoned us to his office.

It took five minutes to brief Westfield on the developments of the last two days, from the time of mysterious Jessie's phone call, to the booking of Teddy Roberts on a weapons possession charge. He listened intently to everything that was said, shifting his look periodically from me to Novitski, and then back to me. Twice he jotted down a note, but other than those momentary distractions, his eyes and ears focused on us and the news he was getting. When the verbal history of the past forty-eight hours was complete, Ben Westfield laid his pen down neatly so that it was perfectly horizontal in the center of the page of his notebook. He then looked directly at the Major. I smiled at the attention he gave to the placement of his pen because it reminded me that this was a man who was more concerned about how his office carpets were vacuumed than he was about the adequate staffing of his department.

"Major, can you give me one good reason on God's green earth why this Roberts hasn't been charged with, at the very least, one count of murder?" the Chief asked in a calm but menacing voice.

I started to answer the questions, but both bosses held up their right hands to silence me. Then Novitski spoke. "The gun is a match. There's no doubt about it, Chief. The hair in the trunk of Roberts' car is similar, and that's all the lab will say at this point, 'it is similar in length, color and thickness to Williams' hair'. And as far as the blood goes, well it is A positive, the same as Williams' type. In other words, we have a lot of circumstantial evidence a this point. On the other..."

"Exactly my point," Westfield interrupted. "We do have, as you say, 'a lot of circumstantial evidence'. A whole lot of it, Major! In fact, I would say we have enough of it to charge this Teddy Roberts person with the killing of at least Williams, if not the other two."

"On the other hand," Novitski continued. "This suspect lends his car to half of the dopers in and around Monroe Avenue. We can't get one person to say they ever saw him in possession of the gun." Novitski paused and leaned forward in his chair to emphasize his next point. "And, after fourteen hours of interrogation, he sticks with his story."

"What the hell does that matter?" Ben Westfield asked with a pseudo-laugh. "He's a liar, that's all there is to that. Maybe he's a very good liar, but pure and simple, he's a liar."

"What matters, Chief, is that both Lieutenant Amato and Detective St. John have talked to this kid extensively and they think he *is* telling the truth. If they believe that, after spending half a day with the kid, I have to put some credence in it."

"Oh come on now, Major," Westfield said with a grunt and look of distaste. "If he didn't do it, then how the hell does he get the gun, the hair and blood, all that 'lot of circumstantial evidence', in his possession and in his car?"

"I'll let Lieutenant Amato go into that for you," Novitski said.

"If I wanted to hear from Lieutenant Amato, I would have asked Lieutenant Amato," Westfield said evenly. "You're suppose to be running that place down there. I want to hear from you!"

You son-of-a-bitch, I thought. You keep me waiting here for almost three hours, and now you won't give me a speaking part? Another power play, Chief-ie? Another example of how this is *your* department and how you can make my life miserable. The words never left my lips, but they were written on my face.

"I thought as long as you kept him here on overtime for two-and-a-half hours that you might want to hear directly from him, Chief," Novitski said in a business-like manner. I marveled at the man's ability to hide his emotions. Not waiting for Westfield to bite, the Major continued. "We are apprehensive about the informant, the caller named Jessie. His information was too good, too perfect. Besides that, he's taking unusual precautions so as not to be identified. We're concerned about him, his motives, and his possible involvement in the killings."

Ben Westfield, if he even heard the information, disregarded it. "I want this Roberts fellow charged with the murder of Williams right now! Then we'll put the entire thing into the Grand Jury along with the other two killings and let them sort out whether or not to level other charges on him."

"Chief," Novitski said in a clear voice. "I am recommending against that action and I want you to make a note of that. If we charge him now, we're being premature. If the Grand Jury doesn't indict him, given the problems with double jeopardy, we will more than likely lose the chance to take a second run at him later on. Give us two more days to track down some things, to get back the final lab reports on the blood and hair and do some interviews and follow some leads. Then, if we don't establish his innocence, and if we build some forensic evidence, then I personally will feel better about charging him at that time."

"All I am making a note of, Major, is that the people of this city are scared to death by these killings," Westfield said dramatically. "They are beating down the Mayor's door, insisting that something be done, and consequently, the Mayor is beating down my door! We now have the man in custody who has done the killings and my two main investigators on this thing are arguing not to free the people from this fear, this cloud of doom, that hangs over them. I don't believe my ears!"

"Can we have two days to run this thing down, Chief?" Novitski asked again. "Roberts isn't going anywhere for now. With the gun and his drug record, we should be able to get a pretty substantial bail set on him. He's locked away and can't hurt anyone from there. The people are safe and we can still take a more thorough look at this thing."

"I'll think about it, but I don't think so," Westfield said ambiguously before dismissing us.

That night I managed to get both of my shoes and one sock off before I leaned back on the bed and fell into a death-like asleep. When I made it back to the office shortly before nine the next morning, I learned that Frank Donovan had already been in for the past five hours so he could talk to Teddy Roberts one more time before the kid went to court and had an attorney assigned to him. The eleventh hour interrogation had netted the detective nothing more than having our alleged serial killer identify a number of people Donovan and Al Verno had photographed while staking out Roberts' apartment. Donovan told us that Teddy didn't know five of the people in the shots, but he was able to identify the remaining seventeen.

"These eight pictures are residents from the other apartments, according to our boy," Donovan said. He then snapped the remaining nine photos down on his desk, one by one, and gave each person a name. "This is George Olivetti, another doper....Greg Fisher, a doper...a guy he knows only as, 'Roger' who he thinks is a burglar...Nancy Sadler, a girlfriend of our guy...a dude named, 'Billy' who, 'just kind of hangs out'...Norma Tardone, a hooker to one and all...Mike Glaxton, a doper...another, 'dude who hangs out and smokes a little reefer' by the name of Gus...and, last but not least, Alex Carson, a doper and a car thief."

"No Jessie in there?" I asked out of hope.

"No Jessie, boss," Donovan confirmed.

I gave the teams a synopsis of my meeting with the Major and Westfield from the night before and then gave them instructions to run down everyone of the people identified in the photos, including the residents, and to try to get names attached to the unidentified and partially identified people in the photos.

When everyone was gone, I called the Chief's office and got Sergeant Polson on the line. I gave him some story about losing my pocket knife and asked him to look around up there to see if I might have dropped it while I was getting my butt ripped by our Chief. Then I slipped in a reminder that we hadn't sat down for a cup of coffee in a long time and asked if he would meet with me at the end of shift.

"Up front, Mike, if you're looking for dope on the boss, I won't discuss him personally," Polson said, laying down the ground rules.

"I wouldn't even ask you to, Pete," I assured. "There's another matter that has my concern, and I need, well, you know how it is, I need to talk to you about something else. Okay? Will you meet with me?"

He begged off meeting me right after work, but Pete agreed to meet me sometime about seven that night. He suggested a little diner, one that was not known as a cop hang out, and promised to give me an hour of his time. I didn't like the fact that a suspect in the case was naming the time and location of the meeting, but I had to live with it.

By the end of the day, the guys came in with odds and ends about the various people in the surveillance photos. There was nothing of earth-shattering importance in all of it, other than each one of Roberts' friends had said he wasn't violent in any way and they never knew him to have a gun. Seven of the group admitted they had borrowed Teddy's car at one time or another. A few of them confirmed they would sometimes keep it for a day or two. None of them owned up to having the car the weekend that Mary Williams was shot. Just as disappointing, none of them knew anything about a guy named Jessie.

I killed a little time at the Robe and Gavel, a little hole-in-the-wall bar over on Fitzhugh Street, that was frequented by court people. A group of about six or eight cops, along with a couple of Assistant District Attorneys, stood in a circle swapping war stories about old cases. The laughter that disturbed some of the more stolid patrons was welcomed by me. It was nice to be in the company of men and women who laughed loudly about death and the fears that drove them to be here in the first place.

Two beers later I was on my way out to one of the suburbs south of downtown Rochester, to find the diner Pete Polson had suggested for our meeting. It was one of those little joints that was suppose to be made out of an old street car, but in fact was a pre-fabbed job of cheap materials. As planned, I got there before him, and slipped my car in a slot far enough away from the door where I could watch my appointment arrive. My wait was less than ten minutes. I was somewhat comforted by the nonchalant way in which Sergeant Polson approached the steps of the place and walked in. I got out of my car and walked into the half-empty diner not more than twenty seconds behind my friend.

The two of us exchanged greetings and then looked around for an empty booth, one that was away from the other patrons. Finding one in the corner, we removed our coats, commented on the weather and seated ourselves. Establishing that neither one of us was really hungry, we ordered coffee and pie and took on positions to convince each other we were relaxed about the rarity of our social meeting. Department gossip passed the time until we had both finished our pieces of pie, drained our cups, and had them refilled. Finally, with twenty minutes gone by, it was time to get down to business.

Being that I was the one who asked for the meeting, it was going to be up to me to open the conversation. Understanding the unwritten rule, I leaned forward, rested my elbows on the table and then dropped the first question.

"So, Pete, with you being up on the sixth floor, do you get much of a need to check records on people from time to time?"

"Yeah, sure, from time to time," he said with a hidden smile that was buried in his face without showing on his lips.

"Why's that? I mean, your job is pretty administrative, right?"

"For the most part it is, like you say, a lot of administrative dealings. However, part of that routine is checking records, digging up some information for the boss, asking questions about this and that," he said with a strange look of satisfaction that is worn by people who own a secret they know is coveted by the person to whom they are speaking.

His look told me he was not going to say something unless I was direct, and asked about it specifically. I wanted to get to the main bout, but decided to stay with the preliminaries for the time being. I needed to study the man before me.

"So, how often do you have to go down and pull records?" I asked.

"Whenever the Chief asks me to, Mike," he answered.

"The Chief, huh?" I commented thoughtfully. "Why does the Chief need to do criminal records checks?"

"Sometimes he gets a letter from someone and he wants to know if they have a record. Sometimes it's somebody asking the Department for a favor, or they want him to show up for a function, or they want to do business with the Department, or something of that sort. The man's super cautious, Mike, so he has me run their criminal histories, you know, to make sure he doesn't get involved in something embarrassing."

What Polson was saying made sense, but it also pointed the finger directly at Westfield, and that was strangely unsettling to me. If what he was saying was true, then chances were pretty good Westfield was a killer - or involved with the killer. However, the question that remained was, how could I know if the Sergeant was being truthful? I was jarred out of my thoughts by the realization that the smile on Pete Polsen's face was now very clear, very noticeable.

"What's so funny, Pete?" I asked, somewhat annoyed by his grin.

"Ask me the question, Mike. Ever since her murder I've been waiting for you to ask me if I checked Mary Williams' record, so ask me."

I tried not to show I was startled by his brutal frankness. "Okay," I said. "Did you check her record?"

"Yes I did," he said matter-of-factly. And then he took over. "It was early January of this year, the sixth of January to be specific. The Chief asked me to see if I could locate an old time informant of his, a hooker by the name of Mary Williams, also know as Queen Mary. I went down to Records, pulled her rap sheet, made a copy of the cover, you know, her address, height, weight, et cetera, and then I put it on his desk. A couple of days later he told me she was no longer at the address on her record and he told me to try to run her down. It took me a day or so, but I found her over on Genesee Street. I never talked to her directly, but I confirmed her present, you know, before she was killed, present address."

"This is going to hurt, Pete, but I got to ask you something."

"Ask me whatever you want to know, Mike. I have nothing to hide. The only thing is that when this thing goes down and if you have to arrest Westfield, you make it clear to the courts and everyone that I didn't go running to you, but all I did was answer your questions when you approached me. I don't want anyone thinking I was disloyal to my boss. Okay?"

"Okay," I responded as I tried to sort out this man's need to be perceived as being loyal to a boss that was a killer. "But, like I said, I need to ask something, and it might hurt you, but I have to ask it all the same."

"Shoot."

"Can you prove it was Westfield that asked you to check her record? I mean, how do I know you aren't feeding me bullshit?"

"That's a fair question, Mike. It don't bother me," Polson said just as I realized I had not seen him this confident, this self-assured, in years. "The boss asks me to do a number of things that I'm not too comfortable doing, so I keep notes. Every time he asks me to check a record, pull someone's personnel file, do a little snooping around for him, I log it in my notebook."

"You said he has you doing things you're, 'not too comfortable doing'. Things like what, Pete?"

"Things, Mike, just things. They're not illegal, but I question whether or not they are proper, you know, if they are ethical. They don't pertain to this matter, and it wouldn't be right for me to discuss them with you." He looked at me to get a reaction, and I gave him a slight nod to tell him I understood his position. "Anyway, when he asks me to do these little things, I make a note of them. The other thing I do, is when I pull a record for him, or sign anything that is related to something I am doing for him, I use my three initials and then add a little letter C after my initials to indicate it was done at his request. You go back and check Williams' record and you will see a little, tiny, letter C after my initials."

"So, what you're telling me is that our Chief, Ben Westfield, had you go down and pull Williams' record about three months before she was killed, and then he had you go find where she was living?" I asked almost in disbelief.

"In a nutshell, that's it," he confirmed. Then, after a second or two of reflection, he added, "He's nuts, Mike. You know that, don't you?"

"I've wondered about it...more than wondered, I guess."

"He goes on a rampage and rips me apart for ten, twenty minutes, over nothing. Then, a half-hour later, he asks me why I'm so down. He enjoys mind games. That's why I started keeping notes on everything. I don't want to get dragged into something at this point of my career."

"And," I continued. "The only reason you never brought this information forward is because you don't want to be seen as being disloyal to this guy?"

Polson stirred his coffee before answering. "Mike, that's all I have on the Department. I'm not what you would call a great cop. I mean, you, guys like you, like Donovan, a handful of others, you're good cops. You stand out. You live and breath this job and you've made a reputation for yourselves. As for me, all I have going for myself is that I am seen as being loyal to my bosses and to the Department. Call it strange, or weird, or something like that, but to me, it's important. It's all I have."

We sat silent for a minute or two, each immersed in his own thoughts. Finally, Sergeant Polson spoke up.

"What are you going to do with this information, Mike?"

"Pete, right now, I don't have the foggiest idea. I've got to go to Novitski with it, that much I do know. Beyond that, I really don't know. I'm going to have to think that over real good, real carefully. However, it goes without saying that you have to keep this little meeting and conversation of ours under your hat. Right?"

"Believe me, Mike, I won't breath a word of this to anyone until it's all out in the open. The fact is, even my wife don't know I'm meeting with you. I told her I had to go up to the mall to get a birthday gift for a guy in the office."

Pete picked up the check and apologized for having to leave so soon. I sat there in the diner alone for another hour or so, trying to plot my next moves. Even though a small part of me took joy in seeing Westfield go down in flames, and I relished the thought of putting handcuffs on him, I was sad for the Department and the embarrassment his arrest would bring on all of us, especially the coppers like Sergeant Pat Polson. I had come to the diner to accuse him of murder and he in turn was worried about how others would perceive his loyalty to a maniac boss. Guys like Polson were the heart and soul of the Rochester Police Department, for that matter, any police department. The ones who placed importance on ethics, values, loyalty, and doing the right thing were getting harder and harder to find. They were quickly being replaced by the career cops who do their twenty years as easily as possible and then get out.

This latest development clearly pointed to Ben Westfield as the one behind the killings, but, it did little to clarify how Jessie and Teddy Roberts figured into the whole thing.

I slept very little over the next ten hours. Whenever my body developed the good sense to shut down, my mind shook it awake. There was little doubt, for me anyway, that Westfield was somehow connected with these murders. Williams' record went untouched for almost a decade, then, only a few of months before her death, her murder, to be precise, Ben Westfield gets an uncontrollable urge to locate her. That just didn't wash. Still, it was Teddy Roberts who had the gun that killed her, Lanovara, and Landers. It was Teddy Roberts' car that bore her hair and blood. And, behind it all, was this guy who called himself, "Jessie." He was the missing link in the entire mystery. He knew too much, was a little too confident, and a little too coy. If Westfield was involved in this thing, it had to be a conspiracy, and if there was a conspiracy I would have to show the link between a street punk named Teddy Roberts, a supposed informant named Jessie, and the Chief of the

Rochester Police Department.

Roberts was either one hell of a good liar or he was innocent. Jessie, on the other hand, had to be up to his ears on this thing. He was the one who gave us Roberts. It was he who had cautioned me about Roberts not wanting to be taken alive. And, it was Jessie who had advised me to shoot first when I encountered Teddy. Subsequently, it was Jessie who gave us the murder weapon. The slippery Jessie and Ben Westfield were in bed together on these killings. My bet it was Westfield pulling the strings and Jessie doing the dancing. Could it be that Jessie was William Westfield? Could it be that this killing spree was a father and son event? If that was the case, then Ben Westfield was more devious and mentally corrupt than even I imagined.

There was no way around it, the Chief of Police had to be interviewed. I had to take the same shot at him that I had taken with Roberts...and I owed him the same courtesy I had given Pete Polson. He would have to be confronted! However, how does one interrogate their Chief?

Finally, about five in the morning, my mind and body both gave in and I decided to work it out in the morning. Fortunately or unfortunately, at that early morning hour I didn't know the morning would only bring more questions, more dilemmas, and very few answers.

About eight o'clock in the morning, I called the office to tell them I would be arriving late. I stopped off at the Police Academy on Scottsville Road, just outside of the city limits, and bummed a cup of coffee off the Range Officer before reminding him of a big favor he owed me from a couple of years back in time. With the information in tow, I called the Major and asked him to meet me for coffee and *biscotti* at an Italian bakery on the city's west side. When he tried to beg off, I told him, "Boss, meet me. It's important." Novitski knew that in telling him to meet me, I was asking for something that was urgent.

It took me less than ten minutes to give him the synopsis of my finding Polson's initials on Queen Mary's record folder and my subsequent conversation with the Sergeant. He listened intently, distracting himself only long enough to dunk the hard Italian cookie in his coffee. It was only when I told him what I had learned at the academy that Charlie Novitski's face froze. His coffee-soaked *biscotti* broke and splashed into his coffee.

"You're one-hundred percent sure of this?" he asked without looking down at his floating pastry.

"I saw the records this morning, Major," I said in a whisper. "Saw them with my own eyes and made a copy of them in case the originals get lost in a fire or some other strange occurrence. Ben Westfield registered an off-duty gun with the P.D. back in 1986. It was a .9mm, same make and model as our killer's gun. Then, bing-bam-boom, about seven years ago it comes up missing and he reports it as being stolen out of his car."

"Any chance we have ballistics, a sample round from that gun?"

"Unfortunately not. When he got it, it was way before the Department kept a fired round and casing from off-duty weapons."

"What about the serial number? Is it the same as the murder weapon?"

"No way of telling. The gun we got out of Roberts' apartment had the serial number filed off. The lab doesn't think they can raise the numbers, but they're going to see if the Feds can do it. That could take a few months."

"You were smart to keep this away from the Department, Lieutenant," Novitski acknowledged. "Now I'm going to order you not to breath a word of it to anyone until I tell you. I want a report on this within the hour, a real report this time, and it will be locked in my safe. In the meantime, I have to have a sit down with someone in order to decide how to proceed from here. All in all, chances are pretty good you or I, or both of us, will be advising the Chief of his rights before the end of the day."

We split up in the parking lot of the bakery and then I headed for the Public Safety Building. My sleepless night, and troubled day, got worse when I arrived at the Detective Bureau and learned the press was insisting on a statement regarding our arrest of a suspect in what they were calling the, "Playing Card Murders." Verno and Paskell had been fielding calls from radio stations, the papers, and the television stations all morning.

"Waste-field had his press relations stooge call down a few minutes ago," Paskell told me. "And he wants you to be at a press conference with the Major in just about, according to my watch, thirty-five minutes. I think he's planning on announcing that Roberts is the killer of all three victims."

"Not only that, Lieutenant," Mancini interjected. "But Jessie's been calling for you. I told him you were taking the morning off, so he won't be bugging you again until this afternoon."

I left instructions to have Major Novitski paged and then I caught the first up-bound elevator for the puzzle palace on the sixth floor. Later on, Novitski would give me holy hell about violating the chain of command, but for now I needed some face-to-face answers. Skipping all the protocol, I had Polson get the Chief on the intercom and tell him I wanted a meeting now. When Westfield tried to stall, I grabbed the phone from the Sergeant and yelled, "NOW, Chief! No stalls! We need to meet right now!"

Needless to say, it was not a pleasant conversation. I tried to convince my boss of the idiocy of having a press conference without having charged anyone with the homicides. He tried to impress me with his rank in relation to mine and the public's right to know. I wasn't too impressed with either argument. His threats about having me brought up on charges for insubordination didn't impress me anymore than his other rantings.

"So, how did they get this information about us having a suspect, Chief?"

"Your guess is as good as mine, Lieutenant," he said with that thin smile of his. "But they know it and we would be foolish to deny it to them. You just be there and keep your mouth shut unless I tell you directly to answer some question. Understand?"

"I won't be able to make it, Chief," I lied. "The informant on this thing is insisting I meet him in less than an hour. I've got to get to him and see what he has."

"Forget him, Lieutenant!" Westfield snapped as he slammed his open hand down on his desk. "We don't need the little turd anymore. You just be here and show some damn support for once!"

"You're making a mistake on this call, Chief. A real big mistake!"

At the time I spoke the words, I knew I was right. I just didn't know how right time was going to prove me to be.

CHAPTER ELEVEN

NOTHING GOES RIGHT

The press conference, as far as press conferences go, wasn't all that difficult for me. In fact, I kind of enjoyed it. The Chief took center stage, with Novitski next to him, and told the media dogs he had, "...dedicated the total resources of the Rochester Police Department," and as a result of his effort, the Violent Crimes Unit now had a break on the three homicides. Mistakenly, he thought he could control the momentum and force of the press by leaving it at that. Westfield seemed confused when the reporters took over the briefing and began demanding answers to questions he wasn't prepared to handle. I sat in the back of the room, with my head resting against the wall, as reporters demanded specifics. Major Novitski finally jumped in and gave a flat statement that we did develop a "significant lead" and that we were pursuing that lead now.

When a reporter asked if Teddy Roberts was the killer, Novitski just smiled and said, "If I was you, I wouldn't print that."

When a couple of TV guys tossed questions my way, I simply threw up my hands and told them any information on the case should come from the Chief...and then enjoyed watching Westfield squirm when the questions went to him.

The Chief finally wiggled out of the fiasco by telling the assembly we all had a lot of work to do and they should expect an announcement of an arrest by morning. I could only smile to myself. Westfield was consistent in changing his mind and I consequently questioned if the man had any credibility, anywhere, with anybody. He obviously had decided not to give us the two days we had asked for so that we could run down all of Roberts little playmates. When the meeting with the press was over, Westfield took Novitski aside and ordered him to charge Roberts with at least one of the murders by the end of the day. The Major stalled the order, telling Westfield that before anyone was charged, it was very important that the three of us sit down and talk. The meeting was set for six o'clock that evening.

The day failed to develop anything that tied Roberts to the killings. I hated sitting on the information I had while watching the teams knock themselves out trying to make a link between Teddy and the killings. Knowing that Westfield had caused Pete Polson to locate Marry Williams, and knowing that our illustrious Chief of Police had owned a gun similar to the murder weapon, the man was naturally number one on my list of suspects. However, my men had to be kept in the dark so that Benjamin Westfield's piss poor reputation would not be sullied.

The teams had been hitting the streets for ten or twelve hours each day and tried to nail down a case on Teddy Roberts. It just wasn't happening because, very simply, Roberts wasn't the killer. With the exception of, 'Gus' and 'Billy,' everyone in the surveillance photos had been identified. I didn't see the wisdom of spending anymore time chasing down these nowhere leads. I pulled Donovan and Verno aside and told them to put all of their time into identifying Jessie.

It was almost five o'clock when Charlie Novitski sat down to discuss our up-coming meeting with the Chief. Every word we spoke, every move we made, had to be orchestrated to a fine degree. We both knew we would have only one shot with the man, so nothing could be left to chance.

However, Ben Westfield would stiff us one more time before the day was done. Ten minutes before our scheduled meeting with him, the Chief called down to the Major's office and canceled the meeting, assuring us he would meet with us the next day. I was in the middle of a lengthy litany of profanity when Novitski's phone rang. He pushed one of the buttons and Donovan's voice came over the speaker phone.

"The Lieutenant with you, Major?" Frank asked.

"He's right here, Donovan," Novitski responded. "Hang on. I'll give the phone to him."

"Don't bother, Boss. I'll give both of you the bad news at the same time," the detective said. "Channel 10 just announced on the evening news that we have arrested Teddy Roberts for the murder of Mary Williams, and get this, he's about to be charged with the Lanovara and Landers murders."

"Oh my God," Novitski moaned as he lowered his forehead into his right hand.

"Do they quote any particular source for this information?" I asked.

"They're quoting 'highly placed police officials' while showing footage of you, the Lieutenant, and the Chief from today's press conference," the speaker phone echoed.

After the Major clicked off the phone we both sat there in silence. A couple of minutes passed before we discussed what to do next. I proposed that I go ahead and charge Roberts so as not to embarrass the Department, but Novitski, in an unusual fit of anger, banged his fist down on the desk.

"No way, Lieutenant! That ego-maniac on the sixth floor is not going to dictate matters of integrity to us." Bang! Novitski's ham hock fist hit the wood surface again. "Let the dirty bastards who leaked this crap charge Teddy Roberts." Bang! "If you don't feel right charging the kid, I won't allow you to charge him! Let Westfield charge Roberts if he feels so damn strong about it!" Bang!

The next day, Friday, I carried a head-banging hangover to work. The Democrat and Chronicle carried a page one story about the arrest of Teddy Roberts on weapons charges and again quoted their, "highly placed police officials" and "investigators close to the case" as saying the weapon he was charged with possessing was the same weapon used in each of the killings. The rest of the story recounted the three killings and threw in a couple of quotes made by me earlier in the week. To Joe Citizen sitting at home in front of his bowl of corn flakes, it was apparent I was the news leak.

Reporters from the papers, radio, and TV stations called all day. Each caller was given the same information. Teddy Roberts had been charged with a weapons violation...all other press releases would come directly from the Office of the Chief of Police. I thought that if Westfield wanted to control the investigation, he could deal with the media ghouls too,

It was hard facing the detectives. I felt I had injured them in some way, and they probably sensed it. Whenever a question came up about Roberts I shrugged it off and said, "Ask the Chief."

Major Charles Novitski made two attempts to set up an appointment with Westfield. Twice he was denied access to the man. We were at an impasse. Novitski would not charge Roberts with the murder count if Westfield wouldn't first meet with him. Westfield wouldn't meet with him unless Roberts was charged with Williams' murder.

This case was driving everyone nuts. Now it was unraveling the entire police department. In the quiet moments between the on-again-off-again meetings with Westfield, I drew up my personal list of suspects on the Spades Case. When I was finished, I was embarrassed by some of the names written on the paper. Along with Westfield, Teddy Roberts, our mystery caller - the enigmatic Jessie - and Sergeant Polson, I had included Frank Donovan and Charlie Novitski. After all, it was Donovan who had predicted the killer would "go public" after the murder of Landers and the press story about the L-A-N theory. He also was a Detective...perhaps *the* Detective Landers referred to in his appointment book. And then there was the Major, my mentor and confidant, my boss and counselor. Why had the hairs on the back of my head gone up when, over coffee and *biscotti* , he had instructed me not to mention a word about Westfield's stolen gun? Why did he have to see "someone" about the matter? I fully realized we all had those "someones" we sought to make contact with when faced with a problematic situation, but the remark puzzled me. Besides, Novitski was also Detective, one with a lot of rank, but still a Detective.

I circled Westfield's name a few dozen times before tearing up the list in a hundred or so pieces for fear that someone would see it and wonder if the case was costing me my sanity. It obviously was costing me the trust I had in people I called my friends.

Luckily the weekend had arrived. The two teams on duty would avoid the office at all costs so the media mopes would have to chase their tails. The papers and the rest of the world would have to stew a few days while I caught my breath. To fill the gaps left by the lack of hard facts, the news stations and papers filled their time and space with a re-hashing of each murder and the arrest of Teddy Roberts. Never lacking in creativity, the news people made the old news sound like breaking news.

Besides the welcome break from the case from hell, Diane and I were finally going to have that dinner we talked about.

On Saturday night I picked her up at her apartment. I had planned on going inside the building and knock on Diane's door, but she was already waiting for me by the entrance of the trendy building. I smiled at my date's confident walk. My eyes also caught sight of her outstanding pair of legs that would cause a man half her age to give a double take. Being a gentleman, and perhaps trying to impress her, I rushed around the car and opened her door. As she slid her trim, aerobic-worked body into the car, I caught a whiff of her perfume and over twenty years of memories waifed their way inside

FROM PAGE **1B**

homicide unit from 1975-1980. He served as captain of Genesee Section from 1982-1988.

After retirement, he and his wife of 33 years, Nancy, moved to New Mexico, where Campanozzi is chief of police at the Pueblo of Sandia Reservation.

Campanozzi was known as a bright, methodical investigator, and a leader who was more than willing to roll up his sleeves — sometimes in unusual ways.

For example, in the mid-1970s he invoked the divine in a case of a city woman being investigated for killing her children.

"She was religious and said she wanted to tell the truth, but needed the strength, so we go down on our knees together and prayed to God to

recalled.

After the prayer, the woman duly confessed.

"He was a cop's cop and he was very thorough, and we all respected him," says retired police Sgt. George Ehle, who recalls that even Campanozzi's memos were well-written. "Most of all, he always spoke of the need to care about people."

Added retired police Sgt. Lou Bertino affectionately, "We used to call him the White Knight. He was just a really, really good cop who was absolutely dedicated."

his characters are compilations of people he has known, his material is grounded in reality.

For example, Campanozzi's experience investigating the mob, including the 1970s execution-style slaying of reputed mob underboss Salvatore "Sammy G" Gingello, manifests itself in Ace Amato's fictional dealings with organized crime.

And the idea for *The Killing Cards* was sparked by a real-life Rochester murder in 1976 in which a prostitute was found mutilated, with an ace of spades found stuck in

The killer was just trying to throw us off, but it gave me an idea of what would happen if a serial killer used his killings to create a royal flush with the cards as his calling cards," Campanozzi says.

Campanozzi says everyone always asks whether the Ace Amato character is really him.

"No," he says.

"He's younger, he's shorter, he has a lousy social life, he's divorced and drinks and smokes too much. And he doesn't have as much fun as I have writing these books." □

Heard

...utor training workshop starts June 22. The classes will be 6 to 9 p.m. Thursdays through July 27 at the White House in the Board of Cooperative Educational Services complex at 27 Lackawanna Ave., Mount Morris.

Those who complete the course will become certified tutors of adults in conversational English speaking skills.

There is a $20 fee for materials and registration is required. For details or to register call 658-7970.

Geneva

Theater posting cheaper tickets

The Smith Opera House is

...es.

Longdue's head is chocked full of cases, both solved and unsolved, of high-speed car chases, of running after burglary suspects in backyards and of being called away from a wedding to investigate a case.

The unsolved 1980 double slaying of Bonnie Maykovich and Tom Tabor — found stabbed and shot in their Shelford Road home — stays with him. As a captain, he traveled to West Virginia to interview people who knew the victims. But no clues as to who broke into the house and killed the couple ever surfaced.

What friends and staff members will remember about Longdue is his genial nature, his ability to talk with anyone, his sense of humor

...puterizing the department in 1988, helping get the new court and police department built in 1992 and starting the first senior citizen police academy in fall 1998.

Longdue also set up a complaint system last year with the Center for Dispute Settlement to combat accusations of racial profiling.

"His legacy is that the youngsters he helped are repaying the community in different ways," said Sgt. Richard Tantalo, who sought advice from Longdue about becoming a police officer more than 25 years ago.

"He understands the importance of being able to work with people . . . he hasn't lost sight of that fact."

But on top of the thousands of hours of police work, Tisa

IRONDE POLI DEPART[T]

my head.

Diane Constance O'Leary had caught my eye one Saturday morning almost a quarter of a century earlier as I was walking a foot beat on Hudson Avenue. Stepping into Rasnick's Bakery, all I saw was the smile that adorned her face. My mind blocked out the over-sized apron wrapped around her one-and-a-half times, the flour that smudged her cheeks, and her tousled hair. All I saw was the smile that spread across her lips and sparkled in her eyes. On Monday morning I returned to the bakery and found out from Buddy Rasnick, the portly owner of the bakery, that the girl with the smile was a college student who only worked part-time for him two evenings a week and Saturdays so as to make some spending money. It took two more Saturdays before I got to speak to my future ex-wife. After that first clumsy conversation, another month passed before I worked up the nerve to ask her out. It would take a couple of more months before we finally went on a date. Although I was totally infatuated by the blond-haired, blue-eyed Irish girl, she appeared to be only mildly attracted to me. We drifted apart for a few months, back together for a while, and then apart again. A year after she graduated from Nazareth College with a degree in economics, we bumped into one another at a New Year's Eve party. We began to date again, got serious about one another, and two years later we were married, much to the chagrin of her father and my mother. Mister Patrick O'Leary did not think highly of dagos or cops. As for my mother, well, although she blamed the Jews for killing Christ, she was very confident the Irish and English had put them up to it.

In spite of our parents, Diane and I drifted into wedded bliss. The bliss part lasted about three or four years. The wedded part lasted almost a decade. The long hours I gave the job, the alcohol that poured down my throat, and the foul temper that spilled out of my mouth, all contributed to the divorce. Finally, she couldn't - and wouldn't - take it anymore. When I failed to come home for a couple of nights, Diane left me a note that emphatically described where I could shove the police department and my liquor.

Now that we had been divorced almost as long as we had been married, Diane and I enjoyed a comfortable friendship ear marked by occasional dinners and easy conversation. We had even taken a couple of stabs at putting the pieces of our broken marriage back together again - the last time was slightly over a year ago - but the efforts never worked out. That final failure was perhaps the hardest for me, but out of it, we agred we were pretty good at being friends and fairly lousy at being husband and wife.

I had to admit that Diane had weathered the intervening years much better than I. While my career had stalled, her's had advanced steadily. What booze and smoked had done to wreck my body, Diane's energetic workouts and health conscious living had combined to keep her young and vibrant.

As we drove out to Dick Moll's Place in the little Town of Mendon, New York, I stole more than a few peeks at the lovely woman next to me. The restaurant was a great place for a steak, and besides, it was far enough from the city and its suburbs that I wouldn't be running into anyone I knew. It wasn't that I minded being seen with my ex, I just didn't want our meeting, our date of sorts, interrupted. The drive only took about forty minutes, but it was like entering a different world. Leaving behind the city sights and sounds, we drove east and then south past the suburban town of Brighton. We laughed and talked as the car glided over small, rolling hills that sneaked up on us quickly, and just as quickly, disappeared in the rear view mirror. We talked about nothing of importance. We were together and that seemed enough for both of us.

I pushed open the heavy, old, wooden, plank door of the country inn and again stole a whiff of Diane's presence. Once inside, we exchanged pleasantries with our host, Dick Moll. Diane and I had been regulars at his old place on South Avenue, and the passing years did not erase the memories shared by the three of us. After a drink at the hundred-year-old bar, we were escorted to the remote table in the back room. It was the very table I had requested a week earlier.

With drinks on the table we made small talk about her job and some of our mutual friends. As she talked I looked at her. Diane wore her forty-some-odd years rather well. Her golden blond hair bounced slightly as she moved her head. She had done something slightly different with her hair. I don't know what she did, but I liked it. I liked it a lot! The style seemed to cup her face gently and it highlighted her other features. The thought that she was the best thing that ever happened to me was a reminder to me that our relationship was another thing that I had screwed up. The thought became persistent and passed through my mind several times as we ate dinner.

Finally, with dinner over, Diane set her napkin down on the table and commented, "So, I see you guys have this last string of homicides wrapped up pretty well."

"Not really," I said with a half laugh. "I thought I taught you not to believe everything you read in the papers."

"The way I read it, it sounded like you arrested this Teddy, Teddy Whatever, for the last murder and were going to charge him with the other two."

"The Chief wants us to, but I don't think he did any of the killings."

She looked at me in silence for a minute and finally asked, "So what is it

Michael? Why are we doing this?"

"I don't know," I admitted. "I just thought it would be nice."

"Michael, we only meet like this when you're bored and out of interesting bodies to keep you occupied. If this case isn't wrapped up....?" She let the sentence trail off unfinished. After sipping her coffee, Diane leaned back in her chair, gave me that suspicious look wives give errant husbands, and asked, "You're worried about something, aren't you? It's the same old you, Michael. Everything's bottled up inside you." She paused as if to look inside me, and then said, "Talk to me. What's going on?"

"It's just this case. It's a real mess. I've really screwed this one up."

"*You*? You screwed it up, Michael? All by yourself? That is so typical, so...so typical you!" She paused and asked, "If things go bad, it's because *you* screw them up. And if they go right, oh well, you just got lucky." She stopped long enough to put her hand on mine, and then continued. "Quit blaming yourself for every damn killing."

"I don't blame myself for the killings. But, if they go unsolved, I...well, it's still my responsibility to get them cleaned up. The cases are my responsibility, Diane. It's not like working at Kodak. At the end of the day I just can't shut off the copier, turn off the lights and go home. If things go right there are plenty of people to grab the credit. If they go bad, well then, it's Mike Amato that gets thrown to the press hounds."

"So quit, Michael. Give it up. You have your time in. You can retire anytime you want to. You don't have to go on living this way."

"Maybe after this case I will," I said with some smugness. "I just might put it all away after we get through this one."

"That's bull, Michael!" Diane said softly as if making a private proclamation. "You won't quit after this one, or the next one, or the one after that. You love it! You really do, dear." The words were accompanied with a smile and a pat on my hand. "It's just that you are so afraid of failing, so afraid of making the same mistakes that everyone of us in the real world makes everyday."

"So what do I do?" I looked up and asked her.

"I don't know, Michael. I really don't know. It's up to you. It's your choice, not mine. Choose what you want, and then do it!"

We ordered coffee and then sat without saying a word until it came. Then, with her coffee stirred, Diane continued.

"The bad times with you were during the times when a case was open, when you would distance yourself from everybody. You would get up in the middle of the night and make calls, go somewhere to check on something, and smoke those damn cigarettes. The best times were when you solved a case and you walked around whistling, smiling and joking. But the worst times, the absolute worst times with you, were when a case went unsolved. You were just plain hateful, Michael. Silent. Moody. Impossible to be with. And, do you know why?"

"Why?" I responded to the rhetorical question she was bound to answer.

"Because you got beat. You felt like you lost this, this game. This good guys and bad guys game you play."

If this was our usual argument, it would have been difficult to sit there quietly and listen to Diane. However, this was not an argument. This was a discussion, a conversation between two good friends who were close enough in spirit to talk like this, but too close in emotions to live together.

"I hear what you're saying and you're probably right in some ways. But, it's hardly a game, Diane," I countered.

"But it is for you, Michael! It's not just a job to you, a job where some problems just don't get solved, or some widgets aren't made correctly. It's a game. Granted, it's a very serious, high-stakes game, but still a game."

"What you fail to acknowledge, my dear wife, is that..."

"Dear *ex*-wife," she corrected with a smile.

I nodded at her point and continued. "What you fail to see, my dear ex-wife, is that I do not work with widgets. This 'game' as you call it, is played with human lives. I mess up, and someone walks. If I'm not good enough, then some killer, somebody who took a human life, goes free. If I don't get this guy there are going to be two more bodies out there."

"And that is the weight you carry around with you, Michael. But, as I said before, that's your choice...if you choose to do it! If it's too much for you, then make the choice to get out. If you choose to stay, then come to grips with the fact that you're going to win some, and you're going to lose some. Just quit whipping yourself over it."

As I laid down the cash to cover the bill and tip, my mind went back thirty-five, forty years, to a time when youth learns the lessons they carry through life. Lessons about honor, loyalty, working hard, and striving to get ahead. Those were the lessons learned through the examples of those we loved and respected as they came home from the factories covered in grime and silently taught us these lessons. Honor. Responsibility. Loyalty.

"I know and understand what you're saying," I said to Diane after we were in the car and heading back toward the city. "It's true, and it makes sense."

"But?" she asked as she tilted her head forward and looked over to me.

"But, it's more complicated than that. If I didn't do this, I don't know what I would do. I'm not even fifty yet. I'm getting too old to do this job, but I'm way too young to retire. Besides, can you picture me playing shuffle board or golf every day?"

"No, Michael, I can't," she responded very seriously. "But I can see some of that pain and anger going away, and that would be nice." Diane audibly sighed, and then added, "You know I still love you, Michael, it's just that for the past ten or twelve years I haven't liked you."

"What about tonight? Wasn't I cute, kind, and charming? Wasn't I bordering on uncontrollably likable tonight?" I quipped.

"Oh, you sure were, but that's only because you needed someone to talk to...and you know you can always talk to me. There's something going on in this case that you aren't talking about. I really don't want to know what it is, but, it's tearing you up. Maybe you think it's solved and that frightens you, because the game is over. Maybe you're afraid you haven't solved it, or you solved it with the wrong guy. I don't know and it's none of my business."

"What makes you say that?"

"I say that because you're here, Michael. You're with me, talking like we are."

"You mean I only call you when I have a problem?"

"No, not at all. You only call me when you're bored or frightened. You're a complex, but not complicated, guy, Michael. You reach out for me when you can't deal with the fear, the fear of losing, of being wrong, of being humiliated. You can handle the rest of it, the bad guys and their blood, the guts and brains, the guns and the fights, but you can't handle being less than perfect."

"Is that why we broke up, because I'm a perfectionist?" I asked in all seriousness.

She smiled and answered, "That and because you're a hard-headed dago, Michael." The smile went away before she added, "You just never caught on to the fact that I loved you because you were less than perfect."

We drove the last few miles in relaxed silence. When I pulled up in front of her apartment, I leaned over and kissed Diane's cheek and she returned the sign of friendship.

"By the way," she said with a big smile. "I'm proud of the progress you're making in controlling your language. It's really nice to have a conversation with you without the expletives."

"I'm trying. It's hard, but I'm trying."

Silence filled the car as neither one of us could find the right thing to say that would make the night last. We said good night one more time, and once again we exchanged platonic cheek kisses.

"Tell me something," she said as she got out of the car. "Is this guy after you? Are you the Ace?"

I shrugged my shoulders and shook my head. "Nah, I really don't think so."

"You get this guy, Michael. You be careful and you get him."

And then she was gone.

Monday was one of those hard working, but non-productive days. Twice we thought we had a lead on Jessie and twice it turned out to be nothing. At six in the evening, after a couple of false starts, Novitski and I were sitting in Westfield's anteroom. We had established our plan of attack a day earlier and now sat silently, each one wondering if the plan would really work. Twenty minutes later we were seated in front of the Chief's desk. Westfield was there to order me to arrest Roberts. I was there to get enough on him to throw his ass in jail.

I put the tape recorder on the desk and Novitski opened the conversation before his boss could ask what was going on.

"Chief," the Major said as he pulled his chair in closer to the desk. "Lieutenant Amato has developed some information which leads us to believe you may have had some interest in Mary Williams prior to her death. We want to ask your cooperation in discussing the situation with us."

Ben Westfield looked at the recorder before shifting a frozen stare in my direction. Finally he asked, "What the hell is the meaning of this?"

"Like I said..." Novitski started before he was cut off.

"I know what you said! I want to know what the hell is going on here. What's this recorder doing here? Have you two lost control of your faculties?"

"Chief, what the Lieutenant and I have to discuss leaves no room for misinterpretation at a later time. There have been several misunderstandings in the past day or so over such things as our request to hold off charging anyone for the recent string of murders, and your insistence that we do charge the man we have in custody for other charges."

"You two have a lot of nerve and little brains. I ordered you to charge that Roberts fellow with the Williams' killing and you've done nothing with it. So now you want to record this conversation while you make excuses over not following my orders!" Westfield looked back and forth between Novitski and I as he went through his tirade.

"No, Chief, that's not the subject of this interview at all."

"Then what is it about, Major? Is this some type of inquisition? You know, I expect this sort of thing from him," he said with venom in his voice as he pointed a manicured finger in my direction. "But you disappoint me, Major."

"Chief, you checked Mary Williams' criminal record less than four months before her death," the Major continued, ignoring the inquisition comment. "That is highly, ah, unusual. It's a coincidence we don't feel can be overlooked. Consequently, there is a need to interview you on that matter. Both Lieutenant Amato and I realize the seriousness of this discussion, and in order to protect the integrity of the investigation, and to protect all three of us from getting, ah, shall we say, getting carried away, I thought it best that we record our meeting."

"Are you accusing me of murder? Are you out of your mind, Major?"

"No one's accusing you of anything, Chief. We have legitimate questions to ask, and we hope you will see the importance of this matter, and cooperate with us. Okay?"

"Oh, your motives are so admirable, Major Novitski, " Westfield boomed in a mocking, theatrical voice as his right hand swept the room. "So, go ahead, and ask your questions. Have your fun, Major. Ask your questions, and we'll see who laughs last. Both of you are looking right down the barrel of departmental charges for insubordination, and you're trying to fend them off with your little game. You two are disgusting!"

"This is not being done for sport, Chief," Novitski answered back, his voice a little louder than usual. "There are legitimate questions to be asked, and I trust you have legitimate answers. What would you have us do instead of meeting and talking face-to-face? Would you rather we went quietly along our merry way, and simply put it into the Grand Jury with the Roberts case?"

With my eyes shifting right and left and then right, I felt like a spectator sitting mid-court at a tennis match. I wanted to jump in. Oh God, how I wanted to jump in! However, I sat quietly as Novitski and I had planned, waiting for the right time, the right mood.

"Why did you check Mary Williams' record, Chief?" the Major asked in his normal hushed tone.

"I never checked her record, Major," Westfield answered as he crossed his legs and brushed imaginary lint off his pants. I watched as he held his right hand on his lap with his left hand, as if doing so would help him get a grip on the interview.

"I'm sorry," Novitski nodded in concession of the point. "Why did you have Sergeant Polson check her record on January sixth of this year?"

"Who said I had Polson check her record?"

"Sergeant Polson did. Amato interviewed him extensively last week."

"And why is it you would take his word over mine?" Westfield asked as he pulled his head back and literally looked down his nose at Charlie Novitski.

"He has records to show he did it at your request, Chief," I said, and instantly caught the man off guard with the information, as well as with my entry into the conversation.

"Records?" he asked of Novitski. "What records?"

"A personal, administrative record he keeps in the normal course of his duties," I answered, knowing full well the use of the legal parlance, 'normal course of his duties' would get the arrogant man's attention. Novitski allowed the information to sink in for a second or two and then continued. "And there is the matter of your personal .9mm automatic which you lost seven years ago."

"What about it?" Westfield asked of me before he realized it was my boss who had put the item on the table. Turning to Novitski, he asked his question again.

"Did you ever find it? Was it ever recovered by some agency? Do you have it now?" Novitski asked patiently.

"No. No. And, no," Westfield answered with a smug smile. "Now do you want to double team me with something else?"

"Just the one thing, Chief," Novitski said. "Why did you want Williams' record checked?"

"Major, I am disappointed in you. I have a department to run. I have many reasons for the things I do, and, if I have to add for your edification, I do not have to explain those reasons to my subordinates. I did what I had to do because there was a need to do it. I'm sorry, but you're just going to have to accept that."

"In other words, you're not going to give me an answer?" Novitski asked without emotion.

"In other words, you and your Lieutenant can take your recorder and get out of here, Major. I don't buckle under pressure from subordinates."

"That's your call, Chief," the Major responded. "But I want you to realize that when Roberts gets charged, as per your earlier order, there will be a Grand Jury called to indict him, and you will be subpoenaed to that Grand Jury to explain your interest in Williams."

"Are you threatening me, Major?" Westfield yelled as he got up out of his chair.

Novitski got up from his chair, leaned the meaty knuckles of his left hand on his boss' desk and countered, "I am telling you my course of action in investigating this case. With all due respect, Chief, I am responsible for the integrity of criminal investigations. I will not, repeat, I will not sweep anything under the rug if there is a matter of proper and legal concern about one of those cases."

The two stood leaning at each over the desk as I maintained my mid-court demeanor. It's possible the Chief blinked, but I'm not sure. All I do know is there was some change in him. Something went out of him. Something in his muscle tone, his rigidity relaxed...or weakened.

"I'll need a lawyer to advise me first," Ben Westfield whispered as his eyes went down to his desk top.

"I understand," Novitski said to the deflated man. "When will that be?"

"Tomorrow, maybe the day after."

"You'll let me know?"

"I'll let you know," Westfield conceded with a slight edge of resignation.

Ben Westfield remained there, leaning on his desk, as we retreated to the fourth floor without a word. Charlie Novitski looked as beaten as the Chief. He secured the tape recording in his safe, sighed audibly, and sat in his chair.

"Go do it, Mike," he told me as he leaned his butt on the locked safe, and folded his arms over his chest. "And be careful about it," he cautioned as I opened the door to the hallway.

I went directly to my car and positioned it between two other cars on Broad Street at a parking meter in front of the old Democrat and Chronicle building. Less than twenty minutes later, Ben Westfield's city-owned black Buick passed me. I fell in behind him at a respectable distance. Once in his neighborhood, my car drifted back as he turned right on to his street and I continued south for a block and then circled back. Three minutes later I was parked across the street and three houses west of the Chief's Tudor-style home. I kept my mind free of any thoughts as I watched the lights in the house come on as the angry man moved from room to room in his sanctuary. Finally, the downstairs lights went off and a window on the second story lit up. An hour and fifteen minutes later the house was dark. An hour went by, then two, but Ben Westfield never left the house.

I stayed on the surveillance point another half hour or so, knowing I was wasting my time. My suspect had turned in for the night without taking the bait. I drove around the block a couple of times until I had heat in the car once again and then zeroed in on a pay phone, stepped out of the warm car and called the Major. The report was short and simple. We talked for a couple of minutes about the possibility of Westfield using the phone to handle the business we suspected him to handle, but both of us agreed he would have taken the hint of the tape recorder, and, for fear of a wire tap, would stay away from using his phone for any private conversations.

"No, Mike, if he was going to reach out for Jessie, or whoever he's involved with, he would have done it in person. We got him too nervous for him to trust a phone." There was a few seconds of silence before he added, "It didn't work, so go home and get some sleep. Tomorrow's going to be a bitch."

I went back to Westfield's neighborhood and parked my car a block away from his home. Getting rid of my suit coat and tie, I pulled an old wind breaker out of my trunk and made my way over a couple of fences. Once in Westfield's backyard I checked his garage. I was somewhere between frustrated and relieved to see his car was still there.

It was almost one in the morning before I made it back to my side of the city. I stripped off my suit and was in my underwear, having a conversation with a glass of orange juice and Southern Comfort, when the phone rang. It was one of the 9-1-1 operators.

"This guy, Jessie, is really getting rather nasty about it, Lieutenant," Operator 361 told me. "He's called every ten or fifteen minutes for the past two hours, telling us to find you, or we were all going to be sorry."

"Did he leave a number?"

"No. He said for you to go to your office and wait for his call."

"Well, I just had a long, hard, day, so, if he calls back again, tell him to call me tomorrow. Anything else for me?"

"He's kind of a weird-o, Lieutenant. The last time he called, he said you were supposed to be in your office right then because of the killing."

"What killing?" I asked.

"That's what I asked him. He said something about the king falling tonight, or the king getting dropped tonight, or something like that."

Five minutes later, Operator 361 was on the line again. A shooting victim had been taken to Strong Memorial Hospital at 11:35 P.M. At 1:50 A.M. he expired. The punch line to her call was...the King of Spades had been found in the bloody shirt the doctors had removed from the victim.

Not bothering to shower, I climbed back into the suit that had already experienced one full day of duty. My hopes that this killing was just copycat killing were dashed when I called the 9-1-1 operator back and asked her if she had the name of the our latest victim.

"It's here in my notes somewhere, Lieutenant," she said to the sound of papers being shuffled. "Yes, I have it. His name is Rex Nelson."

At first it didn't hit me, and I asked, "Is that it? Rex? Nelson? You sure it isn't Rex King, or something like that?"

"Well, Lieutenant, Rex is the Latin word for King, you know," the voice said in a nun-like, but not sarcastic manner.

CHAPTER TWELVE

OF KINGS, KILLERS, AND FOOLS

I was getting too old for this crap! With only five hours of sleep over the past day and a half, I threaded my way from the suburbs on the far north side of the city to Strong Memorial Hospital on the south side of town. I used the time to berate myself for having wasted an entire night sitting on the Chief while the real killer was busy stalking his fourth victim. The only thing I had accomplished through my stupidity over the past week was to establish an alibi for Ben Westfield and Teddy Roberts, the only two promising suspects we had developed since the killings had begun. Having been able to clear them didn't bother me. What drove me to fist-pounding rage was that I was failing. I was losing the game. The entire case was out of control, going nowhere, and I was the one holding the reins.

As I entered the hospital, I took a deep breath and blew it out slowly to gain control of my lost emotions. Two detectives from the Department's Downtown Patrol District met me at the door of the hospital. Before I had the opportunity to rip their collective asses, Don McDermott, the senior of the two men, apologized for not having me called in sooner.

"It was one giant screw up, Lieutenant," the Hollywood version of a detective offered as an explanation as he extended his right hand to me. "The victim was shot about three hours ago now, but the ambulance company got the call directly from some unknown citizen. It was called into them as a 'man down', so they go ahead and take the call without notifying our dispatcher. The white coats go to the scene, see blood all over the victim, but go ahead and scoop him up anyway. While they're en route to the hospital, they have their dispatcher call our people. Finally, ten, fifteen minutes later the P.D. gets the info about a man down from the ambulance hacks and the uniforms shoot over to the location, which is a parking lot next to a gay bar on Franklin Street. When our coppers don't see any ambulance or man down, they figure it's a bogus call and go back in service. Anyway, it takes another couple of calls between the ambulance people and our communications people to sort it all out and, one thing and another, we don't get the call to come on down to the hospital for another half hour after that. So, long story short, we get down here and then the nurse tells us the guy is a stabbing victim going up to O.R. and it isn't until just before we call you that we find out the guy has gone toes-up, that he's shot instead of stabbed, and, of all things, that the doctors found the King of Spades in his shirt pocket."

I listened patiently and chewed the inside of my lower lip as McDermott spun the tale of woe. When he came up for air, I pumped the first question. "Where's the crime scene, and what's being done about the scene and the evidence?"

"The scene where the body was found has been established. Like I said, it's the parking lot behind the joint, and it's been sealed off. The card found in his pocket has been photographed by a technician, and along with the guy's clothes, has been gathered for processing."

"Leads? Witnesses? Name, et cetera, for the victim?" I asked while noticing that McDermott's well-coifed salt and pepper hair was still immaculately in place at this late hour of his shift.

"Our victim is one Rex Nelson, male, white, 27," the tall, slender Detective answered as he pushed open a page of his steno notebook with a manicured index finger. "He's got an apartment over on Goodman near Monroe. We called for a team to go over there and begin scouting around. For leads we got shit. Same goes for witnesses. However, the shift boss sent two uniforms to the bar to get identification on everyone still there. We haven't heard anything from them except that our victim is a known fag and way out of the closet."

"What's the weapon?" I asked as heat began to return to my fingers and nose once again.

"From the x-rays I've seen, there aren't any rounds in him, so it's hard to say. But, based on the wounds I saw, I got to figure it was small, like maybe a twenty-two or a twenty-five caliber."

We went back to the hospital's morgue, with only the sounds of our foot steps echoing in the off the walls of the silent passageway. The body was naked now and had that cold, gray, look that death gives flesh. Rex Richard Nelson was a handsome young man, with a square chin and pronounced cheek bones. His left eyelid was still partially opened, exposing a blue pupil looking into eternity. I moved my attention to the gunshot wound in his lower left chest. My guess was the projectile had entered too low on the torso to strike any significant body organ. However, as too many autopsies had shown me, once inside the cavity, bullets tend to bounce around like a fart in an eight-sided jar. Consequently, only the autopsy would speak details about what damage had truly been done by that particular bullet. Reaching under the cool skin of the left shoulder and lifting up on the dead weight, I rolled the body half way over, and there, where the neck meets the shoulder, was the second wound. The slight bruising around it, along with the black flecks of gun powder that had burned their way into the man's skin, told the story of a gun held close to Rex Richard Nelson and fired as he was lower than the shooter, perhaps kneeling and begging for his life, or collapsing after the first shot had done the preliminary damage. His hands and face were clean and free of any marks of a fight or struggle.

"It could be this is just a lover's quarrel between two frigging fags, Lieutenant," McDermott said. "Maybe the guy wanted to make it look like your serial killer, and stuffed the card in his shirt to cover his tracks."

I doubted the validity of that observation, but more so, I hated the thoughts that went with it.

"You guys stay here and nail down every last detail concerned with this body, his clothing, the doctors, the medical treatment he got, who determined what, and so on," I said as I got ready to break for the door. I was going to leave, but I couldn't resist the urge to make a point. "By the way, McDermott..."

"Yeah, Lute?"

"Nelson is a victim, and he's to be shown some damned respect. Okay? You got that?"

I left the two blank-faced detectives wondering what the hell my problem was as I left for the crime scene. Before leaving my apartment I had the dispatcher call in Donovan and Verno, and start them to the scene of the shooting. As I headed for the bar, I had the dispatcher call in Paskell and St. John, and have them report directly to headquarters. In the privacy of the car, I used the cell phone to notify Major Novitski of my most recent embarrassment.

Nattie's is a popular downtown bar that - either by design or by chance - caters to homosexuals. Since the building had been erected in the late 1800's it had served as a furniture store, a dry goods shop, Italian restaurant and finally it became just another vacant building in just another vacant downtown. Having parked my car across the street, I had a chance to take in the ornate lines of the old - but well-restored - building before I pushed my way through the heavy eight-foot door and entered the chaos inside.

Frank Donovan waved me over to where he was at the far end of the bar and gave me a briefing. So far the cops at the scene had rounded up seven people who either knew the victim or had seen him leave with another white male. The bartender, who knew our victim as a regular, did not recall seeing who Rex Nelson was with, but did remember him ordering two rum and cokes for, "...Bill and me."

We arranged to have the witnesses transported to the Detective Bureau and then cleaned up a few odds and ends at the bar before heading for the Public Safety Building, leaving the technicians to do the work that would carry them into the daylight hours. When we got to the cop shop, the Detective Bureau was a zoo. The witnesses had all been separated. Two of them were in some stage of giving statements while one of them was sitting down, describing Nelson's companion to a detective who was making a composite drawing. Two more of the witnesses slouched behind desks abandoned by the day shift Detectives. Another one sat on the floor like a squatter, his head laid in his crossed arms that rested on his knees. The night receptionist handed me six messages as soon as I stepped off the elevator. All six were from Jessie. I went into my office and began to sort things out when, out of the blue, I got a brain fart.

My guys had identified almost everyone of the people we had seen coming in and out of Teddy Roberts' apartment building. Everyone, that is, except for a mug called "Gus" and another one called "Billy". I was betting that the "Billy and me" Rex Nelson referred to when ordering drinks at Nattie's was the same Billy that had been one of Teddy Roberts' visitors the night Mancin and I surveiled the kid's apartment.

Grabbing the Teddy Roberts folder out of the file drawer, I retrieved the surveillance photos we had shot the night we set up the surveillance on his apartment. I showed the stack of photos to the first two witnesses and drew a blank. The bartender was also unable to pick out anyone. And, then, God bless them, three of the remaining four witnesses each picked out the same photo, identifying the man who accompanied Rex Nelson in the hours before his death. The seventh witnesses said he wasn't really positive, but selected the same photo. It was going to be a long night and a longer day.

I had just stuffed the photos back into the folder when the phone rang.

"Amato," I answered.

"This is Jessie," the voice said with an overtone of joviality. "Having an interesting night, Lieutenant?"

"Not too bad. I just hope the city can afford the overtime."

"Kind of embarrassing to have the wrong man in jail, isn't it?"

"You mean Roberts?" I asked innocently.

"I sure do. You're going to look like a fool in the morning when the story breaks that you arrested him for the killings, and then, out of nowhere, the killings go on."

I wanted to reach through the phone and strangle the bastard. Instead, I said, "I'll get by."

"Don't you want to ask me who's going to be next, Lieutenant?"

"Not really," I answered and physically shrugged so he would hopefully sense my lack of care. "However, there is one thing I would like to ask you."

"Sure thing, Mister *Ace* Detective. Go ahead and ask."

Armed with the identifications just made by the witnesses strewn around the office, I asked, with a smile, "Do you mind if I call you Bill?"

Click!

I had finally gotten to the son-of-a-bitch! In that one second he had been thrown on the defensive, and now, for the first time since the killings began, I was playing offense. I was back in the game!

I held the phone for a half minute before I realized there was a stupid smile spread across my kisser. It was the same look I had seen on undercover cops when they make a bust on a case they had been working long and hard. It was the look of satisfaction when one makes the hunter feel like the hunted. Jessie, Bill, or whoever the hell this guy was, had just gotten that feeling. The smile wore off as I acknowledged to myself that, in order to smooth my ruffled ego, I had just blown any connection we had to the real killer. All in all, I really didn't think the connection was totally blown. Bill - Jessie - whoever, enjoyed the game too much. He was having fun. He would call again.

It was slightly after seven in the morning when we finished up the witness statements. The squad gathered in the squad room and wolfed down some pork hot dogs buried in Nick Tahou's Greek sauce, onions, and mustard. It was a fitting lousy breakfast to what was surely going to be a lousy day. Between bites and swallows, we plotted the day's singular activity. Each team was assigned to go back to everyone of Teddy Roberts' friends and try to find out everything and anything they could about the face in the photo, the guy identified by Roberts days earlier as, "A dude named Bill, who just kind of hangs out."

One of the detectives from the Checks and Frauds Unit threw a newspaper on my desk with the question, "You seen this shit yet, Lieutenant?"

The *Democrat and Chronicle* morning edition ran the headline, *"Cops Wrong - Killer Still Free."* The story below it gave a rather decent accounting of the Rex Nelson homicide and then did what newspapers do best, make everyone else look stupid, as they make themselves appear to be the only beacon of wisdom, while ignoring the fact that they had been clamoring for an arrest to be made.

"With the most recent homicide to be dumped on the doorstep of the city's homicide investigators, there comes the realization they have had the wrong man incarcerated for the past several days. While sources close to the investigation have continually promised that a man recently arrested on a weapons possession charge was the Playing Cards suspect, Nelson becomes the city's fourth victim to die at the hands of the killer who is still, obviously, at large.

"Last night, lights in the offices of the police department's Homicide Unit burned brightly as the entire unit was called in to investigate this most recent homicide and hopefully regain some of the credibility the unit once enjoyed. Several attempts by reporters to contact homicide detectives for their input to this developing story were ignored."

I shoved the paper deep into my trash can and commented on the marital status of the reporter's parents at the time of his birth. My anger went out to the wet-behind-the-ears reporter who wrote the story, the publisher for printing it, and the delivery guy for spreading it around the city. As I made my way to the elevators I knew my anger was misplaced but that did little to unwind the knot in my stomach.

Rather than assign the delicate matter to someone else, I made my way across the ever windy Civic Center Plaza to the jail and got Roberts pulled away from his tasteless, county-provided breakfast. The kid gave me a short course on his rights, emphasizing the fact that I couldn't talk to him now that he was represented by a lawyer.

"Look, you idiot," I said in a not-too-suave manner. "I'm here trying to get you off a murder rap. Now you tell me everything you know about this guy, and don't jerk me off!"

Teddy looked at the photo and gave me basically the same information he gave Donovan a couple of days earlier. The only thing he could add was the guy he knew only as, "Bill", hung around Midtown Plaza and that was where he met up with him sometime back in January.

"Did you ever loan your car to him?" I asked.

"I guess, yeah, I think so," the bewildered kid said, still wondering if he should even be talking to me.

"When?"

"I don't know, Lieutenant. Really! I don't know."

"Once? Twice? A lot? For a day? For a week? What?" I fired off rapidly.

"A couple of times, maybe three or four times," he answered, backing away from me, fearful that the animal in me was about spring out at him. "It was for him just to go to a job interview, or go see a friend of his, or something like that. I don't remember. Really!"

"Did he ever keep it over night?"

"I guess so. I mean, he could have. A lot of times, a guy would borrow it, and if it was late or something like that, or maybe for a chick, he might just bring it back the next day."

"We know he was there a few hours before we busted you. Why was he there? What did he want?"

"I don't know. I don't remember, really. He probably just wanted some smoke, you know, to cop some smoke or something like that."

Other than that, the interview was a waste of time. With the amount of drugs this kid had inhaled, injected, snorted, eaten, and probably crammed up his ass, Teddy Roberts' brain had been toast for the last couple of years. I had a couple of dozen other questions I could have thrown his way, but talking to this kid was like pissing in the wind.

The truth of the matter was, in less than twenty-four hours, I would learn it was not a meaningless interview. In fact, that ten minute interview would soon become the most significant one of my failing career.

It was another dead-end day. The guys had knocked themselves out trying to run down a lead on our new suspect, the elusive "Mister Bill", as they called him. The guy was a ghost, an elusive shadow who drifted in and out of Teddy Roberts' circle of friends. Not one of the entire crew could give us any idea of where Mister Bill hung his hat, who he shacked up with, or what he did. Some of the kids even thought he was a Narc, so they had avoided him.

Donovan and Verno even went over to the Midtown Plaza and picked up all the contact cards the security guards had on anyone named Bill, Billy or William...there were a hundred and eighty-four of them. That would be the task that would bring us into the new day.

I was going to fill my coffee cup one last time, but the pot was empty and it really wasn't worth the effort to make more. Straight Sambuca seemed like a better idea, but when I reached for it, the bottle was gone.

"Son of a bitch!" I said through clenched teeth at the realization I must have drained the bottle some earlier night. Heading for my locker in the men's room across the hall, I pulled out a half-empty bottle of Southern Comfort, and carried it back to the office. My cup now filled with the sedative, I looked out the window across the tree tops that filled Cornhill, a neighborhood that was trying to bounce back under the onslaught of the Jessies and Teddy Roberts of the city. Past the trees rose the steeple of the old Saint Lucy's Church, and farther west and north, the taller bell tower of Saints Peter and Paul Church. The two temples stood like fortresses as my city was being torn apart by drugs, whores, pimps, muggers, and an assortment of other sub-humans.

Diane had often complained that the city was my mistress, my whore, that kept me from her. There was some truth in that. The city was my real love. She was an ugly old broad, banged up and over used like a Main Street whore, but now, in the night, she twinkled and she was lovely to behold. I sipped the booze out of my coffee cup and smiled at my romantic musings.

The day was over and it had been a futile one. The case was overwhelming everyone of us and I could only imagine how my guys were doing at home with their wives and kids. Experience told me they were going home every night after ten, twelve, fifteen hours of this bullshit and being met with a cold shoulder from the wife and questions from their kids.

"Where have you been? What have you been doing?" were the questions. "Nothing," was the inevitable answer. And the wedge was driven deeper.

Four corpses, nine bullets, and four playing cards. Five crime scenes. A hundred and sixty-seven interviews. Three hundred and ninety pages of reports. Seventy-one pages of tech reports, crime lab analysis, and scientific ramblings. Two hundred and sixty-six crime scene photos. With all this information stacked up, what did we have to show for it? Nothing! Not a damn thing!

Roberts looked good for a while, but he was cooling his jets in a cell when Nelson got nailed. Ben Westfield was still on the hit parade, but he had me for an alibi witness. If he fitted into this mess in some way or another, it was in a supporting role, but not as the star.

The King of Spades had been slipped into the killer's hand and now all he needed was the Ace. Very likely that would be me. I would be the prize used to fill out his Royal Straight Flush. That was obvious. What wasn't so obvious was, then what? I had run this thought through my mind a hundred different times. What's he do after he taps me? Serial killers don't just stop and then move on to something else. Killing wasn't just a hobby to them, something to be done to fill in some spare time. If this guy stops after he kills me, it's going to be a first in the history of serial killers.

But then again, this wasn't about serial killing, was it? No, this was a private game where one played only by invitation. This entire thing was about me and him, him and me. It was a private war, a very personal one.

I drained my cup and as the smooth, amber liquid slid down my throat and got around the esophagus, the phone rang. When the phone rang, I choked half of the booze back up. My throat did not reject the liquid, my nerves did.

At this late hour there was only one person who would be calling. "Speak to me, Billy-boy," I said into the mouthpiece on a hunch.

There was a pause caused by his surprise, and then, "You've been waiting for my call, Amato?" the smiling voice asked.

"Not really," I said lightly. "I just took a wild stab. Fact of the matter is I really didn't expect to hear from you again."

"Yeah, well I see you up there burning the midnight oil, so to speak, and figured you were working hard trying to save your job after the way the paper kicked your ass this morning."

He sees me? I turned to look out the window, wondering where the hell there was a pay phone on the South Plymouth Avenue side of the building where he could be watching me. I used a finger to pull the curtain open, and said, "Paper's come and the papers go, Bill, but I just roll along." Still looking out at the empty street, I tried to sound bored.

"Don't bother looking for me, Lute. I'm gone from there. Just like always, you're a little too late to catch me."

I remained silent, letting him have his fun, allowing him to build his confidence, hoping his ego would make a mistake like mine had done the last time we talked.

"So now that you know who I am, how long before you think you'll get to me?" he asked without any sense of concern in his words.

"I'm not all that sure you're the one I want, Bill," I said, teasing him.

"Fuck you, Amato! You know it's me!" He wasn't yelling yet, but his voice was up a notch. I was getting to him...and I was loving it! "You seen that King of Spades in the queer's pocket. You seen it and you know it's me, because I'm the only one who can tell you it was there." He waited for a response, and when he didn't get one, he continued, "It kind of pissed you off that I selected that Rex guy for my King of Spades, huh, didn't it? You were all concerned about it being some guy named King, and what did I do? I went out and found me a guy with a name that's the Latin word for king. Pretty slick, huh? You know it is! I beat you again, Amato!"

"You beat shit," I said in disgust. "This case has more publicity than the O.J. Simpson thing. Any asshole could have killed Nelson and put the card on him just to make it look like it's part of this case." Actually, the thought was not that far-fetched and we had talked about the possibility of it being a random killing or a copycat thing.

"You know what, Lieutenant? I'm gonna ruin your day for you. I figured you would come up with some crap like that. So now I'm gonna teach you another lesson. You go look at that King of Spades that I put in Rex's shirt pocket. You look real close at it, and you're gonna see a little pin hole through the King's left eye. Now you go do that and we'll talk more later."

The conversation was over.

The phone hadn't quite rested in the cradle as I left the office and made my way down to the Crime Scene Technician's Office. I got the duty officer to pull the evidence pouches from the Nelson murder, and sure enough, there was the pin hole through the King's left eye! The only thing Mister Bill had been wrong about was that he didn't ruin my night. I left the office knowing, for the first time since the case began, I was on the right track. Things were finally going my way again...at least for the next twelve hours.
Then they were going to take a turn worse...a whole hell of a lot worse.

I was back in the office before nine the next morning. Bobby St. John told me the Major had been looking for me and that I should see him as soon as I got out of my coat. I grabbed a cup of coffee and went directly to Novitski's office. The Major was behind his desk and signaled me to sit down as I cleared the threshold. He started talking before I made it to the chair.

"I talked to Westfield last night at about nine o'clock. He says he won't be talking to either one of us about Williams' file. He claims he talked to the Mayor about the whole thing and that the two of them agree it's a matter that doesn't concern us, and there's no need for him to discuss it with you or me."

Before I could put in my two cents of doubt, Novitski continued. "Then he says he wants both of us in his office first thing this morning. He never said why, but I didn't like the sound of his tone. There's some shit in the wind, Lieutenant, and I don't like it. Do you know what's going on? Did you two have another go around?"

"Whoa! Slow down, boss," I said with a grin. "Nothing's going on between him and me. We haven't even spoken since you and I went up to see him about pulling the Williams' folder."

"Well, then, let's get going. It's nine o'clock now and he wants us up there like five minutes ago."

We rode the elevator in silence except for a couple of, "Good mornings" or, "How's it going?" to passengers entering or leaving the metal box. Sergeant Pat Polsen nodded a greeting to the Major and I, and I could tell by his look that the Chief had ripped into him about telling me the circumstances around the Williams' file.

Before we could sit down, Polsen told us the Chief would see us right away. Novitski and I entered the large office and as soon as I saw Lieutenant Anthony Freedman of the Internal Affairs Section seated to the side of Ben Westfield's desk, I knew this was not a good thing.

"Sit down and remain silent," Westfield said without any attempt at civility. "This meeting will be short and it will be a monologue." Without a pause, he clasped his hands together on his desk the way that Sister Mary Francis had taught us to do in the first grade. Then, dramatics out of the way, he got down to the meat of the subject.

"You, Lieutenant Amato, are being suspended as of right now. There are three departmental charges being lodged against you. Lieutenant Freedman will provide you with copies of those charges along with the specifications of each charge. In a nutshell they are, one, being in possession of alcohol in a police facility and while on duty."

"Ah! So that's where it went," I thought to myself. The super snoops from Internal Affairs bagged it a couple of nights ago.

"Charge two, is conduct unbecoming a member of this department," Westfield continued. "In so far as you did forcefully interrogate an inmate, Teddy Roberts, while he was represented by an attorney and knowing full well he was so represented, contrary to the policies of this department, the laws of this state, and the constitution you are sworn to uphold. The third charge is also conduct unbecoming a member of the Rochester Police Department, in so far as you did illegally, without a warrant, search the premises of Teddy Roberts, which is also contrary to your oath of office. You will surrender your weapon, your badge, your handcuffs, and your identification to Lieutenant Freedman immediately."

"What is this, Chief, get even day?" I asked.

"Lieutenant Freedman," Westfield said evenly. "Take possession of Lieutenant Amato's departmental property NOW!"

Freedman stood and started to apologize, but I waved it off and handed him my ID, gun and badge. With that out of the way, Westfield went on.

"Lieutenant Amato, the only leniency you will be shown is that I will allow you to plead guilty to any one of the charges, give you a thirty day suspension without pay and accept your resignation. If you refuse to retire and take your pension, I will be forced to follow through with all three charges and then fire you. The choice is yours. You will have forty-eight hours to respond."

I remained silent and motionless, knowing that if I was to say something, my hatred for this man would only put me deeper in the hole I had dug for myself.

"Well? Do you have anything to say for yourself?" Westfield asked.

"For now, I'll live by your rules of engagement, Chief."

"Meaning?"

"It's a monologue, remember?"

I could see that Westfield hated himself for opening that door, but I remained as unflinching as a marble statue.

"Major Novitski, you are being charged with failing to supervise. Specifically, a member of your command, one Lieutenant Amato, did possess alcohol in his desk with your knowledge and without you taking any disciplinary action. Lieutenant Freedman will provide you with a copy of specifications. However, you will be allowed to remain on duty until such time as you plead guilty or are found guilty. Do you have any questions?"

"Who will be taking command of the Violent Crimes Unit during the Lieutenant's absence?" Novitski asked, not giving Westfield the satisfaction of inquiring about his charges.

"Sergeant Mancini will assume all command duties for the time being and I will expect you to cooperate with him in every matter. Is that clear?"

"Clear," Novitski responded.

"You're both dismissed," Westfield said with a nod. "Lieutenant Freedman, you will accompany the Lieutenant out of the facility."

I got up from the chair, afraid my legs would not support me. Making my way to the door, in a way that I hoped would look like a strut, I left the inner sanctum. Tony Freedman apologized all the way down the back stairs and even offered to drive me home. I declined the offer and told him he had nothing to be sorry about. He was acting under the orders of a madman, but the madman was in charge, and I had no doubt Freedman had been fair in the investigation. Although I didn't admit it to him, I knew my own screw-ups had made his investigation simple.

I went out through the huge glass doors on the main level of the Public Safety Building, out into the cold early morning air, and crossed over the concrete Civic Center Plaza to Exchange Street. From there I turned left, headed down to Main Street and then turned right. It had been a long time since I had been to the bar at the Holiday Inn along the Genesee River, so I made my way in that direction. By nine-thirty in the morning I was downing my second beer and getting up to call Donovan's pager number.

Standing near the phone, I found myself mildly amused by the fact that I was being suspended, in part, because I found a murder weapon without a search warrant, and in part, because the department had searched my desk drawer for the Sambuca *without a warrant!* I'm sure that somewhere in some legal mind it made sense that bad guys go free if you don't have a search warrant, but cops get punished if you can nail them without a search warrant.

The pay phone rang, and I carried my third beer of the morning over to it. I lifted the receiver and asked, "Frank?"

"Yeah?" he responded with some confusion. "Frank Donovan here. Someone paged me to call this number."

"It's Mike, Frank. Listen to me now. Just dummy up and don't let on to anyone there that it's me." I proceeded to give him the Reader's Digest version of my meeting with No Balls Ben and cautioned him to be careful of what he did and said in front of Mancini. "He blew me in on the search of Roberts' place and he must be the one who gave me up on the booze. My best guess is that he also briefed the Chief on my last interview with Roberts."

"Hey, that's fine with me, Tiny," Donovan said, and I assumed Mancini must be lurking somewhere around him. "Sure thing. I would love to see you and kick around some old times, but I'm really tied up now. How about later, say about six or so. You name it."

"Make it River View Place, about ten. Tonight's your bowling night and I don't want you blaming me if you don't get a trophy this year. I'll call you at the bowling alley. If you aren't there, I'll page you to see what's going on. Keep your head low, Frank. Bye."

I hailed a cab an hour or so later and was pleased to see the sun had found Rochester once again. By the time I made it to my apartment I was whistling...and I really didn't know why. Personnel matters are not made public, but there was no doubt in my mind this evening's news would have a story based on information from a source, "close to the investigation" that I had been suspended. The news jockeys would make it a point to leave out just enough fact, and add just enough speculation, so that the unknowing public would make a link between my suspension and the failure to resolve the killings.

It kind of surprised me that I really didn't give a shit.

I left my suit thrown across the bed and threw on a pair of sweats and an old Rochester Red Wings T-shirt. Popping the top of a beer, I sat down in front of the television and began flicking through channel after channel of talk show nonsense. Finally, I got to the History Channel and then propped my bare feet up on the arm of a chair as I leaned back on the sofa. I had always been a history buff and soon became engrossed in the accounting of the attack on Pearl Harbor. My eyes and ears focused on the television, but my mind did that wandering thing that minds do when they are left alone.

There was a saying about history, something about if you don't know your history, you're bound to repeat it. "Damn true," I thought. History taught us the traps to avoid, the mistakes not to be made again, the way things work out over and over again. From Julius Caesar, to Napoleon, to Kennedy, through to Nixon, all the lessons of the world were there in the lives of these men. History teaches us that when we become so distracted by what might be, we forget to acknowledge the present dangers of Brutus, of Waterloo, of driving through Dallas in open convertibles, and of little lies.

Ah, how wondrous is hindsight! If I had only learned the lessons of other cops who tried to fight the system, who tried to buck the administrators with street cop mentality, then I might still be working today instead of watching history lessons.

However, on the other hand, if history was such a great teacher, what does it tell me about the killings of innocent people like Landers, Williams, and Nelson? What does it speak of on the matter of Frankie Lanovara getting slam-dunked behind an old warehouse off West Avenue? Where in history is the lesson about a maniac killer picking off four people just to humble me?

The beer and the sun were doing a wonderful job of putting me to sleep, and it was there in that quasi-reality world of semi-consciousness that my mind drifted through history, to the days of a young, idealistic detective who really thought that if you were right you could fight city hall and win, and, that if you worked hard then you would succeed. A history of a smiling, young detective and a smiling wife. A history where booze was a celebrant instead of an anesthesia. A history of young cops and young ladies partying in Genesee Valley Park at midnight after a long swing shift, simply because that was all we could afford. A history where young, emerging Amatos, Westfields, Donovans, and Polsons, laughed and joked about the job, rather than being worried about covering their political asses.

And, it was there, in that state of almost sleep, where history and present merged and became one, that a thought made me sit upright in a jolt, spilling the beer on the floor.

The killer was not Jessie! Perhaps Jessie was the motive. Jessie was tied in by means of a warped mind. Jessie was just a name taken by the killer, a name that was meant to be a clue to my hard head. On that first phone call he had said it, "You can call me Jessie, like Jessie James." The real Jessie was dead. Dead and buried. This Jessie was a ghost. However, it was Mister Bill who was indeed the killer. That was clear. That was a fact! Mister Bill, a dude named Bill, he was our killer.

And now I knew Bill's true, full identity. And, perhaps more importantly, I now understood Ben Westfield's connection. This was a father and son tag team. One helped the other. One came to the other's rescue. Ben Westfield had tried to detour the investigation to being a mob thing. Little Billy Westfield did the killings and was having the fun, but his old man was up to his neck in this thing. Even now, just as I was getting too close for comfort, it was dear old dad who stepped up to the plate and nailed me with a suspension.

The bottom line to the entire thing was that I am now suspended and denied the resources of the department. All I had to do now was prove my twilight zone revelations...but I would have to do it on my own.

CHAPTER THIRTEEN

CHECK, RAISE, OR FOLD

I woke up at about seven that night. It took a second or two to shake out the cobwebs and to decide whether my suspension was a nasty dream or a dismal reality. With the matter settled in my mind, I took a steak out of the freezer and microwaved it to a thaw, prepared some mushrooms with bread cumbs and Romano cheese, the way my mother would have done them, and then went crazy with a salad. As I grilled the steak on the tiny charcoal grill on the narrow patio, I found myself whistling. After, with my first good dinner in weeks under my belt, I grabbed a shower.

The brain is an amazing organ that stores millions of pieces of information. It's been said that everything we have seen, heard, smelled, or learned in any other way, is tucked away somewhere in the fifteen billion or so cells of the human brain. Some of the data being held in the brain is easily retrieved and is brought up readily, with little or no effort. Other bits of information become buried and never again surface until they are actively searched for, or in this case, triggered by an event or mental wanderings.

That's the way it is with names sometimes. At a party, when a half-dozen or so new names are thrown at you, only one or two - if that many - may stick. The other ones are still running around somewhere in the folds of your brain, but you just can't recall them. It probably reveals something about my psyche, but that's how it is for me when it comes to remembering cop's spouses. I just can't remember their names. Officer John Jones may introduce me to his wife, but ten minutes later - and forever after - to me she

162

is simply "Jones' wife".

My narrow mind had done the same with name the of Jessica Westfield. I had met her at cop parties perhaps twenty or thirty times, but I never actively stored her name. In my memory's file, she was simply Ben Westfield's wife, "whatzername". She sometimes met the young Officer Ben Westfield when we had our midnight picnics in Genesee Valley Park. At one retirement party, many years ago, she even sat next to Diane. The four of us - Diane, myself, Ben, and *Ben's wife* - carried on a lively conversation, parts of which I still recall to this day. Still I could not, not until last night, have told you the name of Ben Westfield's wife.

Jessica Westfield was a lovely person, both physically and in her demeanor. I seem to recall her sort of staying in the background at a lot of the cop parties. Although never aloof, she struck me as being a little shy and somewhat overtaken by the boisterous cops and their animated war stories. Even after I arrested her son, William, Jessica Westfield never actually snubbed me. If we encountered each other along the way she would offer a very slight, sort of polite smile, nod her head, and move on.

I guess she was about forty or so, maybe even in her late thirties, when she developed cancer and died within months. Her death came within a year and a half of her son being convicted of rape, and it was probably the combination of the two traumatic events that made Ben Westfield the kind of guy he turned out to be.

I never heard anyone, not even her husband, refer to Jessica Westfield as "Jessie". No, that was the invention of her son. That was his way of making the game a little more interesting. He consciously threw me that clue as a freebie. It was another one of those catch-me-if-your-good-enough things he liked to toss into the cat and mouse, cop and convict game we had been playing over the past few months.

After the full meal and refreshing shower, I poured a Southern Comfort over some ice and turned my attention to the day's events and my present, brand new, problem. Sitting back on the couch, I read through the specifications of the charges that Benjamin Westfield, in the name of the Rochester Police Department, had lodged against me.

It appeared that Sergeant Arthur T. Mancini had been a busy little beaver. Besides working as my partner, he had been doing a little undercover work for the Chief. Although not named specifically in the charges, it was easy enough to read between the lines, especially when it came to, "A witness was present when Lt. Michael Amato illegally entered the apartment of Teddy Roberts and although the witness did not observe any weapons near or around the subject Roberts and/or his furnishings, Lt. Amato alleged he saw the weapon in, 'plain view' stuck between the chair cushion and the chair arm."

It's difficult to describe, but I guess I felt hurt, not angry, by Art Mancini's betrayal. Gazing out the window next to my kitchen table I wondered why this cop, who I considered to be a pretty fair investigator, would turn on me like this. Maybe he felt greater loyalty to Westfield's quest to slay the evil Amato dragon, than he felt to me and the quest to get the mope who was killing our citizens. If he did what he did out of a sense of loyalty and duty, I could respect it - not like it - but respect it. On the other hand, if he did it out of a need to feather his own nest, to work his way into my job, I figured I owed him a pretty good punch in the mouth.

It was also interesting to learn that Internal Affairs, armed with an order signed by Westfield, conducted an, "inspection" of my office area and found, "...a bottle of alcohol, specifically, Sambuca, an alcoholic beverage, containing 38% alcohol, in the bottom right drawer of the desk assigned to, and commonly used by, Lt. Mike Amato." Hmmm! Only thirty-eight percent alcohol! No wonder it never got me loaded!

The complaint on the third charge was obviously generated by Mancini or Roberts' lawyer, Warren Leesburg, over the fact that I had seen Teddy for twenty minutes while he was in the county jail and already represented by an attorney. Part of his complaint was that I had, "...deprived Mr. Roberts of an essential, nutritious morning meal which was essential to his health, well being, and nurturing, and which is vitally needed by Mr. Roberts." It would be interesting to pull this little gem out of the hat the next time Mr. Leesburg decided it was financially beneficial to sue the county on behalf of some other puke because the meals were not so nutritious and healthy.

I threw the charges aside and then made a call to Frank Donovan at the bowling alley. I watched a little Pavarotti on PBS before getting dressed and heading out to meet the Detective at River View Place.

River View Place won't be found on any map of Rochester, no matter how detailed the map may be. Except in the vocabulary of cops, the place doesn't really exist. It's a hideout, 'a hole', a place where cops working the late night and very early morning hours go to find some privacy, to meet up with other cops, eat a pizza, and exchange anecdotes that usually begin with, "You ain't gonna believe this one..." Located behind the Genesee Brewery, the spot got it's name because it does, in fact, offer a pretty damn good view of the city's river and gorge.

As I turned off St. Paul Street to the narrow, old, cobblestone street leading to the meeting spot, I wondered if Donovan and I would be interrupting some young cop's quiet time. However, my guess was that today's cops, beaten down by constant petty investigations, headed by young bosses who wanted to make a reputation as a cop fighter instead of a crime fighter, probably don't even know of the existence of River View Place. But, to guys like Donovan and our peers, the place was a chunk of our lives.

I got out of the Corvette and enjoyed the cold night air that now held just a faint hint of spring. As usual, I was early for the meeting, so I lit a cigarette and loaded up two more magazines for my .9mm. Ten minutes later Donovan's headlights hit me.

"The guy's are really pissed about this, Mike," Donovan said as we shook hands. "They all said to tell you they're behind you a hundred and ten percent and that if you need anything, to just let me know." A hundred and forty bucks in folded twenties was cupped in his palm and passed to mine as we shook hands.

As I flipped through the bills, I said, "Tell them I appreciate it, Frank, but I'm really all set. This thing will blow over in a while and we'll get back to normal." I handed the money back to him, but he waved it off, and I smiled my thanks to him.

We talked for a couple of minutes, recounting some of the meetings that were held on this sacred ground. Our laughter was absorbed into the night along with the distant, muffled roar of the river falls. Finally, it was time to get down to business.

"Nothing really happened all day, Mike. It was another day of shoe leather and knocking on doors. We can't get a line on this little bastard, Billy, from no one."

"I get the feeling you're going to throw a 'but' in here," I said with a smile.

"*But*," he added with a bigger smile. "Bobby paged me at the bowling alley and told me that Roberts' attorney says little Teddy has some very important information for us and wants to talk to you like right now."

"Ain't no way I'm going anywhere near that kid," I said raising my hands in protest.

"No, no. We know that," Donovan acknowledged. "Bobby's the on-call guy tonight, so he called Novitski. The Major already cleared it and says it's okay for St. John to interview the kid if his lawyer is there."

"So?" I asked.

"So, Bobby is meeting with the lawyer in about a half hour and as soon as he gets done, he'll call me and we'll meet him."

We killed some time speculating about what Teddy Roberts wanted to talk about this late in the game, but finally gave up on it. The night air was taking it's toll on us, so we adjourned to a little diner on the city's north side and waited there for Bobby St. John's call. Once we had our coffee, Donovan

told me that Sergeant Mancini had given one and all a little speech about
how he was a fair man who could be trusted by them as long as they
demonstrated professional ethics. He then passed along an order from the
Chief that none of them was to have any contact with me during my
suspension. As a courtesy, one that I knew would be rejected, I suggested
we end our meeting right then rather than bring any problems on Frank. He
shrugged it off with his deep laugh and a hearty, "Screw Mancini, the Chief,
and the horses they rode in on!"

I toyed with the idea of telling Donovan about my conclusion that the
mysterious Jessie and the elusive Mister Bill were actually Ben Westfield's
kid, Billy. For some reason, I really don't know why, I held back the piece of
information. Maybe my conclusion about William Westfield was wrong.
Maybe not telling Donovan about William was wrong. It was getting so I
was having a difficult time telling right from wrong anymore. Maybe I was
being selfish and wanted to keep the info for me, alone. Whatever the reason,
I sat on the information.

Ninety minutes later, with five cups of coffee and two trips to the latrine
gone by, Bobby St. John slipped into the booth next to Donovan and, in his
usual serious manner, extended his condolences to me. I laughed and
reminded him I was simply up on charges, not terminally ill.

St. John smiled back and then leaned in to the center of the table, giving
us notice of the privacy needed for his news. The first part of the news was
amusing, but the second part of it was what brought a smile to my face.

"First thing, Lute, is when I told Roberts you couldn't be there because
you were suspended due to the beef *his* lawyer made to the Chief about you
interviewing him, Teddy got heavy with his attorney and threatened to fire
him." Bobby shared another round of smiles with me and Donovan and then
continued. "I had to calm the damn kid down because I don't want him
kicking the lawyer out if he had something important to give us. Teddy told
Leesburg, 'Mike Amato's the only real friend I got'!" After another round of
grins and nods, St. John continued. "Anyway, the lawyer apologizes all over
the place to Teddy, and he promises both me and Teddy he's going to Westfield
first thing in the morning to get the charges dropped. I really wouldn't believe
a thing any lawyer says, but he seemed pretty serious about it, Lute."

"So what's he got for us?" I asked impatiently, knowing that the lawyer,
even if he was dead serious, wasn't going to get Westfield to back off from
the strangle hold he had on me.

"Teddy says after you talked to him, he remembered that this Billy had
been bragging about this fine car he owned, but he said the cops had seized
it when he got busted for hauling dope out of Arizona up to some friends

somewhere around Chicago."

"Where did he get busted?" I asked.

"When?" Donovan popped in at almost the same instant.

Bobby held up a hand with the palm facing us to forestall the questions. "Teddy says he met Billy right around the first of the year, and from what Billy was saying, the bust had to go down around the last two weeks of December, maybe around Christmas week. He told Teddy he was coming through New Mexico on an Interstate and just got past a big city when a state cop pulled him over on some traffic charge. The way Billy tells it, he was carrying about a couple of hundred pounds of the smoke and the cops grabbed it all, plus his car."

"Sounds like bullshit," Frank said. "If he had that much reefer, he should still be sitting in jail."

"That's what I said," Bobby answered after he sipped some coffee. "But Teddy says Billy told him he jumped bail and got out of there."

We hacked the news around a little bit and then I went out to my car to grab a road map. We traced the route form Arizona to Chicago and guessed, if Billy had been telling Teddy the truth, he had to be on Interstate 40 going through New Mexico. The route went straight through Albuquerque, the only major city in the entire state.

"You know what you have to do?" I asked Bobby St. John.

He smiled and nodded. "First thing in the morning I'm on the phone to the New Mexico State Police and see if they have computers or some way of checking to see if a Billy or William was busted with some marijuana during December on I-40 somewhere west of, or east of, Albuquerque."

With the long day and night behind us, and after making arrangements to keep in touch, we parted company in the diner's parking lot. It was going to be essential for them not to get caught meeting with me, or as far as that goes, even to be seen talking to me. The Police Department was rather peculiar that way. Once they cut a member out of the herd, he was to be totally ostracized by the rest of the members. I guess they felt that it kept the Department pure and unsullied by the dirty party.

On the drive back to the apartment, I tried to sort out my feelings. On the one hand I felt kind of up and cheerful, but then again, I felt tense and angry. I supposed the up feeling came from the progress that was being made, and from the notable benefit of not having to put up with the Department's political bullshit, mainly in the form of No Balls Ben Westfield. The down side came from not being able to be the one to solve the killings. I had been taken out of the game. If the crimes got solved now it would be Mancini's doing and that would be a real kick in the ass! I also had second thoughts about not telling Frank Donovan about Billy Westfield. I wanted to hold that information tight to myself for the time being, but I didn't know why.

I mulled over the impact of the charges and the suspension, and was glad my father and mother weren't alive to see the headlines when the news broke about the charges against me. "Conduct unbecoming" would not be words my parents would be able to swallow easily, and my public embarrassment would have cost them a great deal of respect among their friends and relatives.

Personally, the charges were the least of my worries. Roberts' attorney would make himself a poor witness now that he realized I was only getting the kid out of the shit and not really interrogating him. The other charge about finding the gun, "in plain view," well, that was just a matter of perspective and I could argue all day that I was in a line of sight to see it while Mancini was not. The most simple charge, the one about the Sambuco, would be the most difficult to beat and I would probably have to take a thirty day, unpaid vacation on that beef.

As my head hit the pillow, my last thought was concerned with how I was going to keep myself in the game

Strangely enough, Mister Bill was prepared to handle that one himself!

It was just past eight o'clock in the morning when the telephone annoyed me into a waking state. The annoyance went away when I heard Diane's voice. It returned the minute she completed her first question.

"Michael, are you having me followed?"

"What? What are you talking about, Diane?"

"Are you having one of your guys check up on me?" she asked with obvious anger.

"No. No way! What's this all about?"

"There's been a guy following me for the last day. I saw him when I came out of work last night, but I just passed it off. Then I saw him outside my apartment this morning and I got worried, but he disappeared before I could do anything."

"Who is he? What's he look like?" I asked, trying to play down my concern.

"He's young, about your height, kind of neck-length hair. But wait, before we get into all that, he was in the parking lot at work when I got to work and he waved at me."

"Did you talk to him, Diane. Did you approach him?"

"Michael, *really!* I know better than that! I told one of the guards and he went over to the guy. He told the guard he was a friend of yours and you had asked him to look after me because you were involved in some kind of dangerous investigation."

"Did they get his identification? Did they scoop him up?"

"Michael, get real. They're guards, not cops. All they got was the name he gave them."

She was going to make me ask, so I did. "What name?"

"Jessie. No last name, just Jessie."

I covered the mouthpiece and uttered some nasty word or phrase and then said calmly, "Look, it's probably just some flake, some nut. But still, you better be careful for the next few days. Let me pick you up and drop you off. I got time to do it now."

"That's not necessary. Really, it isn't. Kodak is sending me to the Colorado plant for a week and I leave this afternoon with two of the other managers, so I won't even be around."

"Well that's good. I feel better about that. This jerk will probably take off by then," I said as casually as I could.

"Michael?"

"What?"

"Why do you have free time now? Is that you they're talking about in the paper? I just caught the headlines, but it was something about a detective who got suspended for doing something wrong on a case."

"Well, to tell you the truth, I haven't looked at the papers yet, but yeah, that sounds like me."

"What did you do now?"

"It's nothing, just some garbage that Westfield's dragging around. It'll blow over by time you get back. You go and be a good Kodak nerd for the other 'Dak-ers'," I said with a little chuckle. I knew she hated the cop nickname for Kodak employees, but she made light of my comment.

We said our goodbyes after I reassured her a few more times that there was nothing for her to worry about. I had just set the phone down when it rang again. This time it was Bobby St. John.

"Hope I didn't wake you, Lute, but I just wanted to bring you up to speed."

"No, I was already up. What's happening with the New Mexico thing?"

"Well, nothing so far. You aren't going to believe this crap, but I got in here early and called over there. Those guys are two hours behind us, so it was about 5:30 AM there and I get this lady on the phone and she tells me that they're closed!"

"Their records division, or their narcotics division was closed? I don't understand."

"No. The whole damn place is closed. She tells me that there are no New Mexico State Police on duty from about midnight until around seven or so in the morning!"

"You have got to be shitting me! What kind of two-bit, yokel place is it? I never heard of a state police outfit closing for the night!"

"Well it kind of goes along with the rest of this case. Anything that can possibly screw us up, does screw us up." We both shared a laugh before Bobby continued, "Anyway, this gal was pretty decent and she took down the info and then she told me she would make sure one of their narcs called me back later."

"Okay. Thanks, Bobby. I appreciate it."

"No sweat, boss."

"Look, I hate to do this, but I got a favor to ask. There's another little problem. You guys have to give this guy Bill the full-court press. He's been following Diane around."

"He what?" St. John almost shouted into the phone.

"I just talked to her a minute before you called. It's cool for now, she is leaving to go out of town for a week on business, but I need you to make a call over to Highland Section for me and ask their uniform guys to give her place heavy-duty special attention. There's no telling what this shit bird will pull. Tell them she's a friend of yours and she called. Okay? That way you don't have to let on you and me were talking."

St. John and I talked for a few more minutes and I gave him Diane's address and the low down on how one of the guards had stopped the guy that fit Mister Bill's description and about him giving them the name of Jessie.

"He's trying to frost our balls, Lieutenant. This guy just loves yanking our chain."

"Yeah, well, I think it's my chain he wants to pull, and he just might find there's a pretty pissed off bulldog on the other end of that chain."

"Don't do anything dumb about this guy, Lute. If he's trying to smoke you out, you give me or Frank a call and we'll handle it."

"Yeah, sure," I said casually. "I'm technically off the job. What can I do?"

"Do nothing, boss. Kick back and enjoy it for the time being. Let us earn our keep."

"Right, Frank, I'll watch Oprah and Rosie. But do like I asked you, okay? Make sure Diane's place gets watched pretty good. This frigging clown may want to make a grab at her, and even though she's gone and all, maybe they can snatch up the little bastard on something if they find him hanging around her place."

"From your lips to God's ears, Lute. Don't worry about a thing. I'll get it taken care of for you."

With the phone calls out of the way, I put on a pot of coffee, popped an English Muffin into the toaster, and went out to retrieve the morning paper from the apartment complex' main office. I glanced over the front page and then went to the local news. On the second page was the piece that was of most interest to me this particular day. Under the headline, *"RPD Suspends Detective"* was the story.

"Chief Benjamin Westfield confirmed that a lead investigator in the recent series of the Playing Card Murders had been suspended early yesterday morning. The Chief refused to identify the investigator, stating that it was department policy not to identify officers when the matter was a personnel issue of a non-criminal nature. Westfield refused to identify the officer, stating that it was an internal matter dealing with a command officer's conduct and behavior.

"A senior member of the department, who requested anonymity, told reporters the detective is suspected of having a drinking problem, and may have planted some evidence on a suspect who is currently incarcerated and was thought to be the suspect in the Playing Card Murders case. He also indicated the suspended detective was responsible for having recently abused the same prisoner's rights. Chief Westfield would not confirm any of that information, but said he also would not deny that it was accurate.

"Warren Leesburg, attorney for a man recently arrested for possession of a weapon allegedly used in several of the Playing Card Murders, stated that he has no indication his client was abused in anyway, and stated, 'I just talked with my client last evening and he has nothing but praise for Lt. Amato and his detectives'."

I had to smile over that last paragraph. It looked like Teddy had really done a number on Leesburg. The best part about it was that Westfield would really have to wonder what made Leesburg change his tune so fast. Other than that, the morning held no delights for me. The article did everything but name me. I sat down with my toast and coffee, a luxury I did not usually enjoy, and began to glance through the paper, section by section. I had just completed the sports section and the funnies and was on the way to learning that, according to my horoscope, new adventures were going to open up to me. Then the phone rang again.

I walked over to it thinking that maybe the New Mexico State Police had started their work day, and, just possibly Bobby St. John had some news for me. Instead, I was greeted by one of those new adventures of which my horoscope spoke.

"Good morning, Lieutenant Amato!" the singing voice announced, making me hold the phone at arm's length and look at it, expecting the demon to jump out at me.

"And top of the morning to you, lad," I sang back, hoping to sound undaunted by the sound of his voice on my home phone.

"Do you know who this is, *Ace*?"

"Gee, golly," I said as sarcastically as I could. "It sounds like Billy-boy." I was learning to hate this son-of-a-bitch. I wanted to demand he tell me how he got my number, but I knew it would give him too much satisfaction. His ego was his strength, and like most people, his greatest strength was also his greatest weakness. I had heard that ego yelling the other night when he bellowed about how smart he was in selecting Rex Nelson as his, "King" victim. I had to play his ego as my trump card, and not give him anything about which to feel confident. If I was going to force this little bastard out into the open, I had to break his ego, his spirit, his confidence, and most of all, break his balls!

"I'll bet you're wondering how I got your phone number, aren't you *Ace*?"

"Probably off of some bathroom wall."

"My, my, the Lieutenant is trying to play cute with me. Nice! I like that. It makes me all the more motivated to hear you beg right before I kill you."

His voice, a chilling, psychopathic voice, made me look around the room to find my gun..

"Well, here's how I figure it, Billy, my boy," I said in a happy, melodic voice. "It ain't that big of a thing, and you wouldn't tell me if I did ask. So, the bottom line is, I really don't give a shit."

"Oh, but you're wrong, *Ace* Amato. You're very wrong. I will tell you. I want to tell you," he said in a hurried, eager, manner that made me believe him.

"Sorry, I'm not going to ask," I said just as eagerly. Then, just for shits and giggles, I added, "Besides, I'm really kind of busy now. Today's the day I sort my sock drawer and wash out my old condoms."

"You think you're so fucking smart, Amato," he said, and I knew I was getting to him by the way he bit off every word and emphasized it with the profanity.

He was going to play his big card any second now and I had to be ready for him. I hated the mope, but I was starting to enjoy this little cat and mouse exercise with him. I wondered if I should throw his last name into the conversation, but decided to hold off on that and to see where this thing was going.

"Look, if you really don't mind, I have to get busy. You know how hard it is to wash out these condoms when everything dries up in them."

"You got yourself suspended, didn't you, Mister Wise Ass Ace?"

That was one of his big cards, but it wasn't the one I expected. "Yeah, well, I needed a break from all the bullshit. Besides, it's been almost two years since I last got suspended, so I needed a fresh one on my record."

"You really aren't going to ask me where I got your number, are you?"

"Billy, I really don't give a fat rat's ass where you got it. Hundreds of people got it. Every informant I ever talked to has got my phone number. It's no big deal, really it isn't."

"You're full of shit, Amato," he said loudly, almost yelling. "I got it a special way, a way no other guy could have gotten it. I'm not some stoolie of yours. I'm better than that, sharper than that, and you know it!"

"Okay, if it makes you and your Prozac medication feel any better, gee whiz," I said in a bored, lethargic tongue. "I'm really shocked and amazed you got my phone number, you smart son of a gun, you." Following the sarcasm, I asked seriously, "There, does that make you feel more adequate, Billy?"

"You think you're so fucking smart, Amato. Well you ain't smart. You're dumb, real dumb. You're a dumb mother fucker and I'm gonna get you." He was yelling now, screaming at the top of his lungs. I had him now. He was right at the edge of the cliff. All I had to do was give him a little tap, not a big shove, just a little nudge.

"Look, I really would like to continue this chit chat with you, but these condoms are going to be a bitch if I don't get to them very soon. Okay? So do you mind if we just say bye-bye for now. You see, I really don't care and I'm not really bothered about you having my number. Any jerk could have gotten it. It's just not that big of a deal."

"Oh yeah, *Ace*?"

"Wow, Billy! That was a snappy come back! 'Oh yeah?' Boy you must have worked on that little retort for years."

"Listen to me, Amato! Listen to me! Call your wife. Call Mrs. Diane Amato at Eastman Kodak on Ridge Road and ask her what's going on in her life." Bang! He did it! He just slapped the big card on the table. "Call her and ask her how she likes me escorting her to work, and home, and back again."

"Oh, you know what, Billy-boy? She did mention that to me, and I meant to tell you how much I appreciate what you're doing for me there. She's so scared, she's ready to marry some Kodak dude she's been dating. Or, better yet, I'm hoping the chances are you'll kill the bitch for me. Either way, I get out of paying almost eighteen hundred a month in alimony." I hated the lie I was telling, but I had to tell it.

There was silence on the phone. I waited, counting to five slowly, letting the information sink in to him that if wanted to get to me, he had to come to me directly, me alone, not through Diane.

"So," I continued after the pause. "The fact of the matter is, I don't give a shit about how you got my number and I really don't give a shit what you do about my ex- old lady. Bottom line, Billy-boy, have a nice fucking day!"

With the phone set gently in its cradle, I blew out a long breath of air and reached for a cigarette, my hands shaking with anger, hatred and frustration. I wanted to kill this son-of-a-bitch, to beat his face in, to stomp on his guts, kick his balls into his throat, then rip off his head, and throw it and his balls against a wall. I wanted my hands on this little bastard, gripping his scrawny throat, choking the air out of him, having him gurgle and sputter with his last breaths while I laughed in his face. Whatever his little problem was, he had gone too far. Whatever I had done to this little bastard was fair and square. If he had a problem with that he was going to have to face me like a man, not over the phone like some punk street pussy. We were going to meet...and he was going to die!

It wasn't even ten in the morning and my day was already ruined. The somewhat pleasant feelings I had experienced the day before were now gone and I was once again alone with myself. Playing one of those games that one's mind likes to play with one's self, I thought it might be kind of nice to go take a walk. I slipped into a pair of slacks and a baggy sweater, hopped into the Corvette and drove into the city, aimlessly heading for nowhere, but eventually ending up parking in front of a row of shops that lined several blocks of Park Avenue, over on the city's east side.

Once out of the car, I strolled the street casually, looking every bit the part of a window shopper. The little neighborhood was one of residences and shops mixed together along the three or four blocks. It was one of the last nice parts of Rochester, an area that had seen the onslaught of mismanaged city government that was more concerned with covering its political posterior than it was in insuring the city's potential prosperity. The merchants along the street had banned together in the early 1970's, refurbished their stores and re-created a neighborhood that was like the ones that had once been the mainstay of my city. The old neighborhoods of Swillburg, Bull's Head, Dutchtown, and Bay-Goodman were all just memories now, taken over by drug dealers and gangs that the city administration wanted to pretend didn't exist. Park Avenue was the last bastion of neighborhood life left in the city...and the best place to get pastries, ice cream, and *fratatta.*

These thoughts kept my mind busy as I enjoyed a cup of *espresso* and a dish of *spumoni.* But then my mind wandered to other times and other things. Thoughts of Diane and I walking this street twelve, fifteen years ago, floated in and out of the corners of my mind's eye and suddenly I realized how alone I was. I was forty-eight years old, childless, and without the comfort of a companion, a confidant, a partner with whom I could share these feelings. It was kind of ironic, I acknowledged to myself, when I had that partner, that love, I refused to even own up to such feelings, much less share them with her.

I drifted back to the car, enjoying the gallant effort upstate New York was making in trying to cooperate with Spring. The air was still and warm, and there were even signs of the grass taking on its green tones in the dirt that had been packed under a hundred inches of snow for the past several months. The car was pointed back to my side of the city, and as I made the sweep west bound on the Inner Loop, the Public Safety Building looked down on me pitifully from over my right shoulder. I gunned the motor and sped past the angular gray building at 75 miles an hour.

It was the middle of the afternoon when I made it back to the apartment. I was surprised to see my answering machine held seven messages for me. Damn! I was getting to be a real popular guy in my old age. Two of the messages were from Frank Donovan reporting that he had no news, one was from Bobby St. John speculating that the New Mexico State Police must be on a *siesta,* because he couldn't get anyone there to call him back, and one call was from Diane, saying she was safely at the airport, and would call me in a day or so. The remaining three calls were hang-ups and I took some satisfaction in knowing they were probably from Mr. Bill and that I had not been there to talk to him. I smiled at the impact it must have had on his faltering ego when the phone rang and rang, but I didn't pick it up.

I turned on the television and started to operate the remote like it was a typewriter, flipping from one channel to the next and then back to the starting point. Somewhere along the way I drifted off and took a nap.

I was glad no one was there to see me jump up and trip over the coffee table when the phone jerked me out of a sound sleep at about five-thirty in the evening.

"Just want to give you an update, Mike," Frank Donovan said in his baritone voice. "Basically, we got squat, shit, zip, *natta*, nothing, zero. The State Police in New Mexico finally got back to us to tell us they are checking with their people about who might have made the bust on Mr. Bill, but that could take all week. I guess they never heard of computers. As far as they're concerned, us New Yorkers are too damn pushy, at least that's what one of their shining stars told St. John. Bobby let them know the guy we are asking about is targeting a cop for a murder and that got their ass shoved into second gear at least."

"I appreciate the effort, Frank. I know you guys are pushing it hard."

"No sweat. That's why we make the big bucks."

"Why don't you go crash for the night?" I asked. "We had a long session last night."

"Not yet, Mike. I was going to go grab a bite to eat. You want to join up with me?"

"No, I don't think so, Frank. I want to hang on here and catch up on some sleep. Maybe tomorrow night, okay?"

"Okay. I'll call you tomorrow. Maybe by then these hicks in New Mexico will get their shit together and we'll have this asshole's entire, real name."

"I already have a pretty good idea what the name might be," I confessed. "But let's wait and see."

"Do you want to share that name, Mike?"

"Not yet, Frank. There's been too damn many theories thrown around already."

It made me feel better that I had told Frank Donovan I thought I knew the suspect's name. At least now I wasn't keeping him totally in the dark. I went back to the couch and settled back with my hands behind my head. The sun was going down, and judging by the redness of the sky, tomorrow was going to be a pretty nice day, maybe even a great day. Donovan, St. John, Major Novitski, and Al Verno were going to have to wait until the next day to find out Mister Bill's name.

I didn't have to wait. I knew it already. The killer's identity became clear to me the previous night when I took my little trip through history and found how well the lessons from the past prepare us for the mistakes of today. History had taught us that the enemies we make today are the fights we live in our tomorrows. Obviously I had made an enemy, and he was haunting and taunting me so as to avenge his Jessie. It would do no good to try to convince him I was not responsible for Jessica's death, for in his mind, I was the cause of all his life's ills and failings. He had told me that years earlier and I had dismissed it as bullshit, dismissed it until last night when I remembered the times long forgotten when Diane and I, and Frank and Ginny Donovan, along with all the other young cops and their wives, or girlfriends, would party at the park and how a younger, happier Officer Ben Westfield would play guitar and his pretty wife would sing. And Jessica Westfield had a beautiful, lyrical voice. Yes she did!

The other cops, the newspapers and the public would have to wait another day or so to discover the killer's name. But I knew it now... and I knew why he wanted to kill me. William Thomas Westfield, the only child of Ben and Jessica Westfield, along with his father, Chief of Police Benjamin Westfiled, wanted to kill me because in their own egocentric, self-ingratiating, sick, little minds they believed my arresting Billy had somehow resulted in the death of their mother and wife.

Maybe Billy was right. And, then again, maybe he was wrong. In any event I wasn't going to roll over and play dead for this son-of-a-bitch or his father.

William Westfield had his plans and I had mine. The one thing those two sets of plans had in common was that we were going to meet and one of us was going to end up dead.

CHAPTER FOURTEEN

WAITING

I spent the evening cleaning my off-duty weapon, oiling it and checking the action. When I had it and two clips ready for their work, I brought out a little five-shot, .380 automatic I had bought for Diane many years ago. Watching an old western on the late movie, I cleaned the back-up weapon and readied two more clips. I then took an old .38 caliber, Saturday night special out of its hiding place, wiped it clean of any finger prints and left it on the coffee table resting on a towel. The gun had a nefarious history I'm sure, but back when I took it off a street punk ten years ago, it was just another gun, a gun to be kept for special occasions such as this. With my two legal tools of the trade tucked snugly in well-oiled holsters, next to the illegal one resting on the towel, I laid back on the couch and drifted off to sleep.

In the morning I cursed the couch for my stiff neck, put on a pot of coffee and found myself humming *La Donna e Mobile* in the shower as the warm water loosened the kinks in my neck. It wasn't quite ten in the morning when I finished reading the newspaper. With the last of the six cups of coffee in my cup, I cleaned up the dishes from the two previous days, dried them, put them away and downed the last of the coffee.

I sat down on the recliner and waited, but when nothing happened, I began to clean the apartment. In a half an hour I had the place as clean as any man could have cleaned it. More importantly, later on, if a team of evidence technicians had to go through the place, there wouldn't be a lot of confusing finger prints for them to be bothered with.

I sifted through some CD's and selected an Andrea Bocelli disc to be the background as I mulled over the case. With the tenor's voice belting out arias, I paced the apartment and sifted through what I had...and didn't have. First and foremost, this case was never going to court! I wasn't going to let that happen. The justice this case needed was not going to be found in a courtroom. Besides, there wasn't enough evidence to convict Billy or Ben Westfield of the charges. The murder weapon used in the first three killings could be tied only to Teddy Roberts. The blood and hairs from Mary Williams' body had been found in Roberts' car. The few pseudo-confessions I had from Bill Westfield had not been recorded, and the recordings we did have from his calls to the squad room didn't implicate anyone but Teddy Roberts. Sure, I could testify to the calls I had gotten from him when he told me about the pin hole he had put in the King of Spades he placed on Nelson's body. I could even testify to the admissions he had made on the phone when he bragged about how crafty he had been in selecting Rex Nelson as his symbolic king. I could testify to those facts, but it was my word against his. And, being a suspended cop accused of planting evidence and violating the rights of prisoners, my credibility wasn't all that credible these days. Any half-assed lawyer would find it easy to beat me to death on the witness stand.

Again I sat down and waited...and waited. The three bottles of booze on the shelf attracted my attention, but I closed my eyes and forced myself to nap.

The phone rang and when I opened my eyes, I was surprised to see it was one-fifteen in the afternoon. I smiled and let the phone ring. When my voice came on the recorder asking for the caller to leave a message, the phone went dead. My smile broadened.

I thought about taking perhaps one drink, but pushed the thought out of my mind. Distracting myself with the useless crap that was on day-time television, I killed another hour of waiting...and wondering why people who won't talk to each other in their private lives would come on national television to air their hatred for one another.

By three-thirty in the afternoon the phone rang twice more and each time the caller hung up without leaving a message.

It was almost four o'clock in the afternoon when I got out of the recliner and put the bottles of Southern Comfort, whiskey, and bourbon away behind the solid wood doors of the cabinet over the stove. My mind argued that one tiny taste of Southern Comfort would calm my shaking hands, but my common sense countered with the argument that one sip would lead to a gulp, and one gulp would lead to another. I slammed the cabinet door on the three bottles and returned to the recliner.

At ten after four the phone rang again. After the third ring, I heard my voice asking the caller to leave a message and this time I heard Frank Donovan addressing the tape machine. Before he could completely identify himself, I lifted the receiver from the cradle, shut off the answering machine and said, "Yeah, Frank. What have you got?"

"The cops in New Mexico called, Mike. You'll never guess who Billy is."

"It's Ben Westfield's kid, isn't it, Frank?" I asked.

"How the hell did you know?" he asked with some notable shock, and annoyance, before adding, "And, how long have you known?"

"It all came together for me the other night. I don't know," I said with a shrug. "It was something he said that just jelled all of a sudden. His mother's name was Jessica. It just hit me the night before last, Frank," I said, perhaps overstating my case. "I thought it made sense to me, but I wasn't positive. Besides, I didn't want to send you guys on a wild goose chase if it wasn't him."

"Yeah well, anyway, like Teddy Roberts told Bobby St. John," Donovan continued with a tone that let me know he was upset that I had not shared my conclusion with him, "the State cops grabbed William Westfield and fifty kilos of high grade smoke in a car registered to some broad in Phoenix. He was sitting in jail, and through some screw up in the courts, got released on a hundred dollar bond and he skipped out. They're pissed about him walking and are jumping up and down to get him back, but I told them they may have to wait about a hundred years until us Yankees are done with him."

"Have you told the Major?"

"Yeah, he knows. We skipped the boy wonder, Sergeant Mancini, but briefed the Major. He said for us to tell Mancini and to let Mancini come and tell him, but not to let Mancini know that Novitski already has the information. I don't know why, but that's the way he wanted it. Department politics, I guess."

"The old man's way ahead of Mancini. He knows the kid will be afraid to go to Westfield with it and he'll panic and do something stupid. But Novitski has his ass covered and Mancini will have to answer for it later."

"I hate these frigging politics, Boss. It was better in the old days when there wasn't all this secretive bullshit and the only fighting we did was with the bad guys."

There was silence for a few seconds, and I knew Donovan's message was meant to comfort me as well as be a commentary on the department.

"Look, Frank," I said, trying to soothe his hurt feelings. "I wasn't sure it was him, and I didn't want to say anything until I was sure. Besides, I know you guys too well and I didn't want you to get your asses in a sling by going after him. Another thing is, well, there isn't enough evidence to even book him, much less convict his ass."

"We're friends, Mike. That's what we're here for," he said, making his point. "You put your ass on the line for us a lot of times with the bosses. We all put our asses on the line for each other,".

"I know...and I appreciate it. I really do."

There were a few seconds of silence before Donovan asked rhetorically, "You're going after him, aren't you, Mike?"

"I've got to end this thing, Frank. It's gone on too long. Too many people have died. Besides, unless I miss my guess, he'll be coming after me."

"We want to help, Mike. Just give me the word. Whatever you want, you got it. It's the entire squad's case, Mike. You don't have to take it on alone."

I said the words gently, the way they needed to be said so the man would not be offended. "Just stay out of it, Frank. It's my thing. I need to handle it. He wants me, so he's going to get his fill of me."

"Understood. I don't agree, but I understand."

"Thanks."

I slipped a Pavarotti disc into the CD player. The driving melody and tenor's thunderous voice filled the room with *Funiculi, Funicula* as I erased the micro cassette in the answering machine and waited once again. I didn't think the thin, brown tape caught any of the conversation between Frank and I, but I didn't want to get careless with evidence that could be used against me at a later date.

The CD began to repeat itself and I wondered if I had put off the calls from Billy Westfield too many times. Perhaps I had driven him away from me and to another killing of one more innocent citizen who had nothing to do with our feud. The thought frightened me. I had been waiting almost eighteen hours for Billy to come busting into my apartment...waiting for him to kick in the door or pick the lock...waiting for him to move one foot across my doorstep...waiting to put a bullet into his head. If he was armed, it would be a righteous killing. If he was unarmed, well, the old .38 laying on my coffee table would suddenly become Billy's, and it would still be a righteous killing.

Dusk came, and I waited.

It was dark, and I waited.

Luciano Pavarotti sang, and I waited.

The bottles in the cabinet over the stove called to me. Still, I waited. Finally the phone rang.

The wait was over.

I let it ring three times before picking it up. It was now time for him to wait.

"Yeah," I said into the mouthpiece.

"Amato?"

"Yeah."

"This is Billy."

"So?"

"It's time to meet."

"Well, like they say on the game show, Billy, 'Come on down'!"

"No, I don't think so, Ace. You come and meet me."

"When? Where?"

"There's a phone booth about a block away from your apartment on the corner of Dewey Avenue. Be there in five minutes. I'll call you."

As soon as he hung up, I popped the tape out of the answering machine, grabbed a plastic baggy out of a kitchen drawer and slipped the two legal guns into my waste band, one on the right side, one in the small of my back. I thought about taking the drop gun, but decided against it. I was almost out the door before I remembered to grab my recorder and the little suction cup to monitor the ear piece of the pay phone. With less than thirty seconds to spare I was at the phone booth. I parked the Corvette directly along side the phone booth so the son-of-a-bitch wouldn't have a clean shot at me if he was planning a drive-by from the street. Then I propped the glass door of the phone booth open with a rock so I would be able to move out easily if I had to.

The phone rang once, twice, three times. I took my time to look around at my surroundings as I attached the suction cup up behind the ear piece of the phone and let the phone ring three more times before I picked it up.

"Yo," I said cheerfully.

"That you, Amato?"

"Yeah, it's me."

"You going to meet me?"

"Hey, Billy, if you want to meet me and settle this thing, then let's meet. You've been calling me for a week now, so let's put this thing to bed, okay?"

"Do you know where Canal Street is?" he asked.

"I think I can find it."

"In about two hours, that will be midnight, walk down Canal from West Main, and about a hundred or so feet down the street, on the left side, there's an old warehouse. There's a wooden door, a green one, kind of all faded and peeling. Come through that door and walk to the back of the building."

"Are you fucking nuts?" I asked seriously. Then countered the serious tone with, "Sorry, Billy, that was a dumb question. We both know you're nuts. But anyway, are you dumb enough to believe I'm going to walk into a dark warehouse and let you take pop shots at me? Get real, man!"

"Are you afraid, *Ace*?" he asked mockingly.

"I'm not afraid of you and I'm not afraid of dying, but I'm not goofy enough to give you that kind of edge. You want to meet me, you come down and meet me in the street, in a park, in a parking lot, but not some dark place where you can live out some boyhood fantasy. You want to meet me, then you meet me face-to-face, like a man!"

"That's the way it's going to be, Amato."

"Sorry, Billy. Fuck you!" I said and slammed the phone down.

It was a gamble I had to take. I needed to stay on the offensive, and have him meet me on my terms. I stepped out of the phone booth and lit a cigarette. The match wasn't even out before the phone rang again. I let it ring a few times.

"Now what?" I asked as I picked up the phone.

"Okay," he said between gritting teeth. "We'll do it your way. Meet me in front of the warehouse, on the street, the sidewalk, about midnight."

"That might work," I acknowledged. "But let me ask you a question, Billy Westfield. Why are we meeting?"

"We're going to walk and talk, Lieutenant Amato. We're going to talk things out, and then...then I'm going to kill you," he said solemnly. "Besides, I know your just dying, pun intended by the way, to know how I did all this, how I got to all four of those people, and especially about why I did it."

"Sounds kind of drastic, Billy. Why don't we just skip the killing part and you just tell me everything, I'll just arrest you for the four killings and we'll call it square."

"I'll say one thing for you, Amato, you sure do have a sense of humor."

"Humor? I don't think you killing four people is so amusing Billy. I plan on arresting you for those killings, no matter how much you deny doing them." That part about arresting him was for the benefit of the tape recording that would become evidence at my inquest after I killed this little prick.

"Deny it? Deny It? I never denied it, Amato. If you were listening to me a second ago, I just told you I killed them! I killed them to make an ass out of you, and I did it. I made you look like a clown. In a few hours, everyone is going to know what a clown you really are...were. I killed them and you didn't have a damn clue what was going on. People are going to see that you are so useless, you can't even prevent your own murder. Now, are you going to meet me, or do I have to do something to really make my point?"

I checked to make sure the small reel of tape in the recorder was still going around. It was. I high-fived the air. I had the little bastard's confession on tape!

"Do something like what?" I asked, trying not to give away my joy at having his confession on tape for everyone to hear.

"You don't meet me, or you send the cops around to try to grab me and I'll give you pretty little Diane's head on your desk. I mean it. I see one fucking car that looks like a cop car, one bum that might be an undercover cop and I'll disappear. You can hand me all that crap about not having to pay her alimony, but all in all, I know you don't want to have her blood on your hands just because you're too much of a coward to meet me. You won't ever see me again, but I'll mail you your wife's head."

"Ex-wife," I corrected.

"Or maybe, he continued, "I'll kill one of those detectives you seem to like to so much. They're out everyday, so it wouldn't be that hard to get one of them. Anyway, if you don't meet me, somebody is going to die. Like it or not, *Ace*, that's the way it is."

The phone went dead before I could respond. It was just as well. I didn't have any response.

I headed south on Dewey Avenue, toward the center of the city, calculating I could be at Canal Street by quarter after ten. At a traffic light I took the tape recorder out of my pocket and spoke the time, date, and location of the phone booth into it, and then slipped the device into the plastic bag. If things didn't work out well for me tonight, the tape, along with what the guys on the squad knew about the case, would be enough to fry Billy Westfield...if a jury of his peers was so inclined.

I got up around Lyell Avenue before I began to wonder why Billy was giving me so much time to make the meet. On every other occasion when he wanted me to be somewhere, he gave me only minutes to meet a deadline. Now he was giving me almost two hours. Why the change? Does he want me waiting around for him? Did he have things to prepare, to get ready for our showdown? Maybe he was giving me time to notify other cops, so he could justify in his own warped mind a reason not to face me, and instead go after an easier target, such as Diane. Was little Billy-boy afraid to go head-to-head with me? Why this little twist from a guy who had become as predictable as snow in Rochester? Maybe he needed the time to get from wherever he was to the location of our meeting. It could be Billy just wanted me waiting and stewing for a few hours. Maybe he believed what he had read in the papers and thought I would take the extra time to go out and get drunk, and therefore, he would have a little extra advantage when we met.

Billy Westfield knew I was going to be armed when I met with him, and, I was very sure he knew I intended to kill him. Therefore, why had he consented to meeting me outside the building? He must plan on being there well before I got there, I reasoned. He would be waiting in the alley and when I showed up, he would walk out of the shadows and put a bullet in my head, the same way he had tagged Lanovara and Landers. Maybe that was his plan, but I sure as hell wasn't going to allow him to live out that fantasy.

Something tapped at the back of my head, telling me it was stupid to go down to an abandoned warehouse on Canal Street alone, without back up. But I put the thought out of my head. At this stage of the game I was not into rational, conventional thinking. My thinking was being done down in my gut, in my bowels, in that region of the psyche that stores the IOU's of life and throws caution all to hell in an effort to settle old scores. Maybe some day at the academy, the stupidity of Lt. Mike Amato would be taught and an instructor would stand in front of a projection screen showing my bullet-torn body and caution recruits, "This is what happens when you let your balls overload your common sense!"

"No, I don't think so, Billy," I said to the car's interior as I pushed the thought of having one small drink out of my head. "Mike don't need drinks tonight. It would only deprive me of the clear head I need in order to kill you!"

I cruised west on Main Street, past Canal and wondered if this was Billy's present neighborhood. If it was, it gave him access to every bus line in the city and would put him only blocks away from where Landers and Mary Williams got killed, along with less than a ten minute bus ride to and from the killings of Nelson and Lanovara.

Completing my quick, once around survey of the area, I parked the Corvette in the McDonald's Restaurant parking lot on West Main Street. Before leaving the car, I tossed the plastic bag containing the tape recorder on the floor of the car. If I didn't make it out of this thing, the uniform cops would find my car in a day or so and my guys would have all the evidence they needed to go after Bill. After locking the car, I headed across West Main Street, toward Canal Street. My plan was simple. I would take a quick peek inside the warehouse, get familiar with the layout of the place, and then wait in the alley along side the warehouse until Billy showed up. After that it was just a matter of arresting, or better yet, killing the little prick.

My shoulder shoved in the faded, peeling, blue, warehouse door. Once inside I drew my weapon and let my eyes adjust to the darkness. During all my years on the department I had hated late night burglary calls in these huge, old buildings. Besides providing a burglar with hundreds of hiding places, the structures creaked and moaned under their own weight, sending out sounds that made your finger grip your gun tighter as you listened to the pounding of your own heart.

Closing my eyes for a half minute, I got my night vision. My body moved slowly and quietly past a staircase that led to the second floor. I skipped the staircase for the time being and entered a narrow hallway that led to the rear area of the building. I moved slowly and quietly, careful to lift my feet only an inch or so from the wooden floor and setting them down in silent, forward motions that would hopefully keep the old, dried floor boards from creaking. From time to time I stopped my movement as the unmistakable scratching noise of fat rats scurrying for cover came from in front of me.

I froze as the wall I was feeling with my left hand suddenly disappeared from my touch. It took a second to figure it out, but then I realized that I was at the end of the hallway and in a large, open bay of the warehouse. The faint light that came in through the dozens of broken windows allowed me to see that the open area, with cement floors, was supported by a dozen or so, fat, concrete pillars, and except for them, and some garbage piled up in different areas, the place was empty.

I holstered the weapon on my right side and took a few seconds to gain control of my breathing. The thought of lighting a cigarette came to mind but was quickly dismissed. I remembered the bullet that slammed into Arnie Campbell's forehead almost thirty years ago in Nam after he lit a cigarette and the light became a target for a sniper.

I turned and tried to make my way to the entrance of the hall when one of those creaking sounds made my heart jump and I froze rigid in my tracks. The sound came from behind me, from the floor. The second my mind told my reflexes that concrete floors do not creak, I tried to turn...but it was too late.

I heard the snicker, and then the room seemed to go bright with a flash of light as the two-by-four slammed down on me, its force being absorbed by the back of my head and my right shoulder. The blow knocked me forward and my forehead slammed into a concrete pillar before I slid to the floor.

I don't know how long I was out, but when I came to I realized I was sitting, with my legs stretched out in front of me. A shot of panic went through me as I thought my arms were paralyzed, but I quickly found they were simply bound behind me. I kept my eyes closed as I tried to comprehend the situation. With the back of my right forearm pressed against my side, it was easy to learn my gun and holster had already been removed. However, by pressing the backs of my bound hands against the small of my back I felt the small hunk of iron there and took some comfort, limited as it was, in the fact that the little .380 automatic was still nestled in its hiding spot. From an area in front of me, and slightly to the left, I could hear voices. No, not *voices,* but rather just one voice, one anxious, mumbling, voice.

I tried to come up with a plan but quickly determined there was no plan to come up with unless I knew my surroundings. Even if I could get the back-up weapon out of its holster, with my hands tied like this, there was no way I could get a shot at this animal. My mind shrugged and I figured I might as well open my eyes and get the show on the road.

I moaned and moved my shoulders around in a small, tight circle. Billy Westfield took his cue and came over to me. Only then did I realize that he was not mumbling to himself. He was speaking low but insistent into a cell phone, telling the person on the other end, "Tonight, right now. It's got to be now, right now!"

"So how you doing, Ace?" he asked as he folded the lower portion of the phone shut and crouched down in front of me, holding my gun in his right hand and slipping the phone into his jacket pocket with his left hand.

"Not too bad, Billy, considering some low-level punk had to sneak up behind me with a baseball bat in order to put me down."

"Hey, like they say in the boxing matches, 'Protect yourself at all times.' Besides, it was a two by four, not a bat." The comment seemed to amuse Billy greatly and he let out a belch of a laugh. Still smiling he said, "I just out-foxed you again, Amato. I gave you two hours to get here and I knew you would come early to scout out the place. But, I was ahead of you and I was waiting for you. It seems like I'm always one step ahead of you, doesn't it?"

"Yeah, Billy. You're a brilliant piece of work, you really are."

"You just keep up the smart comments, *Ace.* By tomorrow everyone is going to know you were just a bag of wind, a nobody, a piece of shit that I out-smarted every step of the way." I didn't see the smack coming, but the back of his left hand snapped out and caught me solid on the left cheek.

I spit out a wad of red phlegm and looked the kid directly in his eyes. The nuns at Saint Lucy's often told us, "The eyes are the windows of the soul!" If that was true, this kid had no soul. His eyes were wide and strained, but there was nothing there. No emotion, no feeling, no conscience. We remained fixed in our positions for a full minute, maybe more, just staring at each other, exchanging our mutual hatred for each other. He finally moved and I looked past him as he walked away from me. I quickly judged the distance to the window on the far wall to be about eighteen, maybe twenty feet from where I was seated. Looking at the back of his legs, I brought my legs up slowly and adjusted my position.

"You stay put, Amato," he said through clenched teeth as he turned and brought the gun to my forehead.

"To hell with you, Billy," I told him. "If you're going to kill me, then kill me, but I'm not going to sit here all cramped up."

"Oh, I *am* going to kill you, that's for sure, but in my own time, when everything is right."

"Well then, if you aren't going to kill me now, I am going to get myself up in a different position and then you can play big man and smack me around, of course, taking pride in the fact you're beating a guy that's tied up and unable to fight back and kick the living shit out of you." With that I bent my legs at the knees and pulled my heels back toward my butt. Now I was in the correct position I needed to carry out my plan.

After a couple seconds, he asked, "So, tell me, do you have this whole, entire thing figured out yet?"

"Well, I hate to bust your illusions of grandeur, Billy-boy, but yeah, I got it figured out. You aren't all that sharp and the whole frigging thing isn't that complex, you know."

"Oh yeah? Well then tell me, why was I using the name Jessie?"

"It's your mother's name."

"Hey, not bad, Amato!" he acknowledged with a smile. "When did you figure that out?"

"Oh, about the third, maybe fourth time you called us," I lied.

"You're full of shit! You're lying!"

"Fuck you, Billy!" I spat in the most belligerent tone I could muster. "You're not important enough to lie to!"

"What about the rest of it, then? Why do you think I've been killing these people."

"Because you're a sick, whack-o, piece of human shit."

That back hand left of his snapped out again and caught me a second time. "Tell me why I've been doing this, Amato. Tell me!"

"Look, Billy. I'm really enjoying this stimulating conversation and all, but if you aren't going to kill me pretty quick, at least give me a cigarette and then we can chat the night away."

He looked at me like I was the crazy one and then a grin crept across his face. Reaching in my shirt pocket, he took out the pack of smokes, shook one free and slipped it between my lips. I watched him as he opened the book of matches, pulled out one of the narrow cardboard strips and carefully closed the cover before striking. Law abiding asshole, I thought as he closed the cover over the remaining matches. Then, as he pulled the match along the striking surface, I closed my eyes just as the match got up enough friction to light. In the second that it took the flame to ruin his night vision, I pushed myself up with all the strength I could assemble in my legs and heaved my shoulder into his gut, knocking him backwards and down to the floor.

With my eyes now open, I jumped over him and hurled myself toward the window I had targeted earlier. The sound of my gun sliding across the cement floor was mixed with his curses, but, as for me, I was rather pleased with myself that I had knocked the gun out of his hand. One step from the window I leaped upward and forward at the opening. The small patch of ice or water on the concrete floor was enough to take the push out of my leap and I hit the window low. The instant I hit the window frame, I realized I had failed to consider two things...the height of the window from the deck and the condition of the warehouse floor.

My own cry filled the empty warehouse as my left shoulder and the left side of my face slammed against the metal frame of the window. Although the frame gave a little, it did not break, but rather, flung me back into the room. Crashing to the floor on my right side, I tried to roll over and get up again, but Billy was to me by then. His right foot came up from the floor and caught me in the gut, flipping me over onto my back as I heaved ten pounds of air up from my stomach and out my throat. Grabbing me by the hair, he pulled me forward and up to my feet.

Two minutes later I was standing with my back to one of the concrete pillars, a thick rope wrapped around me three or four times, securing me to the post. I coughed up a little blood, spit it out next to his shoes and asked, "So what were we talking about?"

When we both started to laugh, the startling thought passed through my mind that I was as crazy as him. My laugh was cut short when I realized I could no longer feel my second gun in the small of my back. In my aborted attempt of escape, I had lost the gun. Only then did I realize that was the gun I had heard sliding across the floor. Billy was now holding both weapons.

"You were about to tell me why you think I'm going through all this trouble with you."

"Oh yeah, that's right," I said. "Well, Billy, the way I figure it, you're pretty pissed that I busted you for that rape back a dozen years ago and it's been kind of gnawing at you, so you figure you would cap a couple of citizens and along the way make it clear to the press that you're really hunting me. Lo and behold I come up dead, and everyone knows a pretty smart dude got to me and all the good citizens see that I'm not all that sharp of a detective...or something like that."

"Well, not too bad, Lieutenant," Billy Westfield commented, pursing his lips together and nodding. "But, the way it really goes is this. My mother's dead because of you, Amato. You went after me, but you killed her," he said as he began to pace in front of me, raising his voice a notch. "The woman died of a broken heart after you ruined my life with that bullshit rape charge. After that I got thrown out of school, couldn't get a job, nothing, and she just couldn't accept it. I had to leave town because of you and what you did to me. Even then, after I left and all, you couldn't let up. You had me arrested and hassled almost everywhere I went. Then when my old man got to be Chief of Police, it really got to you, so you began to make his life miserable, busting his chops every way you could. You ruined my life, killed my mother, but that wasn't enough, so then you went after my father. You just weren't going to quit until someone stopped you."

"So you're going to stop me, is that it, Billy?"

"Yes...at least in a way it will be me stopping you. I got you here. I put it all together, but someone else is going to have the pleasure of killing you."

"Oh, really? Well, do tell me, who is our mystery guest, Billy?"

"That's a surprise, Ace. Let's just keep it that way for now."

"Okay with me," I said. "I love surprises." I just couldn't resist the temptation to assault his ego one more time...maybe even the last time. "But my guess is that dear old dad is going to be joining us shortly. Right?"

Again we both laughed, but his heart wasn't in it and I could see he was upset that I had spoiled his surprise.

After a short silence I asked, "So, as long as we're just killing time, in a manner of speaking, Billy, do you mind telling me how you selected and got to the other four victims in this little killing spree you've been on?"

"Mind? Of course not, Lieutenant. This took a lot of planning on my part. I want you to know and appreciate that. I gave a lot of thought to making sure I had a good name for each of the playing cards. That pig Lanovara, Frankie Ten Times, was easy. I borrowed some money from him and when he began to lean on me, I told him I would meet him over there where I killed him. I told him I had some dope I would give him for the dough I owed him. He came walking up all big and bad, and I acted all humble and scared, and then shot the bastard."

"And, Landers? What was it about the detective wanting to see him? That was you, wasn't it?"

"Very good, Ace! I'm proud of you," he said almost triumphantly. "Yep, I called him and told him I was a detective, figured that would screw up your case, and I needed to talk to him about some corruption issues in one of the unions. I made an appointment to meet him after business hours. I waited by his car and figured sooner or later he would give up waiting for me and would go to his car. Actually, I wasn't going to kill him. I had another guy named Jack I was going to hit, but then I remembered my old man saying you and the Landers dude were kind of friends, and how him unionizing the cops made it so hard to do anything good with the department. So I figured killing him would help my dad and would make a better impact on you...and the newspapers, too!"

"I know your dad helped you get to Mary Williams, so that's kind of why I tagged him as our mystery guest."

"Not really, Ace. Close, but no cigar, as they say," he commented with a small, tight grin on his evil face. "He helped me find her, but never knew why I wanted her, not then anyway. You see, I remembered him talking about her when I was a kid. 'Queen Mary this and Queen Mary that.' She was some kind of informant of his, and my guess is he was probably also banging her. Anyway, one day I called him and told him I met a kid from Rochester and the kid was saying his mother was a woman known as Queen Mary and that the kid was trying to locate her and all. He always was a sucker for doing good, so he dug up an old address for her, and had some flunky run her down. So, when I was ready to get to her, it was just a matter of getting to meet her, and bullshit her with some hard luck story until we got to be friends sort of."

"And Rex?"

"You ain't going to believe this, but that was just a stroke of dumb luck. I was going to kill a guy named David King over in the Sheriff's Department, but then one night this fag hits on me. When he tells me his name is Rex, well, I figured what the hell, and I nailed him instead. Besides, it was a nice touch. You know, killing a Rex instead of just a simple thing like someone named King."

Billy went back to pacing, recounting how he had moved from Rochester to some place in California and from there to Seattle, and to a half dozen other places, each time getting busted for drugs, or fighting, or some bullshit thing or another, and becoming totally convinced I was having him arrested everywhere he went. While he was tripping down the Woe-Is-Me path of memory lane, I figured the only way I had gotten this guy to mess up anytime during this damn investigation was when I assaulted his ego. Even though I was bound and not feeling too scrappy, I figured I might as well play the ego card again.

"So Teddy Roberts was just an attempt to throw some shit in the game?"

"Exactly, Ace!" he exclaimed with some glee. "You got to appreciate that touch. That took some planning on my part. I had to point you in that direction real careful so you would bite. It took some doing, but I planted the gun in his chair, then called you, told you he had it, and let you do the rest."

"Do you mind if I point out a couple of screw-ups in your plan, Billy?" Not waiting for a response to the question, I continued. "First of all, you got yourself to blame for me busting you on the rape charge, so quit trying to blame me. You and your asshole buddy forced yourself on the girl, held her down and forcefully screwed her. You were a coward then, just like you're a coward now. Back then you had to use a buddy of yours to attack a girl. Now you have to use darkness and sneak up behind me with a board. It was your decision back then, your choice, your actions that got you busted. I just filled out the reports. Not only that, but if your selective memory serves you right, you may recall you even confessed, bragged about it as a matter of fact, when I talked to you." Billy was still pacing as I talked.

"Second point is that your mother, God rest her soul, a beautiful woman in every way, if I may add, died of cancer as I recall it. Consequently, your romantic version of her dying of a broken heart is just so much bullshit. Besides, if her heart was broken, it was you, not me, that broke it." I watched as Billy, still holding one of my guns in each of his hands, put his fists to the sides of his head, trying to keep my words from getting into his head. Good, it was working. Time to go for the punch line.

"Third point I want to make is that no one is going to see you as a hero on this thing. They're going to see you for the pussy you really are. You killed a punk mob wannabe, an old hooker, a grandfather, and a homosexual. That don't take big balls. Then what is it you do for an encore? You sneak up behind me with a board, tie me to a pillar and have some other gutless piece of shit, like your old man, shoot me. All that shows is that you're a pussy son-of-a-bitch without the guts to face me man-to-man." I paused, waiting for a reaction. There wasn't any. I had to push him harder.

"And, just to wrap it all up for your little, defective mind, everyone in the squad knows that you're the killer. They know it's you, just as much as I do. They know about you being wanted in New Mexico on the fifty keys of reefer." That got his attention. "They know about you planting the gun in Teddy Roberts' apartment right before you called us to say it was there. In short, they got you by the balls, boy. Now then, just for icing on the cake, tonight, when you called me at the phone booth, I recorded your confession to me and the tape is in the United States mail as we speak. With that, along with the investigation, they have you nailed to the cross. So, the bottom line is this, the world is going to find out I did out-smart you. I did put the case together. Yeah sure, we made a little mistake about Teddy Roberts, but even that is documented on the tape that I thought it was a mistake to charge

Teddy with the murders. You're old man was the brilliant son-of-a-bitch that wanted Roberts booked on the murders, not me. Isn't that an interesting footnote, Billy? It was your father that wanted him locked up."

Billy had his back to me as I finished my lecture. He began to turn toward me, in a slow motion military, "about face," on heel and toe, and as he did I got a shiver up my spine, for on his face was the widest, most devilish smile I had ever seen on a human face. Only then did I realize I had gone too far. Never having been one to quit while I was ahead, I had pushed the argument beyond the points that needed to be made.

"That's just what I want, *Ace*," he said through the scary smile. "I want everyone to know it was me. I want it to be proven it was me. I'm glad you got me on tape saying I killed those people and that I was going to kill you. You see, you're so fucking smart, you keep out-smarting yourself. It's good that you and your detectives can prove it was me that killed you. It's great! Wonderful!" He now stepped close to me, put a gun under my nose and said in a whisper, "Because I'm not going to kill you. My father is going to kill you! He's going to have the honor and the privilege of killing you. Let everyone think it was me! So what? I disappeared before, and I can disappear again."

His father? No Balls Westfield was going to kill me? It was obvious to me he was in on this thing all the time, but when it came down to pulling a trigger, could No Balls Ben Westfield really do it? The notion didn't sound right, didn't make sense. Ben Westfield hated my guts, would like to see me dead, was a ball-less, desk-riding, gutless excuse for a cop...but he was no murderer.

I tried to sort it all out. What had I missed on the investigation? What little sign, little innuendo, shitty little piece of evidence did I skip over, not see, not perceive?

I gave up thinking and let my body slump into a relaxed lump hanging from the ropes that secured me to the pillar. There was nothing to figure out. In a few minutes, maybe a half-hour, I would have my answers...and take them to the grave with me.

I had begun the day waiting, and I would end the night waiting. Waiting for Ben Westfield to show up. Waiting for Billy Westfield to play out the last act of his self-directed drama. Waiting to die. Waiting.

CHAPTER FIFTEEN

THE VERY END

Up until now, the worst days of my life had been in the jungles of Vietnam. However, tonight, sitting here beaten, bleeding, and bound, I find the thought of a foxhole in that hot, muggy, piece of hell to be an attractive alternative to my present situation. My life as a cop has surely been less than spectacular, and, by the looks of things, the future doesn't hold a lot of promise.

Over the past few months, since this mind-screwing case began, I've been messed with by my Chief, my own doubts and fears, and one very nasty killer. My career, what little there had been of one, is in the toilet. My reputation, such at it was, is shattered. The remnants of my sanity and sobriety are things of the past. My downfall and my imminent death are due to one man...one very vengeful and angry man.

Because of him, I stand here with my head split open, bound to a concrete pillar in this cold, wet, abandoned, rat-infested warehouse. The musty smells of puddled water and rotting concrete fill my nostrils and find their way to my gut. As my stomach wretches I know my only hope for survival is that my host, the maniac with the gun will be stricken ht an immediate, and very fatal heart attack.

I watch the whacko pace back and forth as he rants about all the injustices of the world, the worst of which, at least according to him, appears to be me. My eyes are on him, but my mind keeps drifting back to what has brought me here, to this spot, this night. Maybe I got too close to this case, too emotionally caught up in it. It very simply may be that these last round of killings became too personal. Perhaps I'm getting too old, stupid, cocky, or crazy. Probably it's a combination of all of the above.

With my hands bound behind me, it's quite a chore to hunch up my shoulders up enough to wipe the blood that runs down the outside corner of my right eye, but in making the painful effort, I am at least able to see my tormentor. My head pounds like a kettle drum doing the *1812 Overture*, and passing out seems to be a very attractive and viable option. At least, in doing so, I will be better off than sitting here, fully conscious, a witness to my own murder.

The sneering mental turns toward me, and I see his agony displayed in a twisted face. Anger, sadness, frustration, vengeance, and hate all mingle together to share the energy of the muscles imbedded in his brow, eyes, and lips.

Facing me now, my killer slowly rolls his head from side to side as if stretching his neck in a distorted, slow motion exercise. He extends his right hand toward my shattered body and soul. His thumb pulls back the hammer of the gun. Fear now comes forward to haunt and mock me. It is not death that I fear, for I came to grips with that demon in a jungle more than a quarter of a century earlier when I learned there were things worse than death. The fear I have this night is rooted in the knowledge I have failed to cage the killer. It is a fear that, in death, I will be ridiculed for my carelessness and stupidity. I fear that none will know how hard I tried, and all will suspect that ego has led me to danger and my death.

Fear, not death, is my villain. Death is sometimes a welcome visitor, a benefactor who resolves your other fears, the ones that have pushed you toward a bottle...and away from everything else. I wonder to myself if it is better to be alive and alone or dead and alone.

I look up to glare at the man who is intent on killing me. I try to look him in the eye but my attention locks on the sight of the gun's barrel and I can picture the copper- jacketed bullet that will soon rocket through the tube and blast its way into my skull.

For better or for worse, it is time to die.

Billy Westfield turns away from me once more and runs his hand, still holding my gun, through his hair as he checks his wristwatch for the twentieth time. I watch him move in small circles as I try to sort out the fact that Ben Westfield, the Chief of Police, was behind all this. It didn't seem possible that he could turn this monster loose on the city, the city he was sworn to protect. But then again, who can say what a man's emotions, fears, and hate will lead him to do? Did he want me so badly that he would use his own son to get to me? How could he sit back and let four people die just so he could kill me and then hide behind his son's psychotic behavior? What kind of man makes his boy, his flesh and blood, a fugitive for life just so he can even a score?

I look up from the floor and back at Billy Westfield as his circular path stretches wider and wider. Something's wrong with this picture! Ben Westfield was indeed a pompous bastard, a liar, and a man of little honor...still, he's no murderer. On the other hand, was that his reason for putting that little spying son-of-a-bitch, Sergeant Mancini in my camp? Was he using the Sergeant to keep himself up on our progress, on how close we were getting to Billy?

It had to be an illusion, but I can't figure out what part of the puzzle is the illusion. Was it an illusion that Ben Westfield was connected to these killings done by his over-the-edge son? Or, was it an illusion that he was too straight to become involved in the killing of innocent citizens? I would only know the answers to those questions if and when my Chief pulled the trigger.

I hear some guttural sound, half moan and half whimper, come from Billy as he passes by in his orbit around me. Things are not going right for the kid and I can see he's coming unwound. Although I want to rip his heart out, I know I have to get to him gently, to reach inside of him with words and have him give up his plan before his old man arrives on the scene. I want him to look at me, to see a man, a human being instead of a symbol for his problems and short comings.

"Billy," I say in a quiet even tone. "Come here."

"What do you want, Amato?"

"I want to talk to you. There's a way out for you."

"For *me*? A way out for *me*? You're the one who needs a way out, *Ace* Amato, not me," he half-laughs with a mock, throaty chuckle as he steps toward me and leans in so close that I'm able to feel his breath.

"Billy, I don't think your father is coming. He's not going to come down here and shoot a guy, an unarmed guy who's tied to a pillar, a guy he's known for over twenty years. If you're going to kill me, Billy, you're going to have to do it yourself. If you kill me, I win, but if you leave right now, then you will win. Understand what I'm saying?"

I have his attention, and just as he's about to turn away, he faces me again. "Just what the hell are you talking about, Amato?"

"You kill me right now, while I'm hog tied like this, and you'll never have another minute's peace. The papers will have afield day about how a cop gave his life in the line of duty, at the hands of deranged killer, and all that crap. And, to top it all off, no one will know why those people died, why you did what you did." I pause to see if he's listening.

"And if I don't keep you here so my father can kill you, how do I win then?"

"You leave me here and you go call 9-1-1 and tell them where to find me. Then, you disappear and I'm left here to talk about what happened, to explain what the hell I was doing tied up in a warehouse in the middle of the night. You wanted to destroy me, to humiliate me, right? Right?" When he fails to answer, I ask again, louder, "Right?"

"Right," he confirmed softly and not with too much confidence.

"Then, what better way to do it than to leave me here, just like this, instead of making a martyr out of me? That way you win nothing and I go out in a blaze of glory."

It looks like I'm reaching him, or at least he is thinking about what I'm saying, but then his face breaks into a slow, emergent smile as he puts the gun to the left side of my head and speaks very slowly.

"But I'm not the one that's going to kill you. Remember? My dad, your Chief, he's the one who's going to blow your fucking brains all over this place. I got you, but you're *his* prize. He hates you as much as I do. You make his life a living hell every day he has to look at you and know you were the one that killed my mother. He's the one that..."

The sentence goes unfinished as the sound of rusty hinges scraping against each other fill the hallway leading to the warehouse. Billy leaves me and moves to the hallway in a crouch. He's gone for maybe ten seconds when he returns, dancing back into the room, moving sideways with his right side and outstretched gun facing me.

"Right this way, Dad. Right this way. Take a look at what I brought you."

Ben Westfield follows his son into the warehouse. His eyes trying to peer into the darkness and make sense out of the shadows and shapes they perceive. The Chief walks up to me and his face suggests that he may not a party to this escapade after all!

"Lieutenant?" he questions.

"Good morning, Chief. Sorry I can't salute, but Junior there has got me tied to this thing."

Westfield looks at me and then to his smiling son. Some unintelligible half-words come up from his throat, but it take a few more swivels of his head from me to his son before he manages to formulate a comprehensible sentence.

"What the hell is going on here, Billy?"

"I got him, Dad. I got him for you," the kid says with a gitty exuberance as he points at me with my automatic. "I got him to come here and I got him all tied up so you can kill him!"

"Kill him? You want me to kill one of my own men, Son? Billy, what's gotten into you? Why are you doing this?"

"He's ruined our lives Dad. You know what he did to me, to you, to mom. This...dude...this...this bastard, this rotten bastard, he ruined it all for us, Dad, and he's got to pay."

"Billy, Billy, Son, listen to me. Listen to your father, Billy. Yes, I agree what he did to you was...was stupid. It could have been handled differently, yes, of course it could have. But that's no reason to kill him."

"And what about what he did to mom, Dad? He killed her. He killed her just as sure as if he had a gun or a knife and shot her or stabbed her. He killed mom!"

Ben Westfield looks at me again and something in his eyes ask me to be silent and to trust him. "Billy, you're wrong Son. Mom died of cancer. The cancer got to her. Amato had nothing to do with that."

"She died of a broken heart, Dad. You said it yourself. After all that bullshit with the so-called rape arrest, I had to leave here. I could never get a job here or anything after what he did to me. Mom was so sad, so sad, that she just died, Dad. She died because he ruined us, Dad."

"Billy, listen to me!" Ben Westfield commands firmly. "If she did die of a broken heart, it was you and I who were the ones who broke it, not Amato."

"Kill him, Dad. Kill him. Kill him!"

"No, Billy, I can't do that. I won't do that. I have no reason to kill this man, son."

"Kill him!"

"Billy, even if I wanted to, I don't even have my gun with me. Listen to me Son, please listen to me."

Billy Westfield is getting angry now. His master plan is falling apart and he is embarrassed by his father's reluctance to kill me. Tears stream down his cheeks as he pleas his case and demands that his father shoot me.

"Here, take his gun. Shoot him with his own damn gun," he says as he nods his head and hands over my .9mm to his father.

Ben Westfield steps in front of me, shielding me from his son's shaking hand, a hand that holds the cocked .380 automatic I had tucked behind my belt, in the small of my back, before I left the apartment.

"Billy," Ben Westfield says softly. "You're having a nervous break down or something, Son. Come on now. Settle down and hear me out, Son. You're all distraught, all upset, and I understand, Billy, I really do." Moving away from in front of me, the older Westfield moves behind me, explaining, "I'm going to untie the Lieutenant now, son, and then you and I are going to sit down and talk, and we're going to work this thing out. You'll see, Son, we'll settle..."

"Get away from him, dad!"

"Billy, listen..." Ben says as I feel the rope around my chest and belly slacken.

"I said, get away from him," Billy repeats. His father steps back from me and Billy cries the question, "How can you defend him? Don't you have any pride at all, Dad? This man makes your life miserable. You told me the last time we talked on the phone about his wise-ass remarks and how he is so goddamned insubordinate to you."

"Billy, that's between me and him. Yes, you're damn right he's an obnoxious man, a very difficult man. But that isn't reason to kill him, Son." As Ben Westfield is critiquing my personal attributes, he again moves in front of me.

"You never had the balls to defend me when he arrested me, Dad, and you never had the balls to kick his ass for what he did to mom, and you don't even have the balls to do anything about how he treats you. You make me sick!"

"Billy, I did protect you, Son. Even now, on this thing you've done to these people. After Mary Williams was shot, I thought it might be you that was doing these killings. I prayed it wasn't you, but I thought it might have been. After all, son, it was you that called me from wherever you were living then and asked me to find her. When she got killed, I kind of knew it was you, but I prayed I was wrong and I said nothing, Billy. I protected you, Son, but I can't let you do this. I can't let you shoot another person in cold blood."

The two men stand only a couple of feet apart, but it might as well be the Grand Canyon between them. I can't see Ben Westfield's face, but Billy's face is contorted and he's crying.

"Get out of the way, Dad," Billy commands as he brings up his right arm and points it over his father's left shoulder, directly at the center of my face. Circling to his right, taking his father out of the line of fire, he sniffs up some of the snot running out of his nose and states coldly, "You shoot him, or I shoot him, but either way the son-of-a-bitch is going to die."

Ben Westfield moves forward, my gun still in his hand, but down at his side as his plaintive cry of, "Noooooo!" fills the room. My mind has trouble discerning what is happening, but it appears that in mid-step forward, toward his son, Benjamin Westfield stops and jumps back just as something makes a loud cracking sound. It takes me a fraction of a second to realize that the crack has come from Billy's gun. My eyes tell me Ben Westfield had been shot by his son, but my mind argues the point. I look at Billy as the Chief slumps to the floor. A long moan mixed with exhaled air comes from the older man's mouth, and then, the room falls silent.

"Look at what you did," Billy cries out to me in agony. "Look what you made me do! You made me kill my father!"

The confused, anguished kid takes a step toward his father's body, and then reels to face me.

"You rotten bastard, Amato," he screams. "I'm gonna kill you, you rotten, dirty bastard."

I look into the barrel of the automatic, and as Billy's finger tightens on the trigger, I lose my nerve and close my eyes.

The sound of the shot is like thunder as it fills the room and bounces off the concrete walls and floor. The sound waves wash over my face as the blood splashes over my cheek. After a few quick seconds, in reflex I open my eyes to see where I am shot. Instead of finding a wound on my body, I see Billy Westfield go to his knees and fall forward on what had been the right side of his face.

My mind races to make some order out of what's happening. The gun had exploded and killed Billy! That's my first reflex thought. But then I look around the room. There, to my right, stretched out on the floor, is Ben Westfield. His right hand is still extended, holding the weapon. A thin wisp of smoke is trailing upward from the barrel. In a split second he has automatically reverted to his years as a cop and the code of ethics he had sworn to uphold. When faced with the final decision he had protected the life of another and took the life of his own son.

Crawling on his belly, the father seeks his son's body, finds it, pulls it to his own...and cries.

A half hour later, I'm seated on the rear bumper of an ambulance, having the cuts on my face tended. At the same moment, Ben Westfield is being rolled into an operating room at St. Mary's Hospital and his son's body is being photographed by crime scene technicians.

I wince as the medics mess around with the cut on the back of my head and my eyes survey around the crowd that has assembled. The rotating blue and red lights of the cop cars and ambulance bounce off the faces in the crowd and I realize the faces are meaningless to me. None are friends. There is no one there to offer solace, to alleviate the loneliness in my heart and soul.

My thoughts drift to Diane. I need her but she's still in Colorado and I have no way of reaching her. I was never there when she needed me...it's probably only right that she's not here...now that I need her so badly.

In the distance, I see Frank Donovan pushing his way through the herd of gawkers and I smile. My head gives a small repeated nod when he takes my hand and asks, "How you doing, Mike?" I thank him for coming, as one might do at the funeral of a relative. Then, cop to cop, I provide a one minute summary of the night's activities. The briefing over, we agree it's going to be another long night and arrange to meet in the squad room.

Finally I walk away. Getting into the Corvette, I think about how fiercely I wanted to win this...this game. Now, when it's all over, when the score is posted, there are four dead citizens, grieving relatives, a dead killer, and a cop on an operating table, grieving the son he had to kill in order to save the life of a man he hated.

And only now do I realize it's no game. In a game there is a winner, someone who claims a victory. In this...this thing, there are only losers.

EPILOGUE

Ben Westfield retired from the Rochester Police Department the day after his son's funeral. I attended church services for William. On the way out of the church I nodded at Ben. I would like to think he nodded back. Some of the coppers say Ben Westfield is living down in Florida, others say he's in Canada. I even heard a rumor that he picked up a Chief's job in a small town somewhere in Montana. Wherever he is, I hope he's found some peace.

He came back to the Public Safety Building just one time, to clean out his office. Word went through the building that he was in, so I went up to see him, to thank him for saving my life. In the singular minute we were together, he made two things very clear to me. One, he had no idea what Billy was up to until the Mary Williams' killing and even then he didn't think his son was capable of such an act. He never even knew the kid was in town until the night in the warehouse. The second point he made was that he never wanted to speak to me or see me again. I believed him on both counts.

The new Chief of Police, Charles R. Novitski, was sworn in on a Monday morning, a month after the shooting. That afternoon he gave me a 10-day suspension, without pay, for having the Sambuca in my desk. The other charges were dropped for insufficient evidence. He then promptly fined himself the equivalent of fifteen days pay for failing to supervise me...but, that's the kind of guy Charlie Novitski was. I say, "was" because three months after taking the Chief's slot, he suffered a massive stroke and died nine days later. We gave him a nice funeral. Cops are good at throwing a nice funeral. I got shit-faced over at the union hall after the funeral and popped Sergeant Art Mancini a good shot in the mouth when he tried to tell me how much he respected the Major.

Me? Well, I'm still poking around dead bodies, trying to make some sense out of life and death. I've gotten over my hate for Billy Westfield, but not for what he did. I've cut back on the drinking quite a bit, but you can still get a pretty good *Caffe Sambuca* if you're around my office when I'm burning the midnight oil. It's at those times that I stand at my office window, looking out over the city, sipping the liqueur-laced coffee, and I think about Ben Westfield. For many of the years that I knew him, he never was a real, down and dirty, street cop. But, there in the warehouse, in one split second, when all the bets were down on the table, he came through and did his job according to the oath we all took so long ago. And, in the quiet of night I wonder if I could do what he did.

A few nights ago, over dinner, Diane told me she was still dating some Kodak stiff. The next morning, at breakfast, she admitted her dating was not a serious thing. It's a new experience for me, but I'm learning to hope.

Last night, the squad threw a little party for me, to celebrate my twenty-fifth year on the job. They gave me a nice wooden plaque. On the bottom there's a brass plate with my nickname engraved on it. In the center of the plaque is an Ace of Spades.

We all laughed when they gave it to me.

I guess it's like they say...You don't have to be crazy to do this job, but it sure helps!

By the way, you remember the pick up truck that was watching me when I met with Fast Eddy Cavaluso? Well, I finally got to the bottom of that. You see, what that was all about was...well, hell, that's another story.

GROUND LIONS

The Adventures of Mike Amato Continue!

Lou Campanozzi's second book, *Ground Lions,* will be released by Hollis Books in November 2000.

In *Ground Lions* Lt. Mike Amato investigates the killing of Danny Martin, a former friend who has become a low ranking mobster. As a rookie cop, Amato had tried to save the Martin kid from the tentacles of the streets, but had obviously failed. The investigation leads the Lieutenant back to his old neighborhood, and forgotten friends, where he uncovers information about his own family's ties to the Mafia.

This fast moving mystery leads the reader into explorations of relationships where friends become enemies, enemies become confidants... and nothing is ever as is seems!.

EXCERPT FROM "GROUND LIONS"

Directly ahead, at the far end of the classy restaurant, was my target for the evening - a half-moon-shaped booth in the back of the restaurant. When I got to within five feet of the booth, Charlie "The Twist" Tortero faced me and put the palm of his right hand to my chest like he was some kind of traffic cop. Earlier in the day I had encountered him on my turf. Tonight I was meeting his boss on his turf. He was eager to tie the score over the humiliation I had subjected him to by tweaking his ear.

"I need to pat you down first," he said with a certain air of smugness.

"I think you love me, Charlie, and you're just using this as a cheap excuse to fondle me," I responded with obvious disdain for him and his instructions. "I'm a cop and I'm packing. Live with it and get the hell out of my way."

Charlie took a half-step forward and said, "You..."

"You drop that hand and move aside," I said in my most threatening voice, "or that chubby little arm of yours is going to end up being the fattest suppository known to mankind."

The gravel voice of Vincent Ruggeri came from the booth. "Let the

205

Lieutenant sit down, Charlie. He means us no harm."

"And have a nice day, Charlie," I said as I walked past the stubby man and up to the booth.

Reaching across the table, I extended my hand to the Old Man and thanked him for taking time to see me. Next, I nodded to Eddy Cavaluso who was seated to Ruggeri's left. After sliding into the booth I reached down to scratch the ear of Fast Eddy's mutt, who was under the table, standing guard in the event that any loose scraps accidentally came falling in his direction. The greetings and important signs of respect out of the way, I slid into the booth and took up a position opposite the Old Man and at a slight angle to Cavaluso.

"I've taken the liberty of ordering linguini and white clam sauce for you, Michael. It's a specialty of our host," Vincent Ruggeri said as he pinched his right cheek and lifted his eyes to the heavens. "Of course," he continued with a slight nod, "if you prefer to order something else, please feel free to do so."

I shook my head and said, "I appreciate your thoughtfulness, Mr. Ruggeri. The linguini and white clam sauce will be fine." It would have been an insult for me to order anything other than what Ruggeri had already ordered for me. Although I didn't like Ruggeri and his chosen vocation, I was not here to insult him.

The Old Man snapped his fingers in the direction of a waiter standing ten or fifteen feet behind him and then pointed down to the plate and then at me. A minute later, a platter of linguini, topped with a dozen good-sized clams on the half-shell, was slipped in front of my chest and my wineglass was filled with a ruby red wine. I let the drifting steam that carried the aroma of mixed herbs drift up to my lips and then drew them deep into my nasal cavities with a long, silent sniff. I smiled my satisfaction to my adversary and lifted my glass of wine to his and exchanged the customary, *"Salute!"* before tasting the meal.

For the next twenty minutes or so we ate and made light conversation about nothing special. Sitting there in front of the most powerful crime figure in Rochester, it struck me how well preserved the man had remained since my youth.

Vincent Ruggeri's full head of thick hair had turned snow white. It was combed back and the thickness of it gave one the impression of a lion's mane. The years had provided the solid, neatly dressed, elderly man with a few lines and wrinkles which had eroded their way into the corners of his eyes, but otherwise Ruggeri had remained unchanged from the time I was a boy. His hands still appeared to be as huge as Easter hams, although they were now spotted with the brown dots that come with seventy-eight years of life. His unmistakable raspy voice sounded as if the man gargled with peanut butter. I remembered it greeting my father, *"Buon' giorno, paisano,"* as my dad and I entered the neighborhood saloon on frequent Saturday afternoons.

Vincent Ruggeri spoke. "I understand you expressed a desire to speak with me, Michael."

I nodded to the man and noted how precise was the language learned in a Jesuit Seminary more than a half century earlier, and how it had remained with him through the years. "I need to ask you a question or two."

Ruggeri spread his arms the width of his chest and left the palms up as he said, "Ask."

"A friend of mine was killed and I suspect one of your friends may have been responsible for his death."

"I am very sorry about the loss of your friend," he commented with a slight bow of his head. Fast Eddie Cavaluso added his sympathy and I nodded my acceptance to him.

"With all due respect, *Signore,* your sympathy is welcomed, but it's meaningless if you ordered his death."

"And why would I do such a thing, Michael?" he asked as he leaned back in the booth and furrowed his bushy, white eyebrows.

"Oh, I don't know," I said. "Maybe you would do such a thing because he was deep in your organization's shorts and some of your friends were getting worried about what he knew. Maybe you would do it because he had developed a good inside track on the rats who hang around your gambling joints. Maybe you did it simply because some of the low-life animals who frequent your joints feared he was a snitch and they convinced you that a dead snitch was better than a live, breathing snitch."

The man looked me deep in the eyes as he said the words, "Michael, I was in no way responsible for your friend's death. I say that to you in all honesty." Then he added, without looking so deeply, "I am not saying I would even know if one of my 'friends,' as you call them, did this terrible thing. However, sometimes those who think I have powers I do not really possess, come to me and ask me if I would approve of them doing certain things, or they ask me if I will bless some of their endeavors, legal or otherwise." He looked down at the coffee cup that was devoured in his right hand and added, "Naturally, I do not condone matters of an illegal nature, and I tell them so." Looking back into my eyes, he added, "But no one came to me regarding a need to injure your friend."

The Old Man's tanned, muscular arms came forward and he now rested the full length of his forearms on the table as he smiled sympathetically at me and leaned forward to talk to me in a low, private voice.

"The Greeks were the true origins of modern civilization. We would like to think it was the Romans, but it was not. The Greeks are the cradle of our system of government, democracy, and justice. If you look at the great philosophers, they were all Greeks. They were intelligent people, and they were intelligent because they observed and they reasoned."

My face must have spoken what my mind was thinking...What the hell does this have to do with anything.

Ruggeri held off my non-verbalized question with an extended beefy palm tapping the air in front of him in a gesture that I should hold my question. "These ancient people observed a lizard who was indigenous to their land. Over time, they came to respect the little reptile. The lizard was small, but it was naturally shrewd. They called the lizard, in their own language, the 'Ground Lion.' In English, the two Greek words became one word... 'Chameleon'." The Old Man leaned close enough for me to smell his cologne as he continued in his guttural voice, "All men are chameleons, Michael. The chameleons change their color in order to survive. If they are on the fence post, they are brown. When they move through the grass, they become green. Men, men like us, like your father, change their colors so that they may survive and prosper. This is not an evil thing. It is simply a fact of life. *Sopravvivere!* It is survival!"

Again I took a quick peek at Cavaluso who continued to study his cup of coffee.

The Old Man hesitated long enough to sip his espresso and then leaned forward again to say, "I know this to be true. These men here, the men you mock, are chameleons. They will change colors and become your friend, or the friend of those bastards in the FBI, if that is what they need to do in order to survive. I know this about my friends and you should know it about your friends. All men are chameleons. You may need to look around you, Michael, and ask yourself this, 'Who do I know, and trust, and travel with, and call my friend...and who among them is a chameleon?'"

Look for this Lt. Mike Amato mystery this November!

ABOUT THE AUTHOR

Lou Campanozzi was born and raised in Rochester, NY. After military service, he returned home and joined the Rochester Police Department. During his 22 years with the department, Lou worked undercover in narcotics, commanded the homicide and robbery squad, and served as a District Commander on the city's west side. After retiring as a Captain, the Campanozzi family relocated to Albuquerque, NM where they now reside.

Lou and his wife of almost 35 years, Nancy, have two grown children and three grandchildren. Besides writing murder mysteries, the author is also a Police Chief on an Indian Reservation in central New Mexico. In his spare time, Lou enjoys opera and oldies, gardening and golf, touring historical sites, and woodworking.